13/7 50p

C000064513

Acclaim for Through It C

"Trebor Healey delivers coming out as apocalypse—tender, destructive, punk. He tore down a worn-out block of queer lit and built it back up. Sweet, sad, gritty, and real."

—Michelle Tea, Author,
The Chelsea Whistle

"I read passages of this novel out loud again and again, absorbing the truth beneath its lyrical language. Trebor Healey understands the beauty and cruelty that spill forth when men dare to express love to one another. He holds up a magnifying glass to the human heart, and his gaze is unblinking."

—K. M. Soehnlein, Author,
The World of Normal Boys

"Trebor Healey's compelling tale of crisis around a family illness and an unexpected first gay love is poetic and reflective, angry, rowdy, funny, and triumphant. *Through It Came Bright Colors* depicts two very different, intertwined love stories, very nearly sacred and profane. A well-known poet, Healey's passionate, lyrical, and muscular fictional debut is filled with characters and story."

—Felice Picano, Author,
Ambidextrous: The Secret Lives of Children;
Men Who Loved Me; and
A House on the Ocean, A House on the Bay

"Love hurts, hurt heals—that's the crystalline message at the core of Trebor Healey's complex, accomplished coming-of-age story about a cautiously queer suburban kid whose heart is unexpectedly squeezed hard by a young junkie's quicksilver mind and beautiful lean body. Neill's life-affirming attraction to life-weary Vince is doomed from this wise novel's very first line—but their fumbling struggle for physical love, emotional connection, and mutual maturity is mesmerizing. The searing implosion of their passion is no surprise, but it shimmers with the compelling honesty of real lives, while Healey's refreshingly original tale hums with the potency of poetry."

—Richard Labonte, Reviewer,
Book Marks; Q Syndicate

NOTES FOR PROFESSIONAL LIBRARIANS
AND LIBRARY USERS

This is an original book title published by Southern Tier Editions, Harrington Park Press®, an imprint of The Haworth Press, Inc. Unless otherwise noted in specific chapters with attribution, materials in this book have not been previously published elsewhere in any format or language.

CONSERVATION AND PRESERVATION NOTES

All books published by The Haworth Press, Inc. and its imprints are printed on certified pH neutral, acid free book grade paper. This paper meets the minimum requirements of American National Standard for Information Sciences-Permanence of Paper for Printed Material, ANSI Z39.48-1984.

Through It Came
Bright Colors

HARRINGTON PARK PRESS
Southern Tier Editions
Gay Men's Fiction
Jay Quinn, Executive Editor

Love, the Magician by Brian Bouldrey

Distortion by Stephen Beachy

The City Kid by Paul Reidinger

Rebel Yell: Stories by Contemporary Southern Gay Authors
edited by Jay Quinn

Rebel Yell 2: More Stories of Contemporary Southern Gay Men
edited by Jay Quinn

Metes and Bounds by Jay Quinn

The Limits of Pleasure by Daniel M. Jaffe

The Big Book of Misunderstanding by Jim Gladstone

This Thing Called Courage: South Boston Stories by J. G. Hayes

Trio Sonata by Juliet Sarkessian

Bear Like Me by Jonathan Cohen

Ambidextrous: The Secret Lives of Children by Felice Picano

Men Who Loved Me by Felice Picano

A House on the Ocean, A House on the Bay by Felice Picano

Goneaway Road by Dale Edgerton

Death Trick: A Murder Mystery by Richard Stevenson

The Concrete Sky by Marshall Moore

Edge by Jeff Mann

Through It Came Bright Colors by Trebor Healey

Elf Child by David M. Pierce

Huddle by Dan Boyle

The Man Pilot by James W. Ridout IV

Shadows of the Night: Queer Tales of the Uncanny and Unusual
by Greg Herren

Through It Came Bright Colors

Trebor Healey

Southern Tier Editions
Harrington Park Press®
An Imprint of The Haworth Press, Inc.
New York • London • Oxford

Published by

Southern Tier Editions, Harrington Park Press®, an imprint of The Haworth Press, Inc., 10 Alice Street, Binghamton, NY 13904-1580.

© 2003 by The Haworth Press, Inc. All rights reserved. No part of this work may be reproduced or utilized in any form or by any means, electronic or mechanical, including photocopying, microfilm, and recording, or by any information storage and retrieval system, without permission in writing from the publisher. Printed in the United States of America.

TR: 10.06.03

PUBLISHER'S NOTE
This is a work of fiction. Names, characters, places, and incidents either are the products of the author's imagination or are used fictitiously, and any resemblance to actual persons, living or dead, business establishments, events, or locales is entirely coincidental.

Portions of this novel first appeared in the *Blithe House Quarterly, Lodestar Quarterly, Ashé!, Harrington Gay Men's Fiction Quarterly,* and *Velvet Mafia.*

Cover design and cover photos of traffic light, clouds, and street scene by Daniel Austin Kopyc (www. cricketcage.com). Cover photo of male model by Mark Lynch.

Library of Congress Cataloging-in-Publication Data

Healey, Trebor, 1962-
    Through it came bright colors / Trebor Healey.
       p. cm.
    ISBN 1-56023-451-2 (hardcover : alk. paper)—ISBN 1-56023-452-0 (softcover : alk. paper)
    1. Gay men—Fiction. I. Title.
PS3608.E24 T48 2003
813'.6—dc21

                                   2002012431

For Johnny, Julie, Ira, and Asa
May they find peace

ℭℛ Acknowledgments

For their keen insight and advice on this manuscript, I'd like to thank David West, Jarrett Walker, and Michael Nava. Special thanks to Felice Picano for his generosity at every turn in this process, and to Isaac Cruz, Sera Sacks, and Gerardo Perez for keeping me going.

I am forever grateful to my friends Frank Shawl, Leah Chapnick, Julie Connery, Paula McNally, the late Charles Swarengin, George Scrivani, Peter Limnios, Larry Ackerman, Taro Akita, Chuck Hawley, Philip Horne, the late David Brown, Roger Corless, Robert Hall, and Ernest Posey for their constant support and encouragement. For his life-sustaining letters and undying faith, a special thanks to Horehound Stillpoint.

I would also like to thank all those who have nurtured my work through the years: Jack Davis and the 848 Community Space Collective; Jennifer Joseph and Manic D Press; Winston Leyland and Gay Sunshine Press; Gavin Geoffrey Dillard; Matteo Bianchi; Jerry Thompson; M. I. Blue; Hank Hyena; and the late Johnny D'Hondt. In addition, I'd like to thank the following editors for supporting this book by publishing excerpts: Aldo Alvarez at *Blithe House Quarterly;* Patrick Ryan at *Lodestar Quarterly;* Tom Long at the *Harrington Gay Men's Fiction Quarterly;* Sven Davisson at *Ashé!;* and Greg Wharton and Sean Meriwether at *Velvet Mafia.*

For all the countless ways they've helped and sustained me, I thank my family. And for offering the world and me a picture of profound courage, as well as inspiration for this book, I thank my brother Terry Healey.

Sometimes I go about pitying myself when all the time I am carried on great wings across the sky.

Ojibwa Song

∝ Prologue

Vince went like a dam in the end—one with his enormous, beautiful, Lenin-esque, Che Guevara of a face painted on it, rupturing and disintegrating in slow motion, swallowed by water. But it wasn't water in his case; it was junk. And the river was a needle, and when that dam broke our whole story disappeared into the tender, exposed vein in the crotch of his elbow.

Peter got morphine once after surgery, and he said, "Yeah, I can understand."

He's a dam too. But the river in him washed over us, washes us still.

He's ringing his bell for me now. He rings it when he needs me at night. My mother would gladly run to him, but he can't handle her overconcern anymore, so he's let it be known that the bell rings only for me.

The bell is old and brass, painted in blues and greens and shaped almost like a bird claw. It has a hollow, faraway sound like the bells they use in Catholic churches when they lift up the host—*this is my body.*

He's grinning when I reach his room after padding down the stairs in the dark, but his grin isn't big like most people's. He has scars, big, red, and keloid, and they've had to cut some of his nerves besides, so it's a baby's smile, uncoordinated—the kind of smile that makes you cheer and want to tell people about it.

I smile back, fearing my smile looks sorry, and I get him up out of the wetted bed. Half-blitzed on Percodan, he had tried to sip some water and spilled the entire glass. I help him over to the old kitchen chair in the corner, where he sits, holding his legs close together and his head tilted to the side and forward as if to cradle the hole in his cheek where the tumor had been—the hole it had returned to, once again to grow. Cancer abhors a vacuum? A fallow field? Cancer spits at my silly clichéd metaphors. Cancer's a cad and does whatever it wants.

"English bed-wetting type," I mutter mock-disgustedly in a French accent, mimicking a character from *Monty Python and the Holy Grail*. I always try to make it fun, but inside I'm my mother too, sorrowful and vaguely horrified. He starts guffawing as I proceed with my little pantomime because he can't laugh right either with his still-sutured scars and cut nerves. He starts to say "Stop, stop" because it pains him to laugh and he's rearing his head up to ease the discomfort, like a little kid wriggling away from a belly tickle.

"OK, OK, I'll try not to crack you up," I concede, but I know through the pain I've made him happy and I'm glad. I'm like my father that way, ready with a joke. I don't know what's best—I know only that I want to make him happy. If it comes to that, I want him to be laughing when the great toilet bowl of the world pulls him down.

I help him struggle out of his pajama shirt and pants, and throw them in a pile on the floor near the door, then turn to get a fresh pair from the dresser, which takes me back ten years because it's that same old dresser from when we were kids and no one was ever sick and I wasn't even aware of being gay yet and our parents, if we thought of them at all, weren't little and fragile as they seem to have become now. We were safe then. Well, relatively. There was still my vicious older brother Paul, who hounded me night and day. But he's since moved to the East Coast and rarely returns. And after all that's happened this year, our squabbling seems like small change.

But he left a hole too; I can't deny that. It's just that I don't see holes the same anymore.

I pull out the fresh sheets and a pair of pajama bottoms, which I hand to Peter, hoping he'll be able to put them on by himself. I change the sheets, watching out of the corner of my eye as he puts first one leg, then the next, into the pajama pants. He's such a beautiful man, I think to myself, his body so perfectly formed. It's odd to see him struggle—he who'd always done everything physical with such grace and ease. Persistent, he gathers the pajamas above his ankles and then, pulling himself up and steadying one arm on the chair back, he yanks them up with the other hand.

"Pretty good," I cheer, "pretty darn good." And I turn and go to him, steadying his shoulders with my hands, guiding him toward the cleaned-up bed, helping him on with the shirt. Then we get him settled back into bed—his body almost like a third thing between us that together we carefully handle, like a delicate and valuable piece of art. Tucking him in, I lean down on one knee to comb the hair across his sweating brow with my hand, careful not to touch his face so swollen with scars. I have to gulp a breath of air to stave off my tears, which are hanging around, almost loitering, like someone in a room who seems to have something to say but hangs back, shy and unsure.

Well, he's two people too. Cancer does that, I guess. He's still the stoic athlete who heals faster than he should and never cries or complains, a picture of self-reliance whose mantra is "Fall down, get back up again" (some coach taught him that, I suppose); but he's also a little kid again—in the middle of the night, or when the pain is bad, or if he's helpless (showers and too much Percodan)—and wholly incongruous to our daytime hero, wanting to be taken care of and held and stroked and made to laugh. At first I was confused, even embarrassed by it, but then I saw in it an ability to invite and accept love in a way I knew I could never do myself. Yet I felt strong, even as I doubted myself, for it made me useful; he made it easy as a child does. I had a strange desire to thank him all the time, but that seemed as ridiculous as his acting like a little kid, and in my befuddlement I just let him thank *me*.

"What have you been dreaming of, Peter?"

"Mountains," he smiles. He grins widely, and I see the half of his teeth that still remain. He grins because we have a dream of mountains. It's become a bedtime story, recounting all the places we've backpacked together and thinking up new ones still to come.

"Peter, we'll go packin' as soon as this is over. How about it? You wanna? Hike way out there."

"Yeah, let's go packin'; that would be great," he replies, as if he were rehearsing his lines in a play because this is a ritual, this dream.

"You just stay busy thinking of a place to go, Peter. Anywhere you want," I respond, taking my cue, as I further tuck him in.

"Tell me, Neill. Describe a place."

I pause to think for a minute, and it all comes flooding back. All those places we'd gone last summer, to get away from home, school, work, or all those things closing in on us as we grew older. Actually, I think *he* went just because he liked it there; Peter was easy. But for me, it was about getting away from people, the world. I was queer and angry and unable to do anything about it back then. I'd longed for a world that loved me anyway, despite it, which wasn't what I was seeing in Republican America, at church on Sundays, or amid the bantering of the "in crowd" at school. What *I* loved about the mountains was that they *were* that world.

So it's easy for me to tell him about a place and a once-upon-a-time.

"There's a place, Peter, where you've never been. It's a meadow called Bear and the bears are thick as bees there—scared me to death when I first saw it." He grins at my gross exaggeration. "The pines, as usual, standing around; snow on the peaks; slopes of fir; and the mules ears grass and wild onions bunched up along the stream . . . Bear Meadow must have been a good mile across at its widest, and it was arced up, swollen, like a pregnant belly. It was bright green, the grass was—chartreuse almost—and the sky was vivid blue. I'd been out for a week or so, scrambling over three passes, camping by lakes where you could see the submerged logs and rocks lying twenty feet below, or along rushing streams, rocky and messed with boulders, going who knows. And no food lost to bears, Peter—imagine that!" He offers a wan smile of acknowledgment. "Anyway, I'm coming through this watershed when I see it ahead of me up through these boulders. I got a full pack, fifty pounds; blisters; I'm slogging loud through the pine needles, anxious now to get there—loud enough so that the first bear that saw me wasn't surprised. Just right after that exhilarating feeling of MEADOW! I noticed him: *BEAR!* He was looking right at me as I stopped and swallowed. He was sitting on his haunches next to an eaten-up, rotten old cedar log lying in the grass. He'd been digging in it, I figured, for ants or termites or something because he was licking his paw like they do when they dig in logs. He was comic and terrifying all at once. But he just sat there as I froze in terror—he didn't move; he didn't startle; he just kept chewing ants and licking his paws, unperturbed like an old Buddha—the sky damn blue, Peter;

damn blue—and me petrified. I never know what to do with fear like that in a place so beautiful and so full of peace. I just started backing away. . . ."

By now, Peter is breathing the soft breath of sleep, and he's probably missed the best part. He'll catch up with it in his dreams, I hope. I take my own story's advice and back away, turning off the lights and half-closing the door, catching the one tear that gets loose and smearing it across my cheek, sniffling it up so Mom won't suspect anything when she whispers for me upstairs, ever unable to sleep through that bell.

"He's OK, Ma—just spilled his glass of water. I changed the bed. It's all taken care of." A feeble "Thank you, honey" floats out of the darkness as I pull her door to a near close and head to my own room. There's moonlight across my bed, tangled with the shadows of the softly swaying branches of the big oak outside my window, and it's as if there is a sort of map laid out upon my bedspread. I lie there wide awake, following its rivers and trails, dreaming a place, still intoxicated with my love of the mountains that's gotten all mixed up with my love of my little brother and, more recently, with Vince. I long to get back up there, high above the world, where things are clear and there's room to sort it all out.

On our last trip together, long before cancer and Vince, Peter and I had gone up over the rim of Yosemite, far up Illilouette Creek, the massive face of Half Dome at our backs, watching over us, its clipped bell-curve shape mimicking an image of the Virgin Mary in her mantel—silent, present, like a last ruin of the faith we'd been raised with.

We'd climbed in silence up out of the valley, huffing and puffing. At first we passed many hikers along the forested trail, but they thinned out rapidly the higher we climbed. Occasionally we stopped to rest, and then we'd look back down behind us through the trees to the valley as it receded farther and farther away until it was only a toy world, almost unreal. It was amazing how quickly we got above it, how quickly it became a little model railroad world with tiny trees and cars and little people and even a miniature river—and the big stones were probably just little rocks placed here and there, the whole distant valley and its immense sheer walls a plaster of paris creation.

When we reached Illilouette Falls—they dropped 2,000 feet, nearly to the valley floor before being lost in a tumble of boulders and granite terraces that followed the canyon down into the valley—we turned inland and headed up the creek to where no one but the "serious" backpackers went, off to find our sanctuary. Inland from the rim the forest grew denser, pines spiraling into the sky, the scattered debris of stone and fallen trees surrounding us. Now there was only silence punctuated by the quiet sounds of distant birds, creaking branches, the occasional chirp of a chipmunk or snap of a branch, the forlorn wind in the high tree tops.

Hours later, we set up camp along the creek, just under some overhanging stones behind which lay an enormous sloping meadow of flowers and sparse grass among sand and gravel and downed, blanched-white, barkless pine logs. Peter made a Frisbee course out of the big pines and scattered boulders, and we played into the afternoon. It was the endless space around us that relaxed us as our voices echoed and our muscles relaxed after straining all day. There were no limits to this game and we could have thrown our Frisbee around over 100 miles with nothing but empty wilderness to impede us. It was an Edenic world, spacious and unhampered by cancer and dogma, hatred and mean older brothers, the past and all things that tried to contain us.

With dusk we cleared areas to lay our sleeping bags under the sheltering pines and big rocks. I watched Peter as long shadows and golden light slowed everything down so that each act, each movement or gesture, took on a significance rarely noticed down below. He'd gone to hang our food in a tree to prevent its capture by bears. I stayed behind to build a fire but turned to watch him without his knowing it. I watched him tie a rock up in a thin rope and then toss it high and up over a branch. It took him a few tries, and once the rock came loose from the rope and nearly beaned him on the head. He jumped aside comically, never seeing me laugh. When he got the rope up over the tree branch, he evened it out and tied one bag to one end, hoisting it high up by yanking down on the other end of the rope. I watched his biceps flex, holding the rope taut. Then he put the rope in his mouth, holding it there so he could proceed to tie the other bag. He saw me then, and smiled around his clenched teeth. I thought almost instinctively with such suddenness: *I love him; he's such a person.* It sounded ridiculous, but that's all I could think of. There was something so utterly and unselfconsciously human and animal about him. I never saw him get frustrated—as I so often did on these trips—with ropes and knives and cut fingers and binding, temperamental straps on shoulders. His body worked with it all patiently, watching me almost with wonder when I'd fight myself.

He had nothing to fight—not then. The Lord giveth and the Lord taketh away—the cheap, Indian-giving bastard. Yet what never failed to surprise me was how, far from leaving a hole, all this loss left a window, a doorway—and through it came bright colors; through it come bright colors still.

❧ I

I'd heard about Vince long before I'd met him that fortuitous day six months ago. Peter knew him from the waiting room at the radiation clinic.

"He's kind of a punk-rocker type with a bad attitude, but he's kind of funny too. He always makes cynical remarks in the waiting room, like, 'I don't want some idiotic funeral; I want them to throw me in a ditch by the side of the road when I die,' or 'What do you give yourself, Peter—a week? Two weeks?' It's funny, but it bums me out because he's the only other young guy there and I think he should have a better attitude. He just gets sarcastic when I tell him he can get better. The only reason I even got to know him was that he was asking everyone for a dollar the first time I went there. They were all saying no and I just felt like we were all in this thing together . . . so of course I'd give him a dollar. I've given him three dollars now."

"What does he need a dollar for all the time?"

"He takes the bus." Peter shook his head. "Can you believe it? Nobody comes with him, ever. He lives in some residential hotel downtown and takes a bus to the hospital for radiation. He's totally depressed and broke—on welfare, I guess. But he's smart. He's got a lot going for him if he'd just realize it. I think you'd like him—he kind of reminds me of you."

"What's that supposed to mean?" I asked defensively.

"No offense; I only meant the smart part." It was a politic answer. I knew Peter saw a parallel in our negative attitudes and, I supposed, the kind of questioning, sarcastic, or just plain cynical intelligence that was at the root of my potential or my demise—it was still too soon to tell, being that I was only twenty-one. "Maybe you'll come with me sometime and you can meet him," he offered.

When we walked into the waiting room the next week, Vince was the first person I saw. He looked right at me—or through me—and my throat filled up. I'd more or less put him out of my mind after Peter mentioned him the week before, and since the topic of him hadn't come up on the ride over, I was caught off guard. I looked away; I looked back. It was odd the way he stared at me and how I stared back. It seemed almost as if we knew each other already, even recognized each other but couldn't figure out where from—as if we'd been looking for each other for a long time. I wanted to turn to Peter and say, "That's him!" but that was actually Peter's line, and he delivered it without the exclamation.

Vince was tall and thin with dark brown almond-shaped eyes over a slightly upturned nose. He had black, dense eyebrows that were off-set by his hair, which was dyed a vivid flaming orange and cut short. On his neck, just under his left ear, was an elaborate and expressive tattoo, a sort of cross between a spider's web and Chinese calligraphy. As such, it had the quality of both repelling you and attracting you at the same time. He had on a pair of badly stained, too-short khakis that revealed his mismatched socks and ratty old Converse sneakers. He wore a white T-shirt with big black letters that read, What Would Satan Do? An arresting intelligence shone from his eyes and he had an almost invasive awareness about him, as if he knew more about you than he should. I felt suddenly naked. I wanted to stare back at him but feared I'd either blush crimson or get swallowed whole. I knew I wanted to know him—wanted him to be my friend in the greedy way children want someone they admire to be their friend.

I suspected he was queer from the minute I saw him. He likely guessed the same about me. Queers always recognize one another, but with Vince it was a kind of recognition beyond even that—right down to the cellular level. I hesitated in the doorway momentarily and then, taking a deep breath, I entered the room. Vince, forever a doorway.

That's when I realized that Peter's cancer had blown the lid off my repressed sexuality along with everything else. And there stood Vince in the clearing smoke—the drill bit of his eyes, the fire that flamed off his head in L'Oréal liquid amber. A part of me then, and for a long time afterward, tried to resist his pull, but he seemed to snap off my ribs like dry twigs, and out ran my heart. Could falling in love be a relief? I suppose when you've fought its possibility for so long, it's got to be.

Though the room was crowded, there were of course open seats next to Vince. He defensively said, "Hi" when Peter introduced us, as if he might be thinking Peter had previewed him for me. In time I'd understand it was simply Vince's irritation with all things polite or cordial. I said something inane, like "Pleased to meet you."

"So, who are you?" he asked me, the introductions now over.

"I'm—uh—Peter's brother," I responded, pointing my thumb at Peter. I was at a loss since Peter had just introduced me as such.

"No, I mean like what are you; like what do you do with yourself; what are you into?" he clarified.

I looked at Peter briefly, who looked at the floor, perhaps momentarily regretting that he'd put me in this position. At that moment "You" would have been the best answer to Vince's question, but I was way too nervous to be in any way suave, and I'd always been too introspective for repartee besides. "Uh, just a guy, ya know . . . a college student. Or I was until recently . . ."

"Well, we're all cancer patients." He motioned his eyes around the room. "Ain't it grand?" A big wry grin spread across his until-now guarded expression. I hadn't seen it coming, like a left hook, and I reeled before attempting a response.

Lamely, I offered, "Yeah, I know."

There was an awkward silence and then Vince began to comment on the bad art hanging on the walls—harmless mauve flowers, well-coordinated abstracts that matched the furniture, and various portraits of cats.

"Sure doesn't make you think of radioactive isotopes or malignant cancer cells, does it?" he remarked, his eyes scanning around the room. "Why don't they have fractals or pictures of magnified carcinomas? Maybe we'd all learn something, see the truth." He raised his voice slightly, looking at Peter and me provocatively as the others in the room began to fidget. He proceeded to tell us that he had had testicular cancer—in too loud a voice—which meant they'd removed one of his balls. "The doctor offered to give me a fake one made out of glass, just like a glass eye. I laughed in his face and asked him what made him think I'd want a cold ball of glass in my scrotum." He paused momentarily for emphasis, before continuing. "He thought I might be concerned about my appearance and what women would think. He said it was a cosmetic issue. I told him I was a fag but not a drag queen, so I'd pass on the cosmetics." He laughed sardonically, and we nervously laughed along with him, but all I could focus on was that he'd just confirmed my suspicions about his being gay, which put a lump in my throat that I tried to swallow, suddenly more nervous *knowing* than when I'd only suspected it. Vince went on: "I told him I didn't give a fuck what anybody thought, and if it bothered them, they could go to hell."

Peter looked at me nervously as if to say, "See what I mean about the bad attitude?" I was still struggling with the lump and managed only a sheepish smile.

I was enthralled by both his brazenness and his honesty. I was surprised that Peter hadn't mentioned to me that Vince was gay, since he seemed so obvious about it. Either Peter hadn't seen it as a big deal or, more likely, it somehow hadn't come up between them. Then again, perhaps Vince spoke of it now for my benefit.

An uneasy silence passed before Peter broke the impasse by asking about Vince's radiation and speaking of his own complications. He mentioned that at one point the doctors had wanted to remove his right eye.

"Yeah, well, the glass eye they probably had lined up for you almost ended up in my scrotum," Vince wiseassed, laughing at his own joke. Peter laughed too, but with embarrassment as an elderly woman across the room tipped her reading glasses to get a better look at the loudmouthed punk. Vince was on a roll and proceeded to dis the medical establishment, from receptionists and administrators on up to technicians, nurses, and surgeons, recounting their persistent ignorance in matters of survival and health. "One doctor insisted on lecturing me on safe sex. When I asked him if oral sex was safe, he said no, the mouth is basically one big open sore." He guffawed. " 'Well, no fucking kidding, and you're a case in point!' I told him. Fuckin' idiot."

Just then Peter was called in for his treatment. As he walked away—and I watched him disappear behind the door—I felt a sudden shame that I'd sat here with this strange, attractive boy, listening to him *dis* the complex and painstakingly built system of knowledge that had saved my little brother's life. Perhaps I should have protested? And so I began our first of a seemingly endless series of arguments.

"Modern medicine does help people, though. It saved my brother; it works sometimes."

"Sure it does," he said sarcastically, "for a while. Or if you're willing to be maimed. I should've just let myself die. Look at us: I've got one ball; your brother's face is a mess—what's left of it. I mean, look around you: Is this really what people want?"

"I don't think my brother's face is a mess, and he's getting reconstruction after this besides. He wants to live; that's what he wants. That's what all these people want."

His eyes flashed coldly. "What the fuck do you know about it?"

I felt suddenly as if I'd overstepped his bounds. After all, he did have cancer, and who was I to lecture him on it? So I scrambled and began backpedaling. "Hey, man, no offense. I know you've been through a lot. I shouldn't speak for my brother or anyone else."

He relented as well. "Your brother's keeper, I understand. He's a poster child; I can't argue with what he stands for." I was silent, unsure where he was taking this. "He's a good guy, though, your brother. He's a lot cooler than most of the selfish fucks in this room. He doesn't," and he raised his voice still louder, "begrudge me a buck when I ask for it." A few nervous coughs nearby conveyed discomfort, accentuating the thickening silence around us.

I didn't want to fall in love so publicly and with such difficulty, though it seemed strangely out of my hands. I offered him a cigarette as a ploy to escape the others.

"Now those cause cancer; I can't possibly accept such a ludicrous offer," he mocked me, speaking in a condescending and officious tone, which he suddenly clipped with a smile. What was it in his smile that made me forget the malice I'd seen in those same eyes a moment before? Was it a tenderness much more convincing than all that bile? Or was it just his duplicitous charm that overpowered me? The constant contrast. Perhaps it was my intense attraction to him, which saw all of his expressions and moods as beautifully rendered—when he'd shown anger, it seemed a perfect, sublime anger, burning clean and blue; when he was defensive, it was as endearing and arresting as watching a little boy aware of an injustice. He seemed to hop from one mood to the next—joking, scowling, enthused, despondent, disarmingly vulnerable—displaying a sort of poetic range that covered all points on the emotional spectrum. It made him seem huge, epic, more vital than anyone I'd ever witnessed. His anger scared me too, but the minute he smiled I felt completely safe.

He smiled again when he said, "But yeah, I'd love a smoke."

The only problem was, I had no cigarettes. I'd said it out of desperation but without forethought.

But Vince was already up and walking toward the door, so I followed him out. I must have looked somewhat stunned, searching my mind for an explanation as to why I'd offered him a cigarette I didn't have.

He delivered me of my anxieties, though, as he pulled out a pack as soon as he got out the door, which opened onto an outdoor corridor running the length of the building. He seated himself at once as he lit up, performing the whole trick in one graceful movement as I awkwardly tried to gain my composure.

"Neill," he said slowly, almost seductively, looking up at me, "as in Armstrong?"

I chuckled nervously, relieved by his humor. "No, as in O'Neill minus the O."

"So you're not the man on the moon?" He shook his head back and forth, sighing. "After all these years I've looked for him." I felt suddenly eager, and I wanted to say I'd be Neil Armstrong; I'd be his man on the moon if that's what he wanted. I'd put on a fucking space suit—one small step for you, Vince; one giant leap of faith and courage right into your arms for me.

I gave him my sorry smile, the one I'd perfected watching Peter. I looked down then, but soon I found I was staring at his hands, having almost forgotten where I was and that I was talking to a stranger.

"Hello?" He was smiling at me again, patting the wooden bench next to him so I'd sit down. I smiled back quickly and went to sit down. I realized I was simply following his orders without even thinking. His power—which I suppose I could also call the power of my attraction to him (whose power was it really?)—was exciting and compelling, but it was also overwhelming, domineering even, and somehow unfair. He was a man with a gun, waving it around, and I was the bumbling security guard, unable to free my weapon from my holster. I excused myself.

"I gotta go to the bathroom," I blurted, then got up and headed for the men's room I'd passed earlier, back down the corridor.

I instinctively turned on the tap to splash cold water in my face the minute I got there, hoping to calm my nerves and get a handle on things. I took a deep breath and for the first time in all these months of Peter's illness I felt suddenly alone and apart, and able again to see where I was, as if I'd awoken from a kind of sleep. Since Peter had gotten sick, I'd put myself aside, dropped out of school, followed the orders of cancer, if you will. I'd stuffed all my personal anxieties about being queer into some drawer and forced it shut, figuring I could get back to my endless obsessive ruminations about my tragic homosexual fate later. I'd told myself that I needed to keep my energies directed toward Peter and my parents. I'd been almost relieved by his illness that way, as though I'd been granted a reprieve from my own seemingly insoluble problems now that they were so clearly secondary to someone else's.

And then Vince. That drawer had popped open violently, as if he were some kind of fag-in-the-box. I looked in the mirror, my mind once again orbiting the enormous black hole of homosexuality. I braced myself for the cold slap of hopelessness that would render me once again a self-pitying ruin, looking for some place to hide—but it never came. A wick, but no match in sight.

I was surprised and bewildered. I racked my mind, but all I could see was Peter's face, scarred and swollen. And when I looked into myself, it was as if there wasn't as much there as before he got sick. I felt empty, but in a good way—a burdensome bucket of water or mud dumped. Perhaps when they took the cancer from Peter's cheek, a whole bunch of other things went with it. He was the root of a sickly tree, and the rotting fermenting fruit I'd carried on my branch had suddenly fallen off and split open, and all that was left were the released seeds.

Which was I: the seed or the shell? Either way, I had a vague sense that those seeds were heading somewhere, just as I had a similar sense that the emptiness would be filled. His brows were dark as dirt; his eyes invaded me. Well, maybe both the seed and the shell, then.

When I pushed open the door, Vince was already standing and waiting for me, having finished his cigarette. I wondered then how he knew I hadn't wanted one, or was he just so self-involved it hadn't occurred to him? I'd never trusted my own heart; I wasn't about to trust another person.

He motioned his head that he was going in, and he entered before I'd even reached the door. I had gained a little equilibrium throwing cold water on may face and I aimed to try to keep it. So I stopped at the magazine table as I walked back into the waiting room and grabbed whatever was on top, resolved to take charge of the situation. Vince looked at me and at the magazine as I approached. It was *Time*. "Propaganda, huh?" he commented offhandedly.

"Uh, well, I guess. I wanted to finish an article I'd started at home," I offered, unsure of myself again, all my resolve evaporating before the orange flames streaming off his head, and overwhelmed by his presence and my own shakiness.

"Give me that," he commanded sarcastically, grabbing the corner. I handed it to him without thinking. I let out all the line. I panicked inside. I knew I needed to get ahold of myself, that I had to stand my ground with him.

"Hey, give me that back." He handed it to me without any resistance and got up to get his own magazine. He came back with *Newsweek*.

"Let's see how many lies we can count," he said slowly, grinning. He was challenging me, but it was all done in such a disarming and friendly way—and besides, he wasn't calling *me* dishonest (or was he?). I thumbed quickly through to an article on the Persian Gulf War.

"Forty thousand children slaughtered, do they mention that?" He said matter of factly, leaning over to see my magazine. "Gulf War syndrome," he read. Then more loudly, he asked, "Anyone have Gulf War syndrome here?" He paused. "Guess not," he added, smiling. What could I say? I smiled at his humor, and then I just looked at him, smitten. He seemed so unaware of his beauty and brilliance, as if it weren't his or any part of him, which made it all the more enticing. It was as if it came through him, the door of him (*Maybe he's empty too,* I considered briefly). Or, like fire, it wasn't really there, it was just something that happens between the wood and the air—or his scalp and the hair dye. His energy was unnerving, and I knew it wasn't just me who saw it. In this crowded waiting room, he was a presence. Though few would acknowledge him or *it,* those of us who did looked at one another knowingly without speaking. I noticed all the others who were in on it avoided him with determination. I was young and thought them cowards. And, of course, I was queer. Whatever the myriad reasons of my surrender, I didn't know then what they knew or perhaps suspected.

And though I do know now, I have no regrets. It was as if all the people of the world were an audience, and what was up on the screen was not important. It was just another *Godzilla* or *Titanic* movie. He was that single person struggling toward the aisle through a row of seats, climbing and tripping and excusing himself (would he actually bother?), while everyone sat enraptured by the film, which existed like the skyline of a city, weirdly still and somehow dead, though everybody knew something by God was going on there—*wasn't it?* Sitting in this theater of life, the backs of the multitudinous heads before me, I saw him struggling—the one moving thing, his eyes looking back at my own. He was going somewhere, and so he was a question posed. I wanted to know where he was going and so, as if from a distance, I tentatively began to follow.

I knew I was in love with him then, but it was more than that— I was falling under his spell. He wasn't just some attractive guy but the fact that he *was* attractive *and* he had that fascinating mind, that vast range of emotions and perception—it was the left hook followed by the solid right. And he seemed so alone, so other, so "man from another world"—as if he had a secret that I was suddenly and solely privy to. It was as if he were asking me to climb on his spaceship going to who knows where and probably not returning. It was exciting, but it also made me uneasy and apprehensive.

I got up to get a drink of water, went to the counter and asked for the time, meandered over to the window. Eventually I returned to my seat. He was reading now. He left me alone, perhaps sensing he was in danger of scaring me off—or was that just my wishful thinking? Maybe he was just interested in whatever he was reading and it had nothing to do with me.

Peter came out a few moments later. I stood up and smiled, and then Vince asked me for a dollar. Before I could respond, the nurse called his name: "Vincent Malone."

It didn't feel as if I'd given my mouth permission to say it, but out it came: "We'll give you a ride, if that's cool with Peter," I said, looking at Peter with my eyebrows up.

"Sure," Peter agreed, as if to say "Why not?"

Vince went off to his treatment, and I sat back down with my brother, who turned to me and said, "Quite a character, huh?"

I swallowed hard. "Yeah, he's a piece of work all right."

"I thought you guys would hit it off," he added good-humoredly. The old lady was eyeing us again, probably wondering who this fool was who'd been charmed by the orange-haired devil.

"I see what you mean though, Peter. He's bitter."

"Yeah, it worries me. I don't think he'll get better with a negative attitude."

"Who knows?" I said, thinking to myself that Vince seemed unstoppable to me. I also hoped and even sensed that I was going to find out for sure just what would happen to Vince, so I saw no need to speculate. I suddenly wanted to thank Peter for guiding me to him. *Silly,* I told myself, but my heart was full and I reached my arm around Peter and, hugging him close to me, I whispered, "I love you, Peter." He blushed—not at love, but because we were in a room full of people. I could certainly relate to that, but I was suddenly exhilarated and so out it came. "This is my brother" I said out loud, triumphantly, smiling and turning to look at him. It sounded stupid, but they all knew what I meant. Even the old lady in the glasses smiled back at us.

Cancer had come to Peter like a rock in his shoe a year ago. It became cancer only in hindsight. At the time, it was a little something on his cheek that bugged him—it tickled; it felt like pressure; it felt like a zit. The dermatologist said it was probably a small cyst or clogged pore that would resolve itself. But clogged pores and cysts can get only so big; rocks in shoes don't grow or send out tendrils.

I can't blame such misdiagnoses. Peter was the kind of kid who exuded good fortune and health; you'd never assume the worst with him. He'd just been elected homecoming prince in fact, and my mother had been sure to tell the doctor so, almost guaranteeing his perfunctory "Keep an eye on it; it's likely nothing."

I had driven the twenty minutes back to my high school from Berkeley where I was beginning my first year of college in order to witness Peter's coronation. Though I'd hated this stuff while in high school myself, I wouldn't miss Peter's moment of embarrassed glory for anything (whatever corny, all-American emotions I harbored were reserved solely for him). So I came and sat there with my parents, trying to lay low in my wrinkled khakis and blue blazer over an unironed white shirt—Mom had insisted this was a formal affair, but it was just a football game to everybody else.

My mother told me I looked great, but since I'd been avoiding girls and dating for years I had no way of knowing whether I was good looking or not. Of course my mother would think so. I preferred to remain invisible.

"So how long's this reign of his anyway?" my father wryly inquired of my mother, attempting to bring her back to Earth. My father had thrown a blue blazer over one of his ratty old Lacoste shirts he used for gardening. This one was green with some sort of chemical dripped down the front of it, leaving big yellow splotches. He was still wearing his suit pants from work, but he'd thrown on his tennis shoes. He looked disheveled; his thin hair kept flopping down his forehead and into his eyes.

Before my mother could answer my father she noticed three girls rubbernecking us from a few rows down, wondering what all the tears and smiles and the fancy dress were about. As if divining the nature of their curiosity, she called out to them, waving and smiling, "I'm Peter's mother—Peter Cullane, the homecoming prince." I was mortified but winced a smile, figuring that was the quickest way to resolve my embarrassment.

"I'm sorry, Frank, what did you say?" She turned to my father briefly. Before he could respond, she was distractedly looking away. "Isn't it wonderful?"

But he was only there for the game—these halftime shenanigans were tiresome. He was proud of Peter's play. Peter had caught two touchdown passes already, before running off the field early to change into his tux. I'd often wondered what it was like to be someone like him. We had all been athletes, my brothers and I. But while Peter had excelled, Paul had simply proved his manhood or toughness with it, and I'd merely just gotten by and swallowed the bitter pill of it. Between Paul and the boys at school, my father and the suburbs in general, sports had never seemed a choice. I figured out quickly that I was hopelessly uncoordinated, so I'd gone out for swimming to save myself the humiliation of what seemed, back then, the ultimate failure.

If it had seemed like a chore to me and a war to Paul, Peter truly loved it. He never held his successes over me as Paul did, so I became a sort of sports fan, but only if it involved him. I'd even go out and watch him practice his high jump sometimes, which is what he loved best. He had such grace; it was extraordinary to watch his body flop in the air like a shimmering trout swimming upstream as he bent backward and sailed over the bar. It seemed so open-ended and unstoppable—his small flight.

"I said,"—and I know he's goading her now—"how long's his reign?" But my mother was looking all around her, lost in the glory, hoping others might notice her and proclaim her Queen Mother. She was an attractive woman, but she looked undignified, all dressed up like this, halfway up the sagging wooden high school bleachers like some suburban Miss Havisham. She'd put on weight in the past few years, but she still looked pretty good with that straight nose and strong jaw, and her handsome hazel eyes always made her look more intelligent than she was. Certain facial characteristics hold up to just about anything and she had a good number of them. In addition to the striking eyes and brows, she had a Marilyn Monroe mole on her left cheek. She'd never needed to use much makeup, but she'd definitely gone overboard with her hair. As I recall, it began a lovely auburn shade similar to Peter's, but over the past few years it had meandered around L'Oréal land and was currently a sort of opaque, reddish brown, like dull Spanish tiles. But it had beautiful waves in it, and she still wore it shoulder length, unlike most women pushing fifty who'd hacked all theirs off in some disheartened concession to menopause or middle-class suburban fatigue.

"Mom, the reign—Dad wants to know how long he's gonna be prince," I nagged her. "Why don't you tell him? Or don't you know?"

"Of course I know," she said boisterously, addressing her husband. "Don't act stupid, Frank. You went to high school," she chastised him. "He's prince until next year when they elect a new one," she hurriedly explained. "And one day, he may end up the homecoming king when he's a senior," she added triumphantly.

"Doesn't Elizabeth have to die before Charles accedes to the throne?" I sarcastically asked my father.

He laughed. "Unfortunately, no, she can abdicate."

"Yeah, but she won't. They'll have to kill her. What do you say, the rack or the guillotine?"

"Well, we can poison her,"—and he paused— "before she poisons us. That casserole tonight was plain awful." I chose not to risk agreeing, but it was a sorry meal: burnt rice with leftover chicken bits and canned cream of mushroom soup mixed in, with a few thawed frozen carrots and peas floating in it.

The mention of her questionable cooking skills got her attention of course. "Oh, Frank, stop it; you know I'm distracted. So I overcooked it. For God's sake, your son's a prince!"

"King for a day," he muttered, but her mind was focused on the field as she intently watched the convertible Mustangs and T-birds now circling the track around the football field, each host to a royal couple. First came the freshmen, two lanky blonds in white formal attire riding in the backseat of a brand-new red Mustang. They hopped out to cheers and climbed up on the dais. Then it was Peter's turn. His "limo," a baby blue 1965 Mustang convertible, rounded the final curve and rolled up before the bleachers. My mother was on her feet, in tears, cheering and waving. I was beyond embarrassment but thought I should stand up too, if not to join her in this joyful moment, then to at least prevent her from falling down through the bleacher or embarrassing herself further in some yet unimagined way.

Peter hopped gracefully out of the back before they opened the door for him—always the track star—and put out his arm for his date, the princess, who now clambered out of the car. Peter was wearing one of those hideous Selix tuxedos, brown with a big fluffy shirt and a red bow tie. His cheeks were ruddy since he'd just had to run into the locker room, shower, and change. He was a handsome kid, and I didn't think that just because he was my brother and my mother kept saying so. He had auburn hair and dark-browed, deep-set eyes. He had full lips too, and his nostrils flared ever so slightly at the base of his perfect male version of my mother's slender long nose. But it was his shyness more than anything that did the trick; that made you forgive him his good looks because you could tell he really didn't know he had them.

His princess, a short and somewhat stocky brunette (*she'll never win a pageant outside of high school,* I thought sadly—*this is your fifteen minutes, Buffy, enjoy it*) who wore a turquoise taffeta dress, lifted her face to the crowd, smiling and waving. Peter, in marked discord to his escort, kept looking down at the ground. He was too tall for his date as well, so they looked particularly awkward as they mounted the platform— she beaming, bright eyed, and looking too short; reluctantly following her, his face flushing red to match the bow tie.

Cancer was to be the bruise on that unblemished apple of the sun. He'd never be the senior king now. No more playing the romantic figure for Peter. High school went on without him, and it seemed they

sort of forgot him the longer he was away. For their love and attention, he would have had to wrap his car around a tree, or been paralyzed on the gridiron while playing for *their* team. But cancer wasn't
like that. It wasn't a public illness; it was a thing of private, invisible,
and irresolute grief; you couldn't put flowers and candles at the desk
he'd left vacated. Cancer wasn't much of a story really, not even a
tragedy. It was something that had to be taken away. It left a hole.

○ɕ III

When we'd dropped Vince off on Sixth Street that fateful day of our meeting—among the winos and the desperate screams of crazed crack addicts in no apparent danger—he asked me for my phone number.

"So, would you, like, give me your phone number?" he implored, leaning his arm on the roof of the car and peering in the window. He seemed both confident and defensive all at once, his brow furrowed as he nervously awaited the answer, a little angry perhaps that he'd even had to put himself out like this—like if he were rejected, he'd be sure to tell you to fuck off when you delivered the bad news. He'd walk away proud and intact either way.

How then could I have not seen the rest of it coming?

I hesitated, shy, flattered, scared. Then I gave it to him, trying my best to be nonchalant as I scribbled my parents' phone number down on a scrap of paper. He smiled back at me when I gave it to him. "See ya." He slapped the roof of the car before turning and entering the glass door of the Baldwin Arms Hotel, a faded art deco palace that I'm sure at one time had been grand.

"You sure you want to be his friend?" Peter asked me as I pulled into traffic.

"Yeah, why not?" I responded, trying to be casual, belying my defensiveness.

"Well, he's pretty fucked up," Peter responded. "Who knows what he's into, living down here. And you know he said all that shit about being gay—I didn't know that. I mean, I don't know—maybe he likes you. It might get weird."

I thought back to my rest room epiphany and knew it was time to tell him, if for no other reason than out of gratefulness for his part in it. And I knew I could tell him, though I also knew there was something final and irrevocable about it, and there was that outside chance he'd be uncomfortable with it. *I don't want to lose Peter,* I heard a desperate voice in my head caution me. But I'd never seen Peter judge anyone, least of all me. Besides, there was another voice too—a similar voice, just as strong, that affirmed: *You don't want to lose Vince either.* I was giddy at having been asked for my phone number; I didn't want to run away from this golden apple being handed to me—indeed, Vince was wholly fuji with his orange hair. Vince was an ignition, a lit match. Peter had been the messenger with the sulfur; Vince would be the spark, the fire, and the journey that became a conflagration. I needed and wanted them both.

"I hope it does get weird," I flatly stated, vexing him.

"What?"

"Peter, I hope it gets weird, and I hope he likes me." I pulled the car over to the curb then, turned off the engine, and yanked up the handbrake, the faded grandeur of Vince's Baldwin Arms Hotel still hovering behind us. "I'm queer, man," I said, shaking my head back and forth, sighing. It was out of character for me to announce such things, ruminary that I was, but I was infected perhaps by the ballsy assertiveness I'd witnessed in Vince.

Peter was caught off guard, blushing slightly as he answered, obviously at a loss, "Wow. Really?"

I could have laughed at his innocence, but I knew at this point any outward expression of feeling on my part would rapidly devolve into tears. I sniffled hard instead, bracing myself. "Really, Peter, and I should have told you a long time ago." I looked down at my lap then. "I was afraid to tell you, Peter. I'm still afraid. And I'm still afraid to tell Mom and Dad." (Paul wasn't even worth mentioning.) "I'm sorry. I don't want to lay anything heavy on you—you've got enough to deal with. And so do Mom and Dad."

"Well, uh . . ." He was still trying to process the emotional news, while I was losing myself in its implications. But the minute I stopped talking I knew I'd lose it, and I finally did. I blubbered some tears and fell into his arms. He was a bit shocked, I could feel it, but he held me close and I recovered quickly. "Hey, it's all the same to me," he kindly offered, looking into my eyes to reassure me. It surprised me, but I also knew that I shouldn't be surprised. It's just that I'd built up such a belief that all people, and especially men, would reject me outright and never trust me again once they knew. Yes, he was Peter, but he was also a man, and my mind, before this, hadn't been able to get around that.

"It is all the same, only different." Then I grinned a sigh of relief, my eyes still puffy from the small explosion of tears—another dam broken.

"How long have you known or, like, when did you figure it out?" he asked, almost shyly.

I thought it but didn't say it: *about ten years and ten blocks from here.* I looked out the window before speaking instead and watched a homeless man limping up the opposite sidewalk, muttering to himself, and I remembered each detail of that long ago summer day.

We were on our way to the beach on one of those few and far between beach-weather days that are almost wholly alien to San Francisco. We were all a bit punchy and rambunctious, having driven nearly an hour from home—the carnivalesque chaos that is family when children are young. From the Bay Bridge and freeway, we exited and drove through downtown and then up the dizzying heights of Pine Street and back down the other side like a roller coaster, arriving at Polk Street, where we hit a red light. I remember my father turning from the wheel, smiling mischievously, to look back toward his boys. It was his joker's face. Then he said it: "Look, boys—look at the fag, over there with the poodle." And he nodded his head toward a man in a blue pantsuit with wide bell-bottom slacks and white platform shoes, strolling along, leading a little groomed white poodle on a leash. He had a bouffant hairdo and he walked daintily, with his feet too close together, as only one kind of man would.

My jaw went slack with dread when I looked at him, and I felt a bolt of fear run from my eyes down into my throat, striking across my heart, tearing it and leaving forever after a scar, before lodging in my gut. Somehow I knew—knew absolutely when I looked upon that man—that we were one and the same in fate. My face must have collapsed into some kind of woe because my mother looked at me with concern and said: "It's OK, honey. Don't be afraid; he can't hurt you."

I stared back at her momentarily and then turned to watch the man recede into the distance. *He is inside me, Mother; he can hurt me.* But I said nothing, sinking instead into my seat and realizing all at once that I was in fact the very thing my older brother had always claimed I was doomed to be. That seemed too unfair, and it felt like a curse; and so I resolved that it could not be a part of me and it *could* be eradicated, sent back to where it came from.

I took a deep breath and answered Peter. "I've always known, Peter. I've always known."

"Shit, I'm sorry," he said, and I could see him thinking backward into the past too, searching out evidence or unintentional crimes. "I hope I never said anything . . ." and shaking his head, "God, how did you deal with that as a kid?"

"Mostly I worried about going to hell—remember how you used to see my saying the rosary?" I smiled through my glazed eyes. "By high school, I was just bitter—and depressed. Turned out that worked best." I grinned sardonically.

"Did you like *do* anything? Like have any experiences?" he ventured.

"No," I said emphatically, "I always hoped it would go away or they'd find a cure."

"So, what's different now? Did you meet somebody?"

"Well, I just met Vince, but it's you, Peter," and I turned to him. "It's you that's different, what you've been through. Everything's different now."

"Yeah, I guess so," he feebly replied, looking out his window at a corner liquor store plastered with lotto signs.

I reached out and grabbed his knee. "You helped me to just face it and deal with it, I guess—get my priorities straight."

He gave me a little sorrowful smile, and softly replied, "It makes no difference to me what you are, Neill." He put his hand on my shoulder. "You're my brother."

I almost laughed, he was such a sweet, innocent kid sometimes. And I almost cried. *What I am.* "We both got a load of trouble, huh?"

"We'll be OK, Neill."

"Well, I've thought about telling you this a few times in the last couple months. I mean, we know each other a lot better now than we ever did as kids." He was sighing and almost looked ashamed. "I just didn't want to burden you, Peter," and I looked directly at him. "You got a lot goin' on and I didn't want to burden you with some secret, and I still don't."

"I'm pretty much better now, Neill; it's OK," and he squeezed my shoulder again to reassure me he was just fine.

"I thought if I told you, I should tell everybody. But I'm not ready to tell Mom and Dad."

"It's OK. I appreciate you telling me, Neill, I don't expect you to just go around and talk about it to everybody right off, you know? I can keep it to myself," and he nodded his head and arched his brows, like a little kid pleading for you to trust him with an adult responsibility or task. "It's not like it's some dark secret; it's just something you don't need to talk about right now. And I'll back you up on that." His brows flexed down a bit and I knew he was going into his fighter mode. "You know, I get real tired of people always talking about my cancer and asking me about it, or if they don't know about it, asking me to explain. And I don't want to talk about it." He looked at me for recognition.

I smiled empathetically, thinking about how he'd lied to some woman once in a grocery store line who was prying, asking him, "Where'd you get those scars?" with that look on her face that had nothing to do with compassion or empathy but unequivocally communicated, *yuck, tell me how that happened, so I know not to let it happen to me.* "Car accident," he'd said flippantly to cut her off. When we left, he looked back at her and called out, "Drive safely," then smiled broadly to show his scarred gums. He then dropped his row of false teeth onto his tongue. She looked shaken, and we both broke into laughter when we got outside: a laughter all the more liberating because it was shadowed by such pain and sadness and fear.

I looked at him mischievously now, my turn to reassure him. "Yeah, maybe we should make cancer our little secret too. They don't have to know." He smiled and his brows visibly arched up, back to where they belonged. I restarted the car and pulled back into traffic as we commenced to conjure up elaborate and silly explanations for Peter's scars, imitating our parents and relatives, teachers and neighbors.

"I've never seen a boomerang do that kind of damage," Peter imitated Mr. Baines, our septuagenarian ham radio aficionado neighbor, while shaking his head back and forth.

"I told him not to work on the carburetor wearing his tie," I mimicked my mother. "Lord, finding him out there, his whole face sucked into the fan belt—oh, it gives me the chills. . . ."

Then he was imitating an anchorman on the eleven o'clock news: "A Walnut Creek teenager with a zit the size of Rhode Island was rushed to the hospital today after he attempted to take matters into his own hands, only to lose nearly a fifth of his face in the process."

We both stopped abruptly then, smiling faintly before falling silent. We even shocked *ourselves* at some point. But making jokes meant we were working together again. I was glad that he was the first one I'd told, and that he knew it. He was like the first face I'd seen after waking from unconsciousness or the coma of middle-class life. I realized then, as I maneuvered my way onto the Bay Bridge, the vast expanse of water opening up hundreds of feet below, that in wanting him to live and fighting to help him do so all these months I had learned—and he was my teacher—that I wanted to live too. That was what was different. My life had been a cocoon of fitful sleep until he got sick. At first, when I saw Peter get "bagged" too, I'd cynically believed my tragic outlook would finally be vindicated. But he'd shown a colorful wing, and I'd stopped thinking and just watched. I remembered then what he'd said to me, not long after the bad news of his first biopsy results, when I'd asked him if he were afraid.

"Well, yeah, but I've been dealt this hand, so now I gotta play it." It was a cliché, but one that people rarely had the courage to truly live up to. I, for one, had in effect thrown my cards back—had forfeited—and had been sitting out the game. Suddenly, there was a bad hand next to me and the player kept right on playing, so I sat up and noticed. Peter displayed a kind of grace in playing his hand out so conscientiously and so calmly, despite the sighs of all the surrounding players. He turned out to be the big brother I'd always wished I'd had.

He showed me by his example how I too could make a go of what I'd surrendered to as a hopelessly flawed hand.

Cancers and queers, and all of them butterflies; my life a cocoon of fitful sleep. He showed me the route out. He showed me in blood and scars; he drew me a map under his eyes, across his own flesh.

∞ IV

For me it really began with the sausage.

I hadn't expected it. I'd been mildly alarmed at how long the surgery had taken. We'd been milling around the hospital all day. When they finished, it had been eight hours, which seemed like an awfully long time to just pull out a splinter. What did we know about the tendrils of tumors?

We'd rushed down to the Post-Op Recovery Room, with its big heavy doors, ominous, like the gateway to the whole grave drama that would ensue. The color left our faces when we saw him. He was barely conscious, and attached to his face where they'd removed the tumor was a sausage of human flesh, cylindrical, bloody, greasy, with coarse, short, bristly stitches sticking out all over it, holding it to his cheek. It led down across his chin and then vanished into a thick padding of bandages on his chest. We were shocked. What the hell was going on? The doctor had said nothing about this when he'd explained the surgery earlier. Had they mixed him up with someone else? My mother had a look of utter horror on her face and began to cry. My father was composed, assuring us everything could be explained, as it was soon enough by a nurse who'd heard my mother's sobs and come to the rescue. She explained the live skin graft that had been pulled from his chest: A *live* skin graft meant that all the skin, right down to the muscle, was lifted up but kept connected so that it would have a blood supply. Then it was stretched, in Peter's case, from his chest up to his face, and finally reattached there. So it was in fact attached in two places, a sort of bridge of flesh, the idea being that this tissue from his chest would replace his cheek, which had been removed, leaving "nothing to work with," as the doctor would later explain. When the graft "took" a few weeks from now, they would unroll the flesh they didn't need and place it back on his chest, where it and the surrounding tissue—supplemented by additional skin grafts lifted from his thighs and shoulders—could be stretched together to fill in what was taken away to make up his cheek. It was ghastly, and more than any of us had expected or were prepared for.

We all commenced to speak reassuringly to Peter, but he was more or less unconscious. He heard us though, knew we were there—which was all that really mattered anyway—but he couldn't communicate or make sense of anything. He muttered dreamily and fell back to sleep.

We walked out dejected and a little miffed. The doctor had only told us he was removing the tumor, and we had wrongly assumed it was maybe the size of a grape or a raisin. What we hadn't understood was that it was fibrous, like mildew, a branching, spidery growth with tendrils throughout his cheek. They'd pulled up his chest because they'd fully excavated one whole cheek, along with half his palate, six teeth, half his nose, and a few pieces of cheekbone. We'd learn all those details in time. These doctors went about it like the Pentagon. They'd tell you they won the battle but never mention the civilians actually killed, the schoolhouses and hospitals leveled, the landmines left behind that decapitated small children playing in the fields. You'd get to find all that out for yourself. But it wasn't as though we could complain or send him back to have it redone. That tissue was gone, bagged up and pumped into the bay or wherever they dispose of such horrors.

At a loss, we went off to eat at a little bistro while Peter regained consciousness. My father and I spent all of dinner reassuring my mother, pointing out the miracles of science, acting like a couple of overconfident med students or politicians, avoiding the painful specifics for feel-good generalities, half the time making things up.

"He's like a house under construction. It never looks like it will end up," I lamely offered.

"Grace, think of how a black eye looks. He'll be back to normal in no time," my father attempted. Then: "It's the latest way they have of doing it; we're lucky that Peter's at a cutting-edge facility where all the latest techniques are used." We were winging it while she remained silent and withdrawn.

I was surprised he was so talkative actually, but I could see her silence was making him worried and he was filling the empty space with words. They were both morphing before my eyes. She only picked at her salad, sighing now and again as if to appreciate our efforts but not changing her withdrawn demeanor in any significant way. As she turned over the tomatoes and spinach leaves on her plate, I half-feared she'd discover some sort of horrific hot dog in there and then we'd have to go into overdrive to combat that omen. My father had a steak, which he cut apart and wolfed down enthusiastically. I was horrified and hoped my mother wouldn't chance upon the thought I was now entertaining. I kept talking right along with my father, not having much of an appetite and just drinking wine and eating bread. *This is my blood, take it and drink it; this is my body, take it and eat it . . .*

Something about the restaurant made me mad. I'd left my brother up the hill in some kind of basement—a castle dungeon—muttering and bloody, while I wiped my mouth with a linen napkin and sipped red wine among the healthy and contented of the city, who all seemed suddenly like complacent dolts, if not cannibals. I said I thought we should have eaten in the hospital cafeteria.

"The food is horrid up there," my father protested. But it wasn't the food I meant. Or was it? I *wanted* to be eating lousy food in an unpleasant auditorium of screeching, metal-legged chairs and laughing orderlies so as not betray him. But, as it turned out, there would be plenty of opportunities to partake of the hospital cafeteria's fare. Peter wouldn't be going home anytime soon after that operation. And then he'd be back again and again.

"He'll never be the same," she said then, not to be distracted by food or our attempts at softening the blow.

"Grace, come on, sure he will. They'll fix him up like new." But what he said fell flat and he knew it as he said it. She'd said what we'd been avoiding thinking or uttering. This wasn't going to be a little scar across his handsome face that gave him some kind of swaggering, sexy mystique. They'd taken his pedigree, deposed him of his prince-dom. Cancer was a bullet that had suddenly become a bomb.

"He's been disfigured by it," she repeated, looking at us blankly. My father and I fell silent then, breathed deep, and said nothing. "I don't know if I can take this," she added ominously.

CR V

He'd called me two days after we'd met in the radiation clinic waiting room, and he asked me if I wanted to hang out. I nervously agreed, wondering what I'd do if he came on to me. I wasn't ready, I told myself. I also told myself I was overdue. *Let's just see,* I finally concluded. After I'd hung up the phone from his invitation, I'd picked it up again and asked the operator for the San Francisco AIDS Foundation, from whom I requested a packet of safe-sex information.

Vince and I met at a coffee shop south of Market Street, in an artsy run-down neighborhood not far from the Baldwin Arms, which was just a few blocks north in what was essentially skid row. He was pacing out in front of the café when I arrived, smoking a rolled cigarette, in a pair of baggy gray Dickies, black Converse hi-tops, and a white T-shirt that read That's Mr. Faggot to You in red and pink letters. I felt like a nerd suddenly, in my standard-issue Levi's blue jeans and preppy, wrinkled oxford shirt. What did he see in me? Maybe it was just physical attraction after all and I was a fool to be falling for him. I felt like a chump in his company. What was it like to be a man who accepted his queerness? I wondered. He seemed heroic, courageous, alive in a way I'd decided not to be or hadn't had the guts for. I felt like a coward. And as such, I'd have to intercept the mail for the next week, not wanting to explain a manila envelope full of instructions on anal intercourse and rimming to my mother.

Attraction is a strange thing. I could list all the places I tried to find the essence of Vince's beauty—its source—in those last few steps I traversed walking toward him: the big, sleepy, brown-black Sicilian eyes; the way his lower lip hung out; the stubble on his chin, next to the soft, greenish, pale olive skin; the protruding Adam's apple; the slightly tanned nape of the neck and the little buds of hair there that were growing back from his last haircut; the kanji tattoo graffitied below his perfect little ear; his slouchy, bony shoulders; the knobby elbows and the long aquiline fingers and their flat nails; each crease across those fingers, the wider knuckles . . .

I cleared my throat, smiled, and nervously said, "Hi." He smiled back, but he looked a little preoccupied, like something was bothering him. "Neill," he said and flicked his cigarette into the street. Then he turned to open the café's door, and in we went.

I was excited by his deep voice as he ordered coffee, my heart rapidly beating along with the techno music playing from the speakers. He had an endearing, defensive way of acting casual when I could tell he was somewhat nervous, perhaps even a little upset. Vince seemed to be on his best behavior today, polite and quiet. Compared to his spirited performance of a week ago, he now appeared almost reserved. The contrast once again aroused me, that range of his. I realized I was hardly even acquainted with him, though his frankness at the clinic made me feel I'd known him for months, if not years. My heart kept up its accelerated beating, an odd mixture of joy, relief, excitement, and fear. He'd look at me, and whatever looked out of his eyes was more than just desire or interest—it was like some kind of challenge, like our eyes were having some metaconversation our personalities weren't privy to.

"Here," he barked, turning from the counter and handing me my cup of coffee. He was looking past me now, over my shoulder, scanning the room for a free table. As I looked down to take the coffee cup, I saw the scars—running up the undersides of both arms—long, pink, and jagged. Beyond the initial shock of them, I was relatively unfazed. Peter had given me a "So what?" attitude about scars and near death—not for lack of sympathy, but because they'd become so commonplace of late. In fact, Vince's scars had the odd effect of making me feel closer to him: they represented one more thing I had considered myself but had never had the guts to do. He'd apparently done so in rather dramatic fashion. I quickly averted my eyes, not wanting to cause him any discomfort. Not that I believed it would. I was in fact sparing *myself* the discomfort of hearing him explain it all in that blunt way he had.

A couple was leaving from the corner by the window, so we hustled over to take their table. Sitting down, I clumsily asked him how he was feeling at the same time he'd begun to ask me how far I'd come from home. We both smiled. He took the initiative and restated his question. I was embarrassed to admit I'd driven in from the suburbs where I was now living with my parents. I was careful to explain that it was only because of Peter that I'd left my place in Berkeley.

I asked him how he was feeling—to change the subject and out of politeness, being that I'd met him at a hospital, after all. He looked fine and answered as much, as if to challenge me with *Why wouldn't I be?* Radiation didn't take as much out of you as chemotherapy did, I knew that, but still it seemed the right thing to say to somebody who was in a serious medical situation.

That's not how Vince saw it, of course. He was the antithesis of a conscientious cancer patient like Peter. For Vince, cancer was an inconvenience, the latest catastrophe in a long line of troubles. It wasn't any more or less important than the job he'd lost, his monstrous family, the grim reality of living in a residential hotel on skid row. He was clearly living by his wits and day to day.

"If I die, who cares?" he said boldly. "But I'm not planning on dying just yet. And besides, it's not like I'm some porn star; I can live minus one ball." It was hard not to laugh, but I could see his humor had an edge that made laughter a risky response, so I just listened. "They tell me my prognosis is good. I only have a few more treatments and then a CAT scan and I'm either a goner or done with it all." He asked me if I wanted more coffee and got up to get us both another cup, obviously uncomfortable with the topic. I found myself admiring his matter of factness, while at the same time concerned at how cavalier it sounded. He was a far cry from the tenuous day-to-day struggles at home—my mother's tears and worrying, my father's black humor and now-constant gardening.

"Oh, Lord!" she'd wail whenever Peter complained of pain or bumped his cheek while brushing his teeth or whatever. I'd come running to the scene like a cop, ready to mediate and deflate the situation, attempt to calm Peter's frustration and my mother's anxiety.

"Geez, just leave me alone," his hands shooing her.

"Are you all right? Let me see; did you break the stitches?"

"I'm fine!" He'd turn angrily away momentarily before turning back to her with renewed patience and even some appreciation, letting her examine his healing scars, if for no other reason than because it calmed her to do so and he knew she meant well.

"Everything OK?" I'd venture upon arrival as Peter commenced to reassure me, and I joined him in reassuring our mother. This was "women's work," as my father saw it, so he waited in the TV room for the report, which it was my job to give.

"He bumped his cheek, Dad. Nothing. He's fine," I halfheartedly imparted, flopping down on the couch next to his big leather chair. He'd rarely respond, but I knew he appreciated me keeping him in the loop in the only way he seemed able to stay in it: from a distance.

When Vince returned with our refills, he asked me what I was interested in and so I answered, "Books," and we talked on and on about them, arguing at times, agreeing at others, but mostly sharpening our own visions with each other's insights. I may not have lived nearly as much as him, but I'd certainly read as much. My heart was beating fast again, not just because of my physical attraction to him but for the sort of dovetail of our minds. It felt like a precious stroke of luck to meet a mind so recognizable and familiar. I never had before.

When he was talking about Burroughs, Vince mentioned that he'd been a junkie, which alarmed me (not only its unknown quality and hint of danger and death, but its express-lane connection to HIV infection—he was both gay and had been shooting up). Then again, it just fed my romantic image of him. He referred as well to his troubled childhood, which consisted mainly of the "old kidfucker," as he called his father, and the "serious cunt," a moniker for his mother. Grim, even sinister, but that was exactly what my world had never been and what Vince had somehow suggested to me from the moment I'd first heard about him from Peter. Oddly or not, it fascinated me.

There was a wind stirring up the purple leaves of the Japanese plum trees on the sidewalk outside, and we watched the branches whipping around. He gulped the last of his coffee and, jittery from its effect, blurted, "Wanna walk?"

I hesitated, tentative again, always turning to look back, second-guessing the road I'd ventured down. There was never anything behind me when I looked, but still things were happening fast and I felt I needed to at least stop for a second while I digested the kid-fucker, the cunt, junk, and the rather boisterous awakening of my dormant sexuality. Then there were those lovely scars that were currently laid out on table so brazenly I had to swallow yet another of the lumps that kept rising to my throat. Maybe I'd had enough for one day, I considered. The panic I'd felt at the radiation clinic seized me momentarily.

"Uh, I got stuff to do today. I should be going."

"Like what? Where are you going?" He looked suddenly hurt, exhibiting once again that maddening and yet irresistible contradictory visage of his. I looked in his sensitive—and somewhat angry—eyes. He wasn't someone you'd ever be able to lie to, not even a white lie. I was a bad liar anyway.

"I don't know. I've got a bunch of stuff to do—a lot of places."

He said "OK," in a clipped tone, and rolled one shoulder, looking away. Clearly, he had picked up that it was a dodge and a bluff. He looked back at me and smiled. "Well, I guess this is it then . . ." But what he was really saying was *All right, be that way. Go ahead and lie.*

Something about that disarming response made me go beyond the limits I normally set for myself. So I took it back, as I suppose he knew I would. "But I can do it all tomorrow, I guess." Thus I set into motion a kind of tension that would continue between us for as long as we both knew each other—and still now, beyond our mutual loss, into the strange personal interior worlds of memory and dream where no one ever truly vanishes—of him coaxing me, and of me, after hesitating, reluctantly following along, a seemingly unwilling accomplice.

We clambered out of the café and onto the sidewalk, throwing on our coats and hunkering down against San Francisco's afternoon wind. We navigated the traffic-congested commuter speedways that crisscrossed the old warehouse section of town and before long had made our way south a handful of blocks to where the streets were once again empty and rarely traveled—potholed, abandoned to the past and to the homeless. Down the empty alleyways between old brick warehouses we rambled, kicking cans along and holding forth on literature, exploring together the bleak and quiet beauty of what had always been my favorite part of town. It reminded me of the mountains and the wilderness: its towering brick walls like sheer cliffs, smokestacks like stone minarets, and the downtown high-rises in the distance lined up like a range of snow-capped peaks. The scattered, broken concrete and rubble were like boulders and scree; enormous fetid puddles in vast, weed-choked fields hinted of alpine lakes in big silent meadows. There were bigger shadows there, wider empty spaces, no one in sight—only Vince.

And Vince filled it. He flowed into it like water; he infused it with himself as he told me about his years hopping trains, recounting all the derelict rail yards so much like those we wandered through now. He was the beaten-up, bent flower surviving among the ash heaps, the loping stray dog we spied ducking under a fence and trotting off across a field. He had the same sort of presence—a vitality among the ruins, an assertion: *still, this lives, this is strong, this is spring and color and life for its own sake*—down among the empty caverns where the floating seedpods of dandelions flitted in dust motes like mirages or lost stars, exiled from the night sky and thus the sentimental collective dreams that made them the subjects of lies.

Vince told me he'd lived for two years on the railroads, traveling from city to city, picking up jobs, living in old houses with students and struggling artists in one up-and-coming former slum after another.

"How come you kept moving?" I fed him questions, more to keep him going than because I really wanted specific answers. I just suddenly wanted him to tell me his whole story.

"Shit would happen—people, roommates, jobs. It all piles up and you've gotta make a break to save yourself." I'd never made a break, but I started to wonder if he was mine, so I nodded in recognition. It sounded romantic to me, since my tactic when things piled up had been to withdraw inward or to go off to the mountains if I went anywhere, from which of course I'd always return. I had never stepped off a cliff, and Vince had stepped off one after another. I suppose Peter, or I should say his cancer, had pushed me off one in these last months and so now I was fascinated with all things falling or fallen.

"What did you do jobwise?" I persisted in my questioning.

"Different things. I've worked at every fucking chain store there is: Blockbuster, Pizza Hut, Tower Records, Virgin—the fucking Gap, believe it or not," he laughed. "I worked in places where I liked the merchandise. And I don't mean discounts," he grinned. "I stole a lot of stuff, so that got me fired sometimes. But usually I just got sick of people—customers, bosses, politics." I just nodded and he kicked a stone in disgust.

"Did you go off on some of your bosses?"

He laughed and then snapped, "Hell yeah," and gave me a big self-satisfied grin. "I'd only do it when there were a lot of people around so I could watch them squirm and try to save face—handle the situation." He rolled his eyes and guffawed. "Vengeance." Then he furrowed his brow and looked angry. "The fucking inane hierarchies of capitalism." Of course I saw his point. I'd had those kinds of jobs at chain stores, so it was hard not to agree. I'd always seen it as something to get through, so that you'd never have to come back to it—like school, the dentist, whatever. If I'd been sad and beaten, I'd also been pragmatic.

"Well, beyond all that crap, what do you want to do?"

He stopped then and looked at me. "You mean, like, with my life?"

"Well, yeah," I chanced, but I already wanted to take it back, thinking I might be putting him on the defensive.

But he looked away, defusing the tension with an almost offhand remark: "I don't know. Maybe go to film school." It had the sound of something that would never happen. I briefly entertained the idea of Vince in an academic setting, but all I could imagine were classroom tirades and expulsions after all he'd just told me. Then again, he'd probably do beautifully on the set from what I'd heard of the auteurs of Hollywood.

"Have you done any college?" I probed further.

"No, are you kidding? I dropped out of high school, took the GED." That put film school even farther beyond his grasp, I quickly calculated, but what really surprised me about his answer was how a high school dropout had become as articulate and well read as he was. But then, it was apparent he was some kind of autodidact, and it was also clear he had a natural intelligence that made me sure the reasons for his dropping out weren't related to his wits. Something shitty had happened to Vince—that was easily assumed, and he'd alluded to it besides. Probably lots of things. I thought back to those names he had for his parents: the "old kidfucker" and the "serious cunt." All I'd really needed to do was fill in the blanks. But, like his scars, it didn't seem a line of questioning fair to pursue. So I wondered and waited.

"What about you?" he turned to me, curious or defensive—I couldn't tell which.

"Well, I don't know. I mean right now I'm sort of taking a leave from school for a while to help with Peter and stuff." He nodded his assent. "I'm doing some temp work—office stuff—near where I live," I added apathetically.

"Oh, man, office work really sucks. I did that once."

"What happened?" I couldn't imagine him in a coat and tie talking spreadsheets.

"Nothing really. They didn't like my tattoo, so I got dumped after the first day. Course they didn't have the balls to tell me that. They let the temp agency handle it." He imitated a faux-sincere receptionist giving him the send-off—"Mr. Malone, um—this is Tiffany from the agency? Uh, Fuckhole Incorporated has decided that you and their firm aren't quite a match. Can we offer you some other opportunities?"

"Yeah, that's it," I chuckled. And after a pause, I added, "Did you ever have a job you actually liked?"

I was surprised by the enthusiasm of his answer as I'd half-expected a blunt no. "Yeah, a couple places. You know, coffee shops, where there were cool people and I could play the music I wanted. The best though was when I worked in a deli in Buffalo owned by this radical dyke. I learned *soooo* much there about macrobiotic food and being a vegan and all that. I used to really be into my diet. Maybe I'll do that again," and he paused, sighing. "Anyway, she was a ball buster in the end—she drove everyone out, so I had a fight with her one day too. She threw a whole fucking potato salad at me—right in my face. There were customers there and everything." He shook his head back and forth and looked to the ground as if to say "what a shame." But I was conjuring it all up in my mind: an enormous bowl that she catapults at him as if thrusting a bucketful of water onto a fire. The vastness of the weight of the stuff hitting his face, gobs sliding off his chest and shoulders; glistening yellow potatoes, pimientos, and mayonnaise smeared across his tattoo—the image aroused me.

He brought me back. "I didn't react, believe it or not. I liked her actually. I respected her and what she was doing with the deli and stuff. I just left. She was having a bad day and I'm an asshole. Fuck her and fuck me. I was depressed at the time. I just didn't care, but I was grateful somehow for all I'd learned from her. It was like I refused to fight back. It was weird. Just a week or so before it happened, I'd gotten held up by a gang of ghetto kids. They surrounded me. It was fucking cold, January in Buffalo. They wanted money. I didn't have any, of course."

He had stopped to hoist himself up on an old cement loading dock, a cavernous empty warehouse gaping open beyond it. Yet his story was incomplete and it begged my question. "What did you do?"

"I told them I had no fucking money and would they leave me alone," he snapped, as if I should have figured it out. Now he was up on the loading dock and entering the blackness slowly, stealthily.

I stood in the weeds watching him, hesitant, not really wanting to follow him but still trying to get to the end of his story. "Weren't you scared?"

"I was depressed. I didn't care." Now his voice echoed as he entered the cavernous warehouse. "One of them pulled a gun and wanted to kill me because I was a smart-ass and because I had no money. The others seemed nervous. I just looked the guy with the gun in the eye—" and Vince turned, his eyes piercing mine from out of the darkness, as if to reenact it, before he continued, "—as he pushed the gun against my temple. And I said, 'Go ahead, do me a favor.'"

"Jesus, you're fuckin' crazy," I shook my head looking away.

"That's what they thought," he said, laughing, coming back down from the dock. "The dude with the gun didn't know what to do. His friends got really flipped out and were saying, 'Come on, let's get out of here—he's crazy; let's go.' But the kid with the gun wanted to blow me away. They convinced him not to. I really didn't care." His face was dead serious again. There it was again—that jump from one extreme expression to another that always left me on edge, unsure of where he was headed next or how he actually, truly felt.

We eventually ended up along the abandoned wharves and piers that loitered about San Francisco's waterfront—casualties of the city's industrial demise. We ended up walking all the way to the Golden Gate Bridge, sharing our stories and counting off the forty or so piers, one after the other, as we moved north along the waterfront, past the touristy garbage malls and faux-fish joints of Fisherman's Wharf, up over the hill of Fort Mason, and then down into the Marina where we walked along the green and marveled at the crass conformity of jogging yuppies and their embarrassingly fashionable outfits. Finally, it loomed before us, that monument to romantic suicide, which always stunned me with its massive and sudden beauty, and saddened me at the same time for the contradictions of its symbolism. Today, I felt it in my heart and smiled toward it, thinking it tells the truth—both sides of it—and that is an act of kindness and courage in this duplicitous, uncaring world.

"The bridge is all right. No amount of tourism can cheapen it," I had to say.

"Yeah, I like it; it's kinda Gothic. But they oughtta paint it black." That made me smile; it seemed almost comic, or corny.

We sat down together in the sand below it, looking up at the architectural glory of its underbelly above the windy, white-capped sea that rolled with big, smooth crests and troughs through the bay's inlet. And that's where he turned to me and asked me.

"So, are you queer, or . . . ?" as he threw a rock into the surf.

He caught me off guard, but what else is new. The drill bit of his eyes—I looked away, dodged him, said I didn't think so, half-hoping he'd press me further. I felt like a coward and I wanted him to help me tell him. I felt a lot of things, sitting under that indestructible bridge, host to a thousand deaths. I felt he held all the cards; I felt afraid and I felt like I was going to cry. And I felt for him a tenderness born of his story and the innocence of the question.

"Hmm," he said, and looked off to sea. Then he started laughing. He turned back to me and put his arm around my shoulders. "I think you are," he said, grinning, as a little kid would say it. I felt another lump rise up and shyly looked at the ground, caught off guard again as he hopped up and said, "Come on."

He didn't bring it up again as we scrambled up the hill to catch a bus and find a cheap Chinese restaurant. He didn't bring it up as we took another bus all the way back to the same coffee shop where we'd begun the day. And then he asked me if I wanted to get a beer. He didn't bring it up four beers into ranting and raving about how awful gay culture was as we sat drinking in the corner of a gay bar. "The music is bad; the whole muscle queen, faux-macho, forever young, what they call an aesthetic . . ." Then he suddenly said: "Can we go to my hotel now?"

"Yeah," I flatly responded. I surprised myself by my answer, but I felt giddy inside, like I'd found something in a store and there was only one left and it was something I must have so I have to rush home and get my money and return posthaste.

I hadn't said much for a while. I liked listening to him. And though part of me kept telling myself I should have been more afraid of him after listening to his sad and fruitless story—he was, after all, the kind of boy I'd been warned against for years—I felt strangely safer and safer the longer I was in his presence. Safe and secure, as I had felt at the hospital. Safe and warm among the ruins. In the doomed places, where hopelessness reigned, I found something better than hope: a world with no future. What relief I felt. The future had always been something to dread, and if I found a world without one . . .

Where do I sign up? My world felt like some kind of boring and average Hilton Hotel I'd been walking through. What if I just left? What if I just walked out one of those Emergency Exit Only doors that made you think twice? Why not, before I was abducted or dragged out by the death police like Peter?

"Bring it on," Peter always said as they rolled him into the operating room, half delirious under the anesthesia. It made me smile and I always felt good about that: if for some reason he died in surgery, a smile was the last thing he would have seen reflected back at him. Bring it on, then.

We walked several blocks back to the Tenderloin to his hotel, which was decidedly not a Hilton. It was a crowded and chaotic part of town, full of milling drug addicts and petty thieves, the greasy masses of the homeless, old black men and screaming transvestites, prostitutes and wronged women. The occasional Cambodian child would weave through it all on a bicycle, smiling, as twinkly-eyed Guatemalan boys sold crack on street corners. Vietnamese and Chinese gangsters, dressed in laundered and pressed black, their hair slicked with mousse, drifted down to do business. An assortment of mostly white bohemians hurried down the streets in cheap but fashionable clothes, glistening piercings, and opaque tattooed arms, in marked contrast to the locals who had no dreams to draw upon their skin, knowing they'd likely never escape this grim ghetto—or maybe they too were just free of the future. If I could have dreamed a world of Jack Kerouac, this was it, and I was ironically—or not so ironically—elated to be heading for a seedy hotel, deep down in the "forlorn rags" of the "railroad earth" from which this magical boy had come, having surfaced only momentarily in that hospital waiting room to fetch me and take me back below to this broken-down Atlantis that dazzled like no palace above ever could.

At the hotel desk, a small booth encased in bulletproof glass, I was refused entrance.

"No guests!" the Arabic clerk barked in his heavy accent, not making eye contact.

Vince irritably pleaded, and the murmuring voices on the plastic lobby chairs began to rise in annoyance. A tattooed teamster of a man began to berate Vince.

"Who the fuck do you think you are? Rules are rules!" he bellowed.

"Fuck you; stay out of my business!" I was shocked by Vince's rejoinder. After all, he was just a skinny little kid. But the burly man just mumbled some insult and ambled away, happy to have made his point for whatever satisfaction it gave him, and in some streetwise way respectful of Vince who, though scrawny, glared with the eyes of someone who would kill you with his bare hands or, failing that, might be packing a weapon. He seemed completely fearless, and I was glad in that moment that I was his friend and not his enemy, although it occurred to me for an instant that he might turn on me one day too.

"C'mon, man, just for a while," Vince continued pleading to the man in the booth. "I'm not one of these low-life losers," he rolled his shoulder, referring to the heavyset man he'd just snapped at. Before the Arab could respond, his head already shaking no, Vince added, "And look at my friend; look how harmless he looks—he's some kid from the suburbs. Does he look like a junkie or a crack head to you?" He raised his voice: "Look at him!" I felt like a chump then, having been suddenly drafted into representing everything I hated about my life.

But it worked. "Twenty minutes!" the Arab barked impatiently, busying himself with some receipts and not looking up.

"C'mon," Vince yanked me by the sleeve, and we hurried toward the elevator.

It too was metal and plastic, which made me think of the hospital. All unfortunate places of refuge tend toward that antiseptic cheap decor, it seems, which made me think it had something to do with disease. Disease preyed upon people here as surely as it did at the hospital. You could hear the hacking coughs of TB, see the scabby arms and faces of the drugged. Who knew what tumors grew fibrous along the water pipes in the bowels of this building, rat infested and cockroach crowded.

He yanked the old cage door open at Floor 6 and we stepped out.

"Shut the fuck up!" Vince snapped as he walked by his neighbor's door. "That guy's always talking to himself," he added for explanation. I was silent, taking it all in, and realizing I was falling deeper by the fathom into his world as I traversed the grim inner sanctum of what Vince called home. I was excited and apprehensive both, but that could describe the whole day spent with Vince, so it wasn't anything new—it had just expanded tenfold and been populated with a cast of extras.

He opened the door to a tiny room with a green indoor/outdoor carpet and a single bed with a checkered orange bedspread on it. In the corner was a sink and next to it a little window that looked out on the alley and reflected in pulsing shimmers some yellow neon sign below. It was a Jack Kerouac wet dream, all right. I'd almost forgotten Vince was there as I took it all in, until suddenly he grabbed my shoulder and turned me around, locking his mouth over mine.

He disengaged himself as quickly as he'd kissed me and then moved to the bed.

"Sorry, I just had to do that," he cracked a lighthearted smile. I shyly smiled back, belying the thrill and my accelerating heartbeat.

"I'm tired; I need to take a nap," he informed me, sitting down to remove his shoes.

I continued to stand, weighing in my mind whether this was a clumsy come-on or the truth, something I would never wholly determine with Vince regarding anything. He was so boldly direct, so blunt, I always fell for what he said as the truth—and it usually was, even if I remained suspicious. After all, only liars tended to be as blunt as Vince.

He laughed at my trepidation. "Don't worry; I won't bother you. I just want to lie down for a while; that's all." But I wanted him to bother me, only I didn't know how to let him know. I watched him lie there, his arms behind his head, his eyes softly closed. I could see the enticing dark Sicilian hair in his armpits within the sleeves of his shirt. I studied him for a moment, taking in his beauty: the dark olive of the skin on his biceps, the softness of his lips under their chapped exterior, the little upturned nose, the mole on his neck and the tattoo, his Adam's apple. I marveled that it was all attached to *his* mind, and I shivered—almost ecstatically—remembering his voice. He opened his eyes then as if he'd read my mind. And I felt like a blank sheet of paper in need of a story—his black eyes were as dark and deep as ink wells; his body, pregnant with motion and muscle, had all the potential of a calligraphy brush. I wanted to bare my chest to him like an empty scroll and watch him fill it.

"Come on," he invited, patting the bed next to him. "Come over and lay down with me." I nervously approached and stiffly laid down next to him, but it was a small bed and, laughing, he pulled me close and hung on to me, saying, "Don't worry; you'll fall off if I don't hold onto you." He laughed again. "You don't mind if we cuddle a little bit?"

"No, no, it's OK," I timidly answered, excited but shy and unsure of myself.

I looked at him as he again closed his eyes, marveling at him. What was it that made him look so precious to me, so fragile? It had something to do with his lankiness, like a lab puppy, with that lazy mouth that hung half open, the childlike determination of his furrowed brow. He was like some little firebrand of a kid, completely fearless—you wanted to protect him from himself.

A wave of fear suddenly washed over me: about not really knowing him; this dismal and dangerous place we were in; his shady past and vague present; his being gay; my lack of experience and my attraction to him. I watched the lonely flicker of the yellow pulsing neon reflection; listened to the mutterings and clinkings in nearby rooms. I felt far from home. Was I ready for this? For any of this? Yet the feeling of being safe with him returned and reassured me, making the ominous wave subside. Others rose up: fears of rejection and of his anger; a fear of my own recent sense of abandon that I was letting flow unchecked, and of which he was a part. Yet each fear rose and fell as if on some new and distant shore, and something steadied and relaxed me. The room slid away slowly, like honey, as I dozed off in his arms.

I awoke suddenly, startled by the sound of a screech down the hallway, and found Vince cuddled up against my chest, looking peaceful in a way I could have never imagined possible. It made me long to hold him forever. I ran my hand through his bristly orange hair, and I knew what smile crossed my face: that sad, sorrowful smile of my mother taking her son up the hill to the high priests of medicine at the hospital, like some necessary sacrifice.

I suddenly had an urge to cry, as I smiled openly and intimately at a man in my arms, completely disarmed and trusting, when for so long I'd been told—and mostly it was I doing the telling—that such a thing was wrong or impossible. I imagined this feeling must be somehow as it would have been for people who had never seen their homeland or their real parents or some long-lost brother—and then, bingo, there they were.

Bang Bang Bang on the door and the Arab's voice shattered our intimacy: "Twenty minutes is up—come out of there!" It was taboo enough to be a secretive homosexual in a straight world, I thought; it felt doubly invasive to have someone banging down the door.

"You gotta go. Sorry," Vince explained, as he pushed me off the bed, a there's-nothing-I-can-do look on his face.

"He won't let me stay?" I half-whined.

"No, he won't!" Vince exclaimed loudly, so that it would be audible out in the hallway. He hopped up, opened the door, and stared boldly at the Arab. Then he turned to me. "Meet me at that same Chinese restaurant in a couple days, OK?" he asked, almost desperately.

"Yeah, sure. Friday?"

"Friday, six o'clock."

I hastily put on my shoes and hurried to the door. Vince grabbed my shoulder, stopping me, and gave me a quick peck on the mouth. I was taken aback that he'd done this right in front of the Arab, but that was Vince. Vince apparently had no shame about his homosexuality, and yet he seemed consumed with shame for the human race and his unlucky fate to be a member of it. I wasn't sure why, but that struck me as poetic and even fantastic—being gay as nobler than even being human. It certainly flew in the face of everything I'd learned or had ever heard. There was something grand about it. It was the beginning of an understanding that, far from being a curse, homosexuality to some people was a great blessing. If that was true for Vince, perhaps it could be true for me too.

I felt an odd happiness then listening to the tinny radio sounds that drifted out from behind closed doors as I followed the Arab down the dark hallway. I looked back before stepping into the elevator, and down there, lit up in the darkness by the reflecting alleyway neon, were dust motes, a fire escape—and, leaning into it, the silhouette of Vince, a darker form among the shadows.

ॐ VI

We got over the sausage, not to mention the huge triangle of exposed muscle and blood on his chest. He lay there with it for two weeks while my mother sat in the corner, knitting or reading. Sometimes she stared out the window, but only while he slept. When she did that, it worried me.

"You OK, Ma?"

She put on a smile to let me know it was nothing or she didn't want to get into it.

My role was Man Friday. I fetched her coffee or breath mints or things she'd forgotten in the car. I felt guilty about it and perplexed, but I actually liked it at the hospital. I didn't miss school or my freedom at all. I suppose I felt I had some value there, or maybe it was just that it was a simple situation in many ways. There were things that needed to get done and everyone appreciated you doing them—it was easy to be useful, to gain a sense of worth.

It was primarily a matriarchy as the nurses ran the day-to-day goings-on. The doctors were like Greek gods or celebrities who passed through now and again but really didn't know that much of what was happening on any social level within the ward. They were the accountants of physiology, the loan sharks of disease. People like my mother kowtowed to them, as did many of the patients' families. It was a whole investment strategy, an appeasement of the gods. Patients, for the most part, were skeptical, and the nurses were—well, jaded.

"Here they come. Look useful—oh, and pretty," Susan snapped sarcastically. She was my favorite of Peter's nurses, and she was referring to some approaching doctor with his gaggle of residents in tow, rounding the corner into the ward. "Hellos" and "how-are-you," waves, backslaps, and basic campaigning ensued as they breezed through to check in momentarily on each of their patients, on their way to the 10,000 other patients on the day's schedule.

Susan had a nose ring and a short, spiked punk haircut; she was the nonconformist of the nursing staff. There were a number of part-time nurses—aging mothers who'd already raised their children; old black women with stories; the occasional male nurse with the gay twinkle in his eye—but the three young women, among whom was Susan, were there every day. The other two were Colleen, the scrappy athlete/cheerleader type, freckled and smiling, and silent Anita, dark haired and dark eyed, a dignified, pious Catholic Filipina, wholly possessed of that quiet beauty that drives men crazy or to poetry—or to art and madness both. All three pretty much fell in love with Peter.

"Adjust those pillows, would you, Neill?" Susan asked as she prepared to re-dress his wounds.

"What do you say, Peter, you want me to use the XL catheter or are you gonna make yourself pee?" she teased him.

"No way, Susan. No catheter."

"I'll run the sink; I'll talk to you, Peter; we can do it," I encouraged him.

"There should be a quart of pee in there by now," Susan pointed out, looking at the pee bucket, her eyebrows raised. "If you don't pee, it's the catheter, and I only use the XL." She smiled a matter-of-fact, albeit sardonic smile, before turning back to some dressings on the rolling metal table next to her.

"I'll go get you some tea, how about that?" I asked Peter.

"OK," he muttered tiredly. "Please, Susan, give me an hour, OK?" She was concentrating on removing his chest bandages, her brows furrowed, enjoying teasing him, seeing how far she could take it.

"Well, Peter, are you just shy, or are you really stopped up?" she asked, not looking at him, concentrating on the delicate task of changing the dressings, with just a slight flicker of mischief in her eyes.

"I'm not shy," he perked up.

"That would be pointless, of course," she replied coyly, laying some new gauze across his bloody chest. "After all, I'm going to be giving you a shower next week when they close up this wound. I can't wait!" And she looked at him with her best vampire imitation as he blushed scarlet.

"Leave me alone," he groaned amiably.

"I can't; I've fallen in love," she stated dryly as she exited the room, with me following on my errand for tea, laughing at her flirting prowess.

In the hallway the wounded wandered, pushing their IV poles, smiling or wincing.

"Fuck, that wound of his freaks me out," she said to me in all seriousness over her left shoulder. "He's so fucking young!" she added, gathering up a pile of charts at the desk.

"Thanks for flirting around with him. I know it makes him happy," I offered.

"He's cute. Are you kidding?" she exclaimed as she disappeared into another room.

Colleen always arrived carrying an enormous shoulder bag. Of course, she had the big voluminous maternal key ring that she flopped like a dead fish on the counter—albeit a dead fish with scales of armor.

"Hi, Neill. How's our champ?" She was so jockish, and so damn maternal although she was only twenty-five. I felt like a little kid or a benchwarmer around her.

"He's getting stronger every day," I volunteered, at a loss for something original to say. I was corny in a way I could never be anywhere else. Cancer brings out the worst and the best in people, or some combination of the two that has an odd effectiveness. We had all become different people—our better selves, perhaps. I wasn't a misanthrope there, and my mother didn't nag or complain about anyone's behavior or whether the nurses' social skills were proper enough. Peter was full of determination and did whatever he could do—less casual and devil-may-care than his usual self. He was anxious to get up and walk but had to wait until they removed his skin graft and closed up his chest.

My father reverted to his coaching mode, as was to be expected. I'm not so sure that was *his* better self, but it did help in its way, curbing his usual eye-rolling cynicism which, considering, had become unpolitic.

I headed off to get Peter's tea and heard Colleen's loud faux-whine in the distance as she entered Peter's room: "Peter, how come you never call me?"

At night Anita would come—Anita, who prayed with him and who possessed a quiet mystery and serenity that Peter told me got him hard.

"I feel kinda bad. She holds my hand and says prayers and stuff, and I'm hard as a rock."

She's a pagan and doesn't know it. I understand it now. But all this came before Vince.

They bathed him; they dressed his wounds. They showed us how. He was the guru, the blessed one, the beloved, and the baby. We all came to know his body intimately, inside and out. They'd pulled back the very flesh on his chest, after all. We knew what was underneath. It was only momentarily upsetting.

In the end, I think his wounds made it easier to love him as they taught me something I didn't know about love. My mother knew it; mothers do. Love was a much more physical thing than I'd ever understood it to be. It lived where his fingers touched mine; it's what made the water bead up on his shoulders and roll off; it's what made his skin warm, glowing and soft. I'd always thought love was some feeling in the mind, but this was the physicality of love: the love of the body, so much simpler; so much more useful. It felt real, substantial, like proof—like what I needed. Cancer gave me that.

ℭℜ VII

When I walked into the Chinese restaurant to meet Vince, he looked surprised, putting down his dog-eared paperback—Durrell's *Justine.* (Wholly appropriate I'd find later. I should have noted it and gone out and gotten a copy to save myself the trouble of living it. But truly, it would have only seduced me further.)

"Wow, here you are. I didn't think you'd even show up," he said, acting pleasantly surprised.

"Why wouldn't I?" I replied, confused.

"After everything I told you?"

I shrugged my shoulders, felt brave for the very first time in his presence. I guess he scared most people away or, if not that, thought me so typically middle class that I'd likely bolt once I got a good dose of him.

We ordered tofu and eggplant in garlic, and he seemed cheerful, excited in an innocent way. His fortune cookie said he'd meet an interesting stranger; mine promised prosperity. Those kinds of prophecies were easy, but they still seemed appropriate in their trivial way.

After dinner, we walked; we talked about books and our pasts some more as we ambled down Haight Street, peering through the windows of closed and darkened shops selling the latest co-opted hippie fashions, greeting cards, or Guatemalan fanny packs. At a thrift shop, we peered inside at dusky treasures.

"If you could have one thing in this window, what would it be? Only one," I emphasized. There were colorful stained-glass Tiffany lamps; mannequins wearing housedresses from the 1960s; necklaces and earrings from someone's estate; rings from defunct marriages or someone's hippie youth when they'd flowered like the spring, before heading back to graduate school and normalcy. There were old silver picture frames, an antique iron, partial sets of golf clubs missing their comrades and an old pair of paratrooper boots. "I like the boots. What about you?"

"That diamond necklace, there, or whatever it is, cuz I could sell it for a good chunk of change." Vince was too mercenary to really enjoy this little diversion, I soon realized, but he was a good sport and we persisted, stopping at thrift store after thrift store, as Haight Street was lousy with them. By the time we got to the end of the street, we'd accumulated in our respective imaginations: Three pairs of shoes, an old black sweater, a handful of jewelry, two cameras, a Barbie, a tacky velvet picture of Jesus, eight CDs, and a glowing Virgin Mary statue. It wouldn't take a genius to guess who picked what.

"I need a drink," Vince eventually announced, and off we went to a hip little bar where we gulped and babbled the hours away, arguing over the merits of conceptual art, punk rock, and Andy Warhol.

Now that we were lit up, we marched up the hill into Buena Vista Park—not a great idea at that hour as skinheads and gay bashers were known to frequent it after dark. "Who says we're gay, and who says I'm not tougher than them?" was Vince's answer to my caution. His fearlessness was infectious. He seemed to know these places—a world I was unfamiliar with—I did things with Vince I'd never allow myself to do alone. With Vince, I was somewhere else, and so I trusted him to guide me. It was a wholly different world with different rules, different threats and dangers. I'd been warned of such people and places, sure, but nothing in my life had turned out as they'd told me; worse yet, much had just plain dead-ended. The old myths were just that—myths. With Vince it was time to see what was under this rock, the one they said never to turn over.

And then we kissed each other intently for a long time against a tree up there in the eucalyptus forest that was dappled with moonglow. He kept looking at me with that furrowed brow, as if trying to figure something out that only kissing me could uncover. I knew then he was interested in me somehow and wanted to get to know me, easing my doubts from the other night in the hotel. Could it be he saw something vast in my eyes too? I couldn't imagine how; I felt so constructed and dead next to him—an empty suburban office building after all its windows had been blown out with a cluster bomb named cancer. Yet I felt a growing confidence now and a tenderness between us that became easier with time; his tough-guy guard increasingly let down.

We eventually returned to the hotel via a raucous late-night bus, my mind racing with *this is it*. Vince had to haggle again with the Arab, but something was different about the exchange. Still, the Arab made no eye contact as he barked, "One hour!"

"Why'd he give us more time, Vince?"

"He knows we're fags." I was perplexed and gave Vince a questioning look. He repeated himself as he yanked open the elevator door and motioned me in: "He knows we're fags; he's being cool, get it?" He looked at me like I was naive. And he was right, because I didn't get it.

"Why would someone be nice to us because we were gay?" I persisted. Vince rolled his eyes with impatience and then explained to me what I would come to learn about places such as these.

"He trusts us now. Last time, how could he know? He just doesn't want people doing drugs or killing each other. But since you came back, and we complied to his twenty-minute order last time—and I kissed you—" now I knew why he'd kissed me in front of him—"he gets the picture and he knows we aren't doing anything that will get him in trouble. He doesn't care if we fuck, any more than whatever slumlord who owns this place does—as long as no one's paying anybody for it." I had to remind myself that I was in his world now—a world I'd been warned to stay away from, that was supposedly "worse." Yet no one cared if you were queer? Didn't think it a big deal?

"That's cool," I said, slightly awestruck at what I saw as the irony of it.

"Live and let live, Neill—ain't it grand?"

He paused to aim the key in the lock: it was dark enough in the hallway that it was hard to see any detail, so he waited for the neon's flash. The lock clicked, and Vince turned to me and smiled coyly.

"Wanna come in?"

"Yeah!" I said exuberantly. He grabbed my coat and pushed me playfully across the threshold.

Vince slammed the door shut with the heel of his shoe once we were inside and, grabbing my back and turning me around, he kissed me passionately as he pushed his hips into mine. I pulled at his clothes, but he stopped me, and then he went to the bed to take off his shoes. I followed suit, not knowing what to do or why he'd suddenly stopped me. He pulled down his pants, under which he wore a pair of white thermal long johns. He climbed into bed with his long johns and T-shirt on and said, "Come on." I was at a loss and confused, but I'd never done any of this before, so I followed his lead, confident we wanted the same thing and willing to comply since I hadn't a clue how to proceed. I stripped to my boxer shorts and T-shirt and climbed in, but he stopped me and pulled off my shirt, baffling me further since he'd kept his on.

"Sorry, but I never take my shirt off," he suddenly said.

"Why not?"

"I just don't. I'm skinny and I don't like people to see my chest."

"You're cute. I like how skinny you are . . ." I fumbled for some kind of appropriate response, hoping to reassure him and in so doing, get him to take it off. I was overwhelmed with a desire to be naked with him, but it wasn't to be.

"It's all about my dad. A long fucking story you don't want to hear." His brow furrowed, warning me not to pursue it.

I did anyway. "No, I do." He rolled his eyes.

I felt my lust wane and my tenderness for him well up in its place as I climbed into the bed and held him, looking into his eyes. "Vince, I really like you; I want to know all about you."

"No, you don't; believe me, you don't." He said it brusquely, as if he was bored by his own story, but I just continued to look at him. Eventually he settled back onto his pillow, rolling his eyes back as if to remember, and before long he began to tell the long sad tale of the origins of Vince. I laid on my back next to him and we both stared at the ceiling and its blotchy brown water stains flashing yellow with the pulsating rhythm of the neon sign outside, conjuring like film images from long ago and far away.

℘ VIII

There were plenty of reasons why I hated my big brother Paul. A lot of it was kid stuff, of course, and hate's too strong a word for it now. If the world had made just a tiny place for faggot boys I suppose our conflict may have never grown into the hideous monster it became. But there was but one road to follow if a boy ever hoped to be a man and it was lousy with sports, guns, fighting, and swagger. I pretty much botched them all, which was a source of endless shame for Paul, who didn't want to be associated with such a brother. He always thought it was his job to fix me, little right-wing conformist that he was. When I think of who Paul was, how could he not have hated me?

Maybe, though, he just loved me. Why else would he care?

Regardless of the underlying motives, he concluded me a hopeless cause at some point and simply disowned me. He had Peter, after all. After he'd made up his mind about me by my eighth birthday, he just told the other kids that I was adopted or had birth defects. I told myself I didn't care; it let me off the hook, after all.

The sad thing was I think I fell in love with him right around then. He was beautiful to me and, like Peter, everything a boy should be: athletic, tough, handsome, roguish, and unpredictable. It only made me hate him more. Paul was a battle I'd never win and a brother I could never disown. Fate even had the audacity of having him save my life once. His power over me seemed relentless, like a cruel god.

Yet Paul wasn't to be my first love. The lifeguard holds that distinction. I met him the very day I nearly drowned and Paul saved my life. I wonder sometimes if the lifeguard was simply at the right place at the right time. How I needed my brother's love that day, laid out on the dock coughing and choking, but all he did was hang back with his friends and mock me. He didn't even thump my back. He'd dragged me to the dock after I'd gone under not five feet from it, but that had been a job, one brother responsible for another.

The lifeguard was the only one who *really* touched me. He'd swum over from the beach, having observed the crowd that was gathering on the dock and staring down at my prone figure. I was on my side, coughing and blubbering tears, and I could see him approaching through my watery, obscured eyesight like a vision. He arrived with big, long strokes, his blond head bobbing above the water as he swam up, and lifted himself onto the dock in one fluid motion. He kneeled by me, patting my back, and asked me if I was OK as I collapsed into sobs. Then he reached out and held me to him.

The boys all began to talk over one another in the way of boys, recounting their frontline witnessing of the spectacle. Paul just glared and said nothing as the lifeguard looked me intently in the eyes, and told me he'd carry me back. He was big, brown eyed, and muscular, and he had the beginnings of a beard, with those patchy dark spots on his chin and upper lip where he'd shaved. I remembered thinking he looked different somehow, as if he was part man and part boy, some kind of magnificent bridge arcing across the grim abyss that separated the two just-as-grim and disappointing poles of maleness.

He climbed down the ladder into the water and gently reached out, asking me to come into his arms. He told me to put my hands on his shoulders and ride piggyback while he swam us in. I followed his instructions, clasping fast to his shoulders, slightly frightened of and fascinated by the otherness of him—a boy who was not a boy—in the dark hair peeking out from his armpits. I rested my head on his warm, smooth back and finally felt secure, contented to ride that way forever.

I must have looked a sorry Venus on the half shell as he carried me to shore, but my heart was full. We swam slowly in, and he'd ask me now and again if I was OK, and I'd answer quietly, "Yes." When we got to the shallow water, he touched down on the bottom and told me I could walk up to the beach with him now. I held onto his hand and looked up at him as we emerged before the crowd of suburban mothers who had gathered on the shore to find out what was happening, alarmed and all a little too rotund in their colorful one-piece swimsuits. I instinctively turned as we got nearer the women and held furiously onto his right leg, which was thin but muscular and sparsely covered with dark hair. I didn't want to let him go. I knew if I did he might disappear forever. He wasn't like anyone I'd met or known before: he wasn't a kid; he wasn't a man; he was something else. Finally, my true big brother, come down, like they said God did, from that higher place called high school. He stood still with his hand on my head as my mother ran across the sand, parting the women, to meet us. She thanked the lifeguard profusely and took me by the shoulders. She pulled me, but I resisted, holding firm to his leg. He leaned down calmly and said it was OK; it was my mother.

"Little boy, your mother will take care of you," he had gently implored, squatting down to my level and searching out my downcast, shame-faced eyes. I didn't know how to say I didn't need her or any of them anymore—that I needed him to take care of me. It certainly didn't feel funny at the time, but what a comic scene it must have been. A little film noir femme fatale I must have looked, clinging to him, not wanting to go to Mommy, like Bogart and Bergman in *Casablanca:* "You're getting on that plane . . . where you belong . . ." But I had none of Bergman's composure or grace and began to wail. I knew I was supposed to feel secure with my mother, but suddenly it seemed clear—though I was at the same time horrified and guilty to feel it—that I didn't care if I ever saw her again.

But whatever he said, I would do, and I sniffled hard and released him. I watched him walk away as my mother dragged me up the sand to our towel like some territory from which she'd feel safe to assess the damage. For the next hour, as she fretted and made me eat and drink, I watched the lifeguard in his chair: the red shorts of him; the bright, shining blond hair; the tan and smooth chest, and the hairy legs that made him not a boy; the friendly way he answered questions; the other high school kids who stopped to greet him. One blonde girl lingered awhile, smiling shyly, and I figured what anybody would figure. *I wish I was her,* I thought sadly. Yet I wanted to be him at the same time. At least *with him* somehow. I wanted to be on his back, riding through the sky or sea, forever being asked if I were all right, and "Don't worry; I'll carry you."

Paul didn't come in from the dock. He simply waved to my mother as if to say he was just fine. Peter played peacefully nearby, digging a little hole in the sand with his red shovel and talking to himself. I felt glad for my little brother then, sure he wouldn't revel in my latest misfortune as I knew Paul was sure to do. I vowed that day I'd never hurt Peter again, so that if I ever had to save him or help him he wouldn't have any reason to regret that I had. What a sorry offer of love, and yet what a fitting prophecy it's turned out to be.

And since I'm Man Friday, I had to go to the airport to pick up Paul.

I hopped in my old VW and, as I got it started, realized I hadn't been alone with Paul since he'd left for college five years ago. On his occasional holiday visits I'd only seen him with the whole family. If he came at all, he stayed a day or two at the most and I gave him a wide berth. I guess you could say we were estranged.

Paul was waiting for me on the curb in front of the baggage claim as I pulled up. He looked slightly different. Still, he had the black shock of hair—boyish—and the ice blue eyes. He looked a little heavier, a little more hunched in the shoulders, a little more tired than I'd remembered him. All told, he was handsome, as he'd always been handsome. Handsome and right—the worst possible enemy.

"Hey, how are ya?" he quipped as he opened the door, but without smiling, like I'd seen him an hour ago. He didn't smile or look like he missed me. He asked me how school was (it wasn't), and I asked him about his work for the congressman. It was all just polite bullshit. But he seemed suddenly smaller to me, shrunken. What had I ever been afraid of? Well, he'd been bigger than me once and the world had been smaller.

I tried. "Man, it's been a long time, Paul," I said with as much friendly enthusiasm as I could muster. "What, a couple years?"

"Something like that," he muttered, looking out the window.

"How do you like it back East?" I tried again.

"It's all right. Cold."

"Yeah, I guess."

"You should change lanes; this guy's not gonna speed up," he said, pointing out a sluggish Lexus floating in front of us like an apparition. So I changed lanes, and as I did, I felt that old longing for our fruitless interminable war to end.

"So how's Peter doing?" he asked in a businesslike tone.

"He's OK, holding up well. It's pretty hideous, his skin graft." I described it to him and he didn't flinch but just nodded. Maybe when he saw it, something in him would change too.

"How much farther?" he asked.

I looked at him as if to say, "Well, that's up to you, Paul." Sometimes I thought fighting was the only relationship we had. "Half hour," I answered in a clipped tone.

We didn't say anything else. I thought of Chief Joseph then and agreed with him, perhaps understanding for the first time why he'd been so famously and oft-quoted.

"This is it," I said cheerily as we turned into the hospital garage. We parked and rode the elevator in silence. I asked him if he'd been to this hospital before. He said no. When we got to Peter's room, my parents stood up smiling, and Peter tried to grin from the bed. I said, "Here he is," referring to Paul and went to sit down, wishing he wasn't there or wishing he *was,* or some combination of the two. I sat quietly while they filled him in and he spoke cheerfully to Peter, calling him a "stud," saying, "You'll be back on the basketball court in no time."

He was staying for the weekend. I kept myself contained. He argued with my parents and deflected most of their questions while he hovered around Peter talking sports and girls. *He'll be thirteen to the bitter end,* I thought. I was relieved when he finally left. I realized I could only *wait* for Paul; there was really no way to pursue him. And that realization revealed to me something about Peter, which nowadays tended to reveal something about love: Peter *let* me love him. My heart having filled these last weeks had nothing to do with him loving me; it was the other way around: I didn't need or want Paul's or Peter's love so much as I wanted them to accept *my* love. Peter seemed to be saying, "Sure, bring it on," and that broke my heart in some crazy way that I hadn't understood until right then, with Paul among us, who had always preferred I keep my love to myself. But love was a loop, wasn't it? Love was a loop like the river, the clouds, and the sea.

ⅭⱾ IX

Vince told me sad tales of Buffalo that night—about its dark winter skies and bare-branched trees, its vast potholed grocery store parking lots, abandoned steel mills and forlorn glass towers rigid in an icy sky. He described the cold, filthy slush along the roadways after snow that cars sloshed through and made a mess of. He recalled too-warm and too-crowded houses during those winters when his parents fought with kitchen utensils—his mother chasing his father with a spatula or a wooden spoon and beating him on the back. Always, his father turned his back to her onslaught, almost stoically at first, moving away, his voice coldly warning her to cease. The children always stopped whatever they were doing, swallowed. All eyes turned toward the kitchen—its Victorian, flowered wallpaper, its sentimental ducks and home-sweet-home insipidness. They're terrified by their mother's wrath, which they can't understand, and full of dread at their father's inevitable breaking point, which always came when he turned finally to face her, his jaw cold and firm, his eyes blank. Then he swung his fist into their mother's holy, yet crazed, face. She screamed and fell, wailing, and they all froze momentarily then bolted as their father ordered them to their rooms.

"One time when I was five, I made the mistake of running up to my mom to console her as she huddled on the ground crying." He turned his head angrily away then before continuing. "The kidfucker clocked me too. They were like pimp and whore, those two. She fuckin' hit me right after he did."

In the basement was a rec room and a bathroom where his father took him while his mother was at church with his two older sisters. His father explained that religion was for girls, not boys. He turned on the shower and undressed himself, nodding for Vince to do the same. Vince said he liked this part of it. He was excited to be naked with his father at first. He knew it was special. And even entering the shower—the warm water, holding his father's thigh, touching his skin—was sweet. It felt giving, an invitation. After that, his father wanted something from him, and then it seemed he'd disappeared into what he wanted as he manipulated Vince around like some kind of chair or toy. He remembered what it was: "It's too big, it's too big," he cried out, as if it would have almost been OK if it hadn't hurt so, if his father had been gentler or at least not so big. He couldn't see his father by then or look him in the face, but he knew how his eyes looked. He knew.

He wanted his mother then, but she was gone at church, which was for girls, and *this,* he was made to believe, was for boys. All he really knew was that something painful was happening, and when he asked his father to stop, his father ignored his plea. He'd always say the same thing when it was over: "If you tell your mother about this, I'll beat you to death."

Then he was alone and frightened and confused.

In the garage was an old station wagon with false wood on its sides. Snow chains lay in a pile in the corner next to spooled jumper cables and slumping boxes full of old magazines. He used to spend a lot of time in the car in the garage; it was a place to be alone—his place. It was a cold place in winter, and even in the summer the vinyl seats were cold like sheets. He would lie there in his seven-year-old musings, staring at the faintly patterned fabric of the roof and making shapes from the minutia of ventilation holes—continents and faces, flowers, trees, and sometimes even words.

By then, he'd already started walking the long way home, making friends so that he could go to their houses after school instead of to his own. His mother harangued him about how cruel he was to avoid her and his sisters, who she claimed only wanted his company. But he was their whipping boy; he knew what they wanted with his company.

"You're just like your father," his mother said with disgust.

"No, I'm not."

"Yes, you are—selfish and rude and uncaring."

"Am not." The spatula stung as it slapped against his forearm. He was caught off guard as she caught fire (that's how he always saw her when she was angry—a woman on fire), screaming—"How dare you talk back to me—how dare you!" and he ran through the house, a mad-woman on his heels, flames licking at his ears, and then the slap of the screen door as it slammed behind him, the decreasing volume of her voice because she always stopped there and he kept going.

At the little desk in the school classroom, he felt for gum and boogers on its underside as the teacher read *Tom Sawyer,* and he began to daydream about parentless boys. In the little cell of his brain where the shower was he thought of his father's words: "You're not like me at all. You're not a real boy. You should have been a girl. You're too soft, too skinny, too much like your mother."

"No, I'm not."

"Yes, you are—whining and devious and disobedient."

"Am not."

He squeezed Vince's little bicep hard then, until it made him cry out. "Don't ever talk back to me."

Mostly Vince was silent when his father talked to him in the shower, thinking of other things, his father's voice a far-off radio or TV. He conjured up visions of floating down the river on a raft, fatherless and full of adventurous visions, as he winced and sniffled his tears, knowing now it was no use to plead. The river would be different than this sterile place—this grim Auschwitz gas chamber that never had the decency to finish the job—with its harsh fluorescent light and loud, falling warm water that had lost the power to clean. On the river, there would be soft dark earth and big trees hanging their heavy branches into slow, deep, moving cool water. Towns would come and go, with white church towers and grand pillared mansions looking across lawns to him and all things that flowed downstream. And nothing could reach him. His parents could pace along the shore like hungry tigers. They could roar and paw the air, but they'd never reach him.

Vince was leaning up in on his elbow, looking through the flashes of neon toward the sink, as if the story rolled on out there forever, like a film. "There were rats in that place," he told me. He was only twelve, but he'd run away again and was squatting with a bunch of teenagers in an old brick building in downtown Buffalo. It only lasted for a week that time. His mother sent the police looking for him, and he knew it wasn't because she cared but because she wanted him punished for betraying her, for making her look like a bad mother. He ran away again when he was fourteen. That time he made it all the way to Rochester. When he asked the policeman why they always took him home instead of to jail, the officer answered that he hadn't committed any crime. So he knew what he had to do.

The next week, he smashed a window open at the drugstore and stole a bunch of candy and cigarettes. He sat at the door under the deafening sound of the alarm (which he hardly noticed since he was used to blocking out loud noises at home), smoking and eating candy bars until the police arrived.

There was a sort of nothingness and peace to his transgression on the empty suburban Main Street of old brick buildings where cars lolled by as he sat, unconcerned with the alarm. He vowed never to come back to this town—ever—and he looked out upon the street, his mouth full of chocolate and peanuts. He was stuffing himself and not even hungry. He looked at the shoe repair across the street, the stationers next to it, the beauty parlor across the parking lot—as if for the last time. He started to cry but didn't know why, and he told himself he didn't want to cry in front of the police. He didn't want anyone feeling sorry for him. They always touched you, wanted to help you. It disgusted him. He knew he didn't want to be touched or helped—he just wanted to get out of there. He snuffled up his tears and decided he would hit the policeman; he would fight him. Maybe he would get shot or slammed down against the pavement. He wanted to be hurt—he liked how it felt substantial, not vague like all this "good and bad," and "you're like your mother," "you're like your father," "you're a girl, blah, blah." He wanted something he could feel against his skin, but he didn't want it to be tender. He wanted it be indifferently cruel, anonymous. He'd been betrayed by what little tenderness he'd known.

Suddenly he wanted his father to fuck him like he used to. He wanted it to hurt and he wanted his father to be cruel. And he wanted to spit in his face and then maybe murder him, beat him with a tire iron or a plumber's wrench. His mother, he thought, deserved a bullet. He didn't want to get too near her. He wanted to blow her away from twenty feet out, keep all that nagging, all that clawing and scratching, at bay. Somehow his father's cruelty was preferable, blunt and abrupt. She, on the other hand, had always scratched at him, slapped him—stinging, skittish pains. She was a mosquito to his father's dog bites. He didn't know if it was just that his father got it over with quicker or if he really hated his mother more. He didn't care.

When the police car pulled up and an officer got out, sauntering over in his slow cowboy cop walk, Vince bolted. He ran faster than he'd ever run before, and he laughed to see the uniformed cop chasing him. *It must be awful trying to run in that polyester uniform,* he thinks, *with all those things hanging off your belt.* He knew the cop didn't want to run, hated this part of it. Vince loved it. He wanted to hurt every adult he could, ruin this cop's day. He felt light, like he could run forever. He ran fast and hard as a kid can; he was scrawny and he dodged and darted, jumped over a low brick wall in the adjacent parking lot, rolled—like he's seen on TV—over a car hood, but flubbed it and ended up falling flat on his back. He lost time and the cop gained on him. Now he was in the park and he was losing wind and he slowed down, but not too much—he wanted the abrupt hit of the cop. He felt the back of his shirt yanked hard from behind and he went flying like a rag doll. He was only fourteen, maybe five feet four, 100 pounds at most. He ate the grass, felt it pressed into his cheek, his whole body pinned and forced hard into the cold lawn. The cop had him face down, cuffing him. He struggled and felt the cop's knee in his back. Then Vince felt his own cock getting hard.

The cop uttered profanities at him, drilled him with questions. But Vince only smiled. He'd gotten what he wanted—fuck what the cop wanted. He was eventually thrown in the back of another car that pulled up. The place was teeming then: three squad cars, five or six cops milling about. He laughed at how he'd beckoned society, authority, to his person. All he had to do was break one window and the strongest nation on Earth showed up to look him in the eye. He felt like thanking the cop who caught him.

This time he ended up in a group home with other juvenile delinquents. That's where he first had sex. There was nothing tender about it. A big black boy wanted to fuck him and they did it in a closet one night. The young black boy was even bigger than Vince's father and it hurt terribly. He bit his lip and took it, noticed that this boy was just like his father—he didn't care if it hurt Vince. And that was just fine.

He didn't know how, but one of the counselors found out and they interviewed them both. It was all, Why? You know sex is against the rules; did he force himself on you?" Blah, blah, blah. Vince said as little as possible; the black kid got kicked out and Vince was allowed to stay. He figured it was either because the other boy was black or because it was easier to pin a rape charge on him—the fucker is always the perpetrator? Vince didn't care; he didn't even know the kid. It was each man for himself, that was clear, and if it was a racist world, well no kidding, things were bad all over.

There was a woman there, Sandy, who took an interest in him. This pissed him off at first but then she offered to let him draw, read, cut pictures out of magazines for collages—all sorts of stuff, and in her office. He knew she had some kind of do-gooder agenda, so he was suspicious, but he craved the privacy of her office as opposed to the fucking jungle of the common rooms where he had to deal with up to ten other adolescent boys, dumb brutes all. He liked to make the collages especially, and she laughed at them as if she "got" what he was up to. He appreciated it, but at the same time warned himself to be careful and stay on his guard. He suspected she was trying to get a foothold.

She came and went, conducting her business while he dismantled *Vanity Fair*s, *Newsweek*s, *New Yorker*s, and *People* magazines.

"Can I see?" she eventually asked. He sat back from the table and she peered over his shoulder and let out a laugh. He had placed two businessmen in an impressionist painting—one of Renoir's group picnics. There were modern objects strewn about amid the fruit baskets and wine bottles: a telephone, a fax machine, computers, electric can openers, Xerox copiers. A Cadillac was parked in the background. She noticed there were pills strewn across the tablecloth, cigarettes in the women's mouths, a gun in one man's hand. She struggled with liking the collage, laughing at Vince's cleverness and satire, while remembering her professional obligation to analyze him. But he relieved her of her confusion.

"Don't tell me what it means, please."

She grinned, sighing. "It means you're way too bright to be stuck in a place like this."

"What's intelligence got to do with it?"

"Everything, Vince. Smart people survive; it's as simple as that." She walked over to her desk, adding, "And smart people thrive. And they find a way to manage their problems."

"And I don't?"

"I didn't say that. I think you're coming along fine, but you can't stay here forever. And you don't need to," she added, as if to imply he might be losing his place.

"Are you kicking me out?"

"No, I'm wondering what you're thinking in terms of your stay here. Are you thinking about how you might find a way to deal with your home situation?"

"I'm not going back there."

"OK. You're smart—" she conceded, but with a challenge. "What are your other options?"

"Endless. Anywhere but there." His resolve touched her, even though it was somewhat pathetic. He didn't have anywhere to go or any power in the situation.

"OK, so, which of these endless options looks best right now for you, at fourteen?"

"Staying here."

"Where's here? In this room?" she queried, slightly alarmed. He didn't answer.

"You don't seem to like it so much out there in the rec room," she said, and she gestured her head as she sat down at her desk, leaning back in her chair. "Technically, you're not supposed to be in here. I thought it would help, so I offered, but I can't let you stay here forever. Do you understand?"

"No." He didn't look at her, holding up a magazine, looking at it intently, and then putting it down to begin cutting something out. It struck her how he was just a little boy, or was stuck in the position of one, and yet physically he was more or less a man. She was almost aroused by the contrast but put it out of her mind. Still, it made it hard to talk down to him, and she suddenly didn't want to.

"Vince, you're a special guy; I made a special move for you. I wish I could move you in here, but I can't. I have to treat all the kids the same and we have rules besides."

"Rules are meant to be broken."

She guffawed. "That's an old cliché, Vince. Do you really believe it?"

"Yes."

"Can you think of any good rules?"

"No." She worried she was losing him again and she hated the feeling. It was always so tentative. You had to tread carefully and guide the interaction before they realized they'd made themselves vulnerable. She hated the whole thing, really. She felt she was always tricking them, and the minute they found out they felt betrayed, which made next time harder. The best method she'd found was giving them some privacy and a chance to do what they wanted, thus Vince and his collages. But both were essentially against the rules.

"Well, Vince, you know what? You're right. I hate this job and its rules." She got up and busied herself looking for some papers. When she found what she was looking for, she sat back down with it and saw from the corner of *her* eye that Vince had been watching her from the corner of *his* eye. He knew something was imminent. "Vince," and she read the file: "Vincent James Malone—pretty name." She rolled off the facts about him tiredly. "Born five, twenty-five, 1970, Buffalo, New York . . . to James Sebastian Malone and Sylvia Maria Cirrencione."

"Cheer-en-choni," he corrected her phonetics.

"Cheerenchoni," she enunciated. "Italian name, correct?"

"Sicilian," he corrected her again. She laughed. "And Malone's Irish," he continued "but he's half Polish too—that's why he's such a stupid motherfucker."

"Hmm," she intoned, pausing. "You know, I'm Polish, Vince." She looked at him directly. "There are lots of people of Polish descent in Buffalo."

"I know."

"Well, don't you think that's a negative stereotype to say Polish people are—I won't repeat—uh, ignorant, say?"

"No, all the ones I've met are."

"I see. Well, you've just met one who isn't. Unless you think I'm stupid?"

"No, I'm sorry; you're a nice lady, Sandy—and smart." He flashed a smile at her before looking back at his magazine.

"Thank you. So what are your stereotypes about Italians and Irish people?"

"Sicilians."

"So Sicilians are different from Italians?"

"Yes, very."

"How so?"

"Louder, meaner, poorer, fatter . . . stupider."

She rolled her eyes. "Well, Vince, where'd you come from then, with all these stupid genes?"

"Beats me."

"Vince, you're too intelligent to fall into the stereotype trap. I guarantee you it won't help you navigate through life."

"So I can't tell you what I think about Irish people?" He smiled. *Dammit,* she thought, *he's flirting.* It engaged her, but not in the way she wanted. She had a sudden impulse of anxiety she'd felt before when a young boy talked with her as a man would. It was a mixture of fear—since many of the kids she counseled were sexual predators—and desire. Some of these boys were so lovable, and, in their way, so powerful.

"Go ahead. Shoot."

"Drunk, obnoxious—they never shut up."

"OK, so let's play a game here. How about some positive stereotypes of these various ethnicities if you insist on stereotyping. It goes both ways, right?"

"Let's see, uh, Polacks have blue eyes?" he offered.

"That's a stereotype, true, but only a neutral characteristic—not really a good or bad thing."

Vince picked up a *Vanity Fair*. "Well, according to these magazines, blue eyes are a good thing."

"Good point, Vince. So you see that the fashion industry promotes stereotypes?"

"I guess so."

"And since you have brown eyes, you must be unattractive?"

"Black eyes."

"OK, let's just say nonblue." But why did she find his contrariness so endearing, almost sexy?

He smiled. "I'm ugly as sin; just ask my Dad." She was treading dangerous ground again. How had it gotten here? Perhaps she should have dismissed this discussion of stereotypes at the outset. She knew it was going to be tricky. She also knew that just telling these boys it was wrong to think that way did little if anything. You had to draw them out. He was going on: "I'm skinny; I have a bad chin, no muscles; I'm too short; and my hair is stupid."

Low self-esteem irritated her, both because it was so common and so difficult to eradicate. In her line of work, it was like roaches. "Vince, this is why I bring up stereotypes. All those things you just said—brown eyes . . ."

"Black."

"Black eyes," she raised her voice, "being thin or lean, lightly muscled, small, having thin hair, a soft jawline—these are captivating to some people and not to others. Do you understand that?" She squinted her eyes and realized she was being a tad condescending.

"Well, if you look at these magazines, they show you what most people think is beautiful."

"I disagree."

"It's right here," he said, and he held up the magazine and fluttered it.

Sandy pointed at it with her pencil. "Vince, somebody produces those magazines. Somebody in LA or New York. Who are they to dictate to everyone else?"

"They're just showing us what we all know is true or we wouldn't look at it." He opened the magazine and held it open to a male model in a Polo outfit to emphasize his point. "Look at these guys; they're cute—and blue eyed!"

"Do you understand, Vince, that stereotypes perpetuate opinions?"

"Perpetuate?" he repeated, unsure.

"Yes, that means carry them forward . . . or promote . . . or it means to keep something going. If you keep seeing it, you'll start to buy it."

"Yeah, yeah, I know. And I know these people are fucking idiots, but I also know what is attractive, and so do they."

She was frustrated. "It's all about changing habits, Vince."

He didn't respond immediately and went back to cutting out pictures. She sensed in time he'd ask, and he finally did but without looking up at her and almost with reluctance. "What do you mean?"

"Well, we get into habits for better or for worse. We live in a society that has a habit for blond, blue-eyed people, just like you are in the habit of using profanity." He rolled his eyes. "The great thing is, Vince, you can change your habits. You can decide—just you, not the magazine or anyone else. You can choose which habits help you and which hurt you. That's really the trick to everything." He was beginning to tire her, and she him.

"Yeah, well, being in this room is a habit that helps me." *He's a smart-ass,* she thinks; *it's useless.*

"And a habit that hurts me. I'm sorry, Vince. I can only encourage you; I can't keep you here. They want to release you." She gestured with the papers in her hand.

"They have a habit of sending me home."

"It's a bad habit, huh?"

"Yeah. What's a good one?"

She looked at him sternly, putting him on notice that she wasn't taking any more crap. "Keeping your nose clean until you're eighteen," she said firmly, "and then you don't have to go back there, ever. I'm sorry the laws are the way they are. You have two parents who can care for you. We can't *prove—*" and she says it slowly so as not to sound too dismissive, knowing he had good reason to feel how he did about home "—that they're unfit. I can't put you in foster care or keep you here or let you go live on your own."

"I'll run away again." She was silent. She almost wanted to tell him to go ahead and do it, but she had professional responsibilities and legal considerations. Sometimes she hated this job. "Vince, we've made a lot of progress here."

"My mother is crazy!" He raised his eyebrows and his voice, almost pleading.

She hated this part; she had to play the heavy now. "Vince, remember I told you that the only real case we had for you was your father's abuse, but he's been gone for years and you don't see him anymore, and your mother doesn't allow him near your house—she has her restraining order—so there is no danger of him hurting you again."

"Oh, she's just as bad," he said cynically.

"We have to prove that."

"Fuck, she hits me." And he was pleading with her again.

"Unfortunately, it's still legal to hit your children—within limits. And your stepfather is a gentle man, isn't that true?"

"Yeah, he's whipped. That's the only reason my mother keeps him." She longed to hug him then, but the old fear surfaced. *Oh fuck it,* she thought. She walked over to him and gave him a big hug, and those damn tears she always tried to hold back welled up as she wrapped her arms around him. But he didn't hug her back.

She let go and composed herself. "I'm sorry, I'm really sorry." She's looking at the ground, ashamed.

"Yeah, sure," he was cold as ice. "Thanks for nothing." He walked out, slamming the door, and she stood there overcome by the sadness and her own powerlessness to do anything to assuage it. Then she saw his collages on the table. At first she thought of running out after him with them, but she feared he probably wouldn't even acknowledge her shout. She could send them to him at home, she supposed, but between him and his mother, she couldn't convince herself they would likely survive. She decided to keep them for him, if he ever decided to come for them. Perhaps though, she was keeping them for herself. As she opened a drawer to file them, she remembered her religious mother who saved every thank-you note ever sent to her, telling her daughter she was keeping them just in case there was any problem come Judgment Day. Such a silly woman, she thought, sadly. She slammed the drawer closed, sat down, and into her hands, she cried.

"Sandy was all right," he sighed then, kissing me lightly and then throwing back the covers to hop over me and go to the sink in the corner, where he peed. He looked wraithlike in his faded long johns, the neon flashing him yellow, then back to black, then yellow again as he finished peeing and shook himself off.

"Come here," he said, turning to me.

I'd do whatever he said, and was up and moving toward him momentarily. He kissed me then and pulled my body to his. And we looked at each other, as our faces flashed yellow, then disappeared, then yellow again. He hungrily began kissing me then, licking my lips and chin, pushing his tongue deeper into my mouth. I just tried to keep up with him, my heart beating—I who'd never been kissed before my first visit to this tawdry room a week ago. I responded with all my pent-up desire and loneliness, and before long he was bracing himself under my onslaught. We wrestled together hungrily, and I started pulling at his clothes. But he disengaged his mouth from mine and abruptly stopped my hands by grabbing them firmly.

I looked at him expectantly, inquisitively. I knew he wouldn't take his shirt off, but his pants too? I was confused.

"I have a herpes outbreak," he said bluntly. "We can't have sex." I'd been so worried about HIV for the past two weeks, I felt like I didn't even know or care what herpes was. But I knew enough to know it was contagious and I appreciated him telling me. "It's on my thighs, so I can't take my long johns off," he said matter of factly.

I was disappointed but only momentarily. I didn't care if we had sex. Neither did the Arab man downstairs, because he never came knocking as Vince and I wrestled clothed for four hours that night, pushing against each other, groping and kissing, embracing. It wasn't really frustrating because it was more than I'd ever done before, and whatever I was drawn to about him seemed to pulse out of his skin and feed me whatever I needed, even if it was only through his hands and mouth. It was enough.

We tired eventually as the sunrise began to mute the neon's flash outside the window, and we slept, waking later tangled like seaweed or string—as if among all the stories we'd shared.

We were still erotically charged, of course, and looking back now I felt closer to him then than later when we always orgasmed together. I'd always heard that sex could make you one with another, but it was in fact not-sex that had bonded us, kept us close. It had been a sort of high tantra before I even knew what that was. I was happy and home somehow, still full of him, and he I hoped of me, lying side by side.

He woke up and kissed me, grinning tiredly.

"Where'd you get that tattoo?" I asked him then.

"Somebody I knew once who used to travel the trains with me," he answered indifferently.

"Does it mean anything?" I thought again of how it looked like it could have been a Chinese or Japanese character—a symbol for something.

"No, he made it up. But it looks like it means something, huh?" He smiled. "That's what I like about it. Keep 'em guessing." He smiled coyly then and pushed me playfully to get me out of bed.

We went out to Golden Gate Park that morning, ambled down sun-dappled trails under enormous wind-blown cypress trees, and deconstructed Western civilization, subject by subject, and then put it all back together again according to us. What we built was something born of what we tore down, like Watts Towers in Los Angeles—the detritus of civilization reorganized and mounted upward to a fabulous spire, this time made of him and me. It was our unique and personal tower, like all love affairs tend to be, for better or worse.

We ended up near the museums in the afternoon—the neo-Egyptian de Young; the neoclassical Academy of Sciences; the all-glass Victorian Hall of Flowers, a vision through the distant trees. There was the dilapidated art deco bandshell wrapped in cyclone fencing, a victim of the last earthquake. A long rectangular plaza of pollarded elms in uniform rows filled the space between these structures, their leaves just beginning to sprout anew on the pollarded branches that looked tight as fists where they ended in bulbous knobs. I felt kind of sad for the trees, the way they'd been planted in rows and pruned to a deformity—someone's idea of beauty. But there was something charming too in their raised fist defiance.

I was exhilarated suddenly, and I felt elated as well to be in San Francisco because I knew I could do what I wanted to do next: kiss Vince deeply, right on the lips in the middle of a city park, among the milling crowds. Our passion remained unspent—call it pruned—and so it was forever replenished. We were the pruned boys with a pruned sex life too. We made out for glorious, long moments as every turn of his head revealed new muscle movements, rippling beneath his neck's pale olive skin; every blink of his eye launched a sigh in my heart that ripped through me as loud as a crowd's sigh, ten thousand strong. The pout of his lower lip, the boniness of his shoulders, the furrow of his brow as he looked at me wondering, his matching fascination obvious—all of it cut through me, pushing up lump after lump into my throat. And he kissed them all.

We got up and walked, holding hands, tangling our fingers together with the sexual tension that still coursed through us. We went all the way out to the ocean. *That's twice now,* I thought. The bridge was north of us, inside the entrance to the bay, far around the point of Land's End. Only tankers rode the line of the horizon from here. We ambled along the ragged shore, in the wind and the late sun, and we kicked about through the surf's refuse: discarded blue and orange styrofoam from far-off buoys; polished pieces of blue and green glass, and broken sand dollars; stones, driftwood, and the heaps of frothy by-products from some unknown pollution; shattered remains of crabs, and the snotty entrails of washed-up jellyfish; long bulb-studded strands of kelp unanchored and ambushed by flies. All lost things, having drifted off from somewhere and ended here.

Three weeks after they'd attached it, Peter was carted away to have the sausage put back where it belonged. "We'll miss it," Susan quipped.

His surgeon treated it like it was routine, and I suppose as a part of the process it was, but to see him return with a now-intact face and body was, after having witnessed him trapped in that "cocoon" of flesh, both a relief and a bit of a shock. He kept changing form, and we were bracing ourselves this time, realizing that whatever scars he returned with now would be the scars he'd have to carry for good, whereas all the gashes and stitches we'd gotten used to had been reassuringly temporary.

"Want some coffee, Mom?" I ventured, as we both sat nervously awaiting his return. It was a bad idea, but I was at a loss. Probably the last thing she needed was more stimulation.

"No, hon, I just want my Peter." And the tears welled up in both our eyes as I thought to myself, *Whoa there, keep it steady; no need to go for the cheap shot.*

I took a deep breath. "OK, Mom. Come on, he's gonna look great. Just remember the scars are gonna be big in the beginning, like the doctor said. You know, they swell." She was nodding as if to say, "I think I can do it." "And remember when he talked about plastic surgery and all that, down the line? They'll be able to erase a lot of his scarring." But I was losing her again, probably because I was alluding to horrors that painted ghastly pictures in her mind. She bent her head into her hands. "Ah, Mom. Come on, Mom," I implored as gently as I could. I was used to reassuring her like this, and then once she was up and running again, I'd bring in a nurse and sneak off to go cry my own tears out in the men's bathroom, a safe distance from her.

They rolled him in, finally, and he was trashed on painkillers and whatever else they gave him. Mom was up and smiling and grabbing the pillows as they shimmied him off the gurney and into his bed. He was grinning like a drunken fool, seemingly having a good old time. It broke my heart and I got shaky again. I couldn't believe what a balancing act this whole fucking thing was, and I wondered whether I could stay up. I wanted to just gloriously fall off the wire, be done with it. And I was just his brother. God, what my mother must have felt. I vowed I would somehow outlive her just to save her from ever going through this again.

She was all excited then, thanking the nurses—it was as if it was a kid's birthday party and he wasn't even sick—and the fear I witnessed on her face a moment ago was completely gone. She was so grateful that he made it back once again alive from wherever they kept taking him.

It was when he dozed off that the trouble began again. It was then that she entertained the darker fantasies she kept in check when he was awake and watching her. It was then she started her sighing and unsteadiness.

"I don't know, Neill; I don't know if I can take any more."

My father'd taken to saying "Not now, Grace. Besides, you don't have a choice" when she'd get this way, but it was my job to provide what he couldn't, so I resisted the temptation to use the tough-love approach, even though it did seem appropriate now and again.

It was time to get her moving, I figured. "He's OK now, Mom. Let's let him sleep off the drugs. Come on, let's take a walk."

She gave me her sweet sigh of a smile, appreciative of me in a way I'd always taken for granted until then. Now I knew what I meant to her. Cancer taught me that too.

We wandered around the ward, talking to the other patients and staff. My mother was a chatty, sweet lady and everyone naturally took to her. She was already showing up with baked goods for the nurses and staff. And she left no one out, hounding down orderlies and janitors on other floors who had done her some small kindness and loading them up with gingersnaps or Toll House cookies for their kids.

There were a lot of nice people on that floor and they helped me take care of my mom. Maybe because it was the floor for "special cases," which we soon learned was a euphemism for "hopeless cases" generally, the staff was more attentive and kinder. It could have just as easily gone the other way, though, I considered, leading instead to cynicism and burnout. Whatever the case, we gratefully accepted their warm welcome, figuring we'd be there for a while. Maybe it was just that: They knew they were stuck with us for a month, so we might as well make friends.

Peter had something to do with it too. He was like the great young hope of the sixth floor, the star victim. He was younger than most of them, after all, and he was what they called "a trooper." Everyone unanimously believed that Peter would beat the odds, which weren't so good since his kind of cancer, it turned out, usually occurred only in people over seventy years of age. My mother hoped it meant he was some kind of old soul, while the rest of us just figured he had youth on his side and thus a well of strength unavailable to the old folks, so the hell with the odds.

"My boy's the wild card," my Dad would say, his eyes twinkling. "I've seen him on the field; I know what he's capable of." He was slipping more and more into sports metaphors, which was how he'd always handled crises. In past years, he'd always say it was "Round five in a fifteen-round fight" when he was arguing with my mother and she was threatening to divorce him. We knew they were empty threats generally, but we also knew his sports metaphors meant he took them seriously, even if she never saw them that way.

And now she was on my arm as we walked, and the sixth floor looked nothing like a locker room or spring training camp. If anything, it struck me as more like a thoroughfare through a neighborhood. It woke up and slowed down with the sun each day, and there was always some kind of local news or gossip making the rounds. We'd almost always see Ryan, a bald teenager with Hodgkin's disease, rattling along with his IV pole, rocking out to his Walkman. We didn't know him very well because he rarely took the earphones off. He'd told me one day in the sunroom at the far end of the hall that he thought heavy metal made a sound that cancer cells couldn't fight, so he was listening to as much of it as possible to save himself.

He always waved to us, though, smiling as he ambled by, accompanied by that tinny sound emanating from his earphones as he circumambulated the floor, IV pole in tow. We gave him the thumbs up and a smile in return.

I'd take my mother room to room, just to get her out of herself. She liked Mrs. Granger, an ex-schoolteacher pushing eighty. She'd had three kinds of cancer and dozens of surgeries in the last ten years and had so far survived them all. She was one of those upbeat types, wholly unafraid of death but still fighting for the sake of her little grandchildren who sat quietly by her side every weekend.

There was a paraplegic morphine addict named Stan who lived next door. We'd visited only once and hadn't been back as he'd usually insult anyone who tried to cheer him up. My mother was an early victim. He'd called her Mary Poppins. He'd rail on in a sort of humorous satirical monologue about the food and hospital bureaucracy, occasionally throwing in ribald sexual commentaries regarding the nurses. He was often asleep, and we'd heard he was in some sort of awful pain that perplexed the doctors so much so that they put him back on morphine after every surgery. Not surprisingly, he'd become addicted over the course of his troubles, and one of the floor's dramas was his ongoing "rehabilitation," which varied day to day in a sort of *is-she-or-isn't-she?* gossip that circulated around the floor. He would throw terrible fits when no doctors or attendants were in sight, but his oddly seductive and charming approach toward the nurses got him the needed shot (which they were forbidden to give him) often as not. I shouldn't have been so disinterested in his plight—it might have helped me later with Vince. But as it was, I considered opiates to have nothing to do with me and wondered only briefly how he pulled it off, figuring I'd never know besides, since the nurses who snuck him shots were never going to cop to having that kind of legally indictable mercy.

There were, of course, those bright-eyed nurses who flirted with Peter and me—young men were in short supply on the sixth floor and Ryan wasn't really available—and gave my mom back rubs and moral support. The young interns and residents would make their rounds in the afternoon or early evening, talking of sports or snowboarding or something young and male. They'd always add beer to Peter's menu—in a kind of dude solidarity—which he could never drink, so I got to drink it. We laughed a lot about that. It would be late at night, and I'd be hanging out in his room with him watching TV, going back and forth from the nurses' station refrigerator to get my next beer from the shelf with his name on it. What a party.

"No matter how much the insurance company sticks it to us, at least one of my sons is getting drunk on their nickel," my father wryly remarked.

He was only there in the evening and he immediately turned on the TV if it wasn't already on. He avoided my mother's gaze as he hated that tragic sigh of hers—it made him impatient, jumpy. We'd suddenly become pals so he wouldn't have to field her tears. But I wasn't interested in sports so all his jabbering about the Bears' basketball program was one-sided. But I did the best I could. I knew I couldn't take him for walks around the floor—all those ill people gave him the creeps. He was focused on Peter, he said. "You gotta keep your eye on the ball." *Oh brother,* I thought.

Sometimes he pulled out medical bills, wowing us with the figures. "That first surgery was twenty grand! And this last one, they denied my claim!" And he guffawed: "They called it cosmetic surgery." I'd nod my head, thinking, *Yeah, my brother's a regular Cher over there in the bed with those big ugly scars crisscrossing his cheek.*

Then there was my father's research. He was collecting books and articles on Peter's particular cancer. My mother thought it was morbid, but he saw himself as the coach and he had to study the opponent. Even Peter rolled his eyes when Dad would leave the room for the bathroom, or at the end of the evening when he'd beg me to ride home with them so he wouldn't be her captive audience. Sometimes I did; sometimes I just slept on the floor or in a chair. Sometimes Susan brought me a cot, and a couple of times she even gave me a room.

And Dad was on his own for the next twenty-four hours. *Who is he?* I wondered, lying one night on my sleeping bag on the floor of Peter's room. He was like some man who'd been hanging around—like Reuben in the Partridge Family—a kind of manager more than a father. He was a sort of comic sidekick to my mother. He fulfilled his practical duties certainly, fixing things and establishing his authority around the TV, but emotionally he was usually dead on arrival. He'd done his stand-up vaudeville nightly for two decades, so he was no stranger to any of us, but we didn't really know him any better than if he had been performing up there on stage and we were just a familiar audience. He really was a clown, with all the mystery that the role entailed. Who knew what was under all that face paint?

I'd given up finding out a long time ago, which felt very sad to me just then.

In the silence, punctuated now and again by the beeps of the nurses' station or Peter's fitful breathing (his mouth was like a hole of blood and rags), I remembered those few times when I'd felt close to my dad.

He used to talk about all these toys from his childhood. We loved it and knew it was all a setup. He'd do this kind of thing, over and over again, mentioning some old treasure, getting us all worked up, and then saying there was no chance we'd ever find it—which left us all obsessed. We'd beg him to take us to Aunt Mary's then so we could look, but he'd throw up his hands, pleading it was no use, all the time probably knowing exactly where the said item or items were.

Aunt Mary lived out near Golden Gate Park in a little row house she'd bought before World War II. She'd raised my father, who'd lost his mother at birth and his father in the war. Aunt Mary kept nearly everything, and her little house swelled with family mementos until her basement became a literal storehouse of heirlooms. We'd discover something new every time we visited, and it had become a part of the ritual of whatever mysterious item he'd introduced of late to head down the steep back stairwell into the basement to try our hand at finding it. One time I remember it was the milk tops he'd collected as a kid, which he'd formed into armies and baseball teams, each according to brand name.

Down the long, steep stairway we'd go, the darkness lit by a single swaying bulb hanging from the ceiling. Downstairs it was dark and windowless, and we were small, and the stairs were high and steep, and my father always told us to be very careful—he was sure Aunt Mary would someday fall down these stairs and break her neck and not be found for days. He always said things like that so we didn't ever believe him and weren't disturbed or concerned. In fact, it just excited us the more as it promised a thrilling danger to the journey.

Lined up in leaning rows across the moldy cement floor were the stacks of boxes we would plunder, digging and discovering myriad items from old shaving kits and dime-store novels that belonged to our grandfather to tin soldiers and notebooks full of my father's childhood drawings. We'd each run to show him our latest discovery as he waxed nostalgic about rationing and blackouts during World War II, and all the people now long dead he used to know. He'd chatter away about Rossi Playground and igniting firecrackers stuck out of tomatoes and throwing them into cars; rolling tires down Stanyan Street into traffic; the kid who got his eyelid caught by a friend's fishing pole when he cast out into Stowe Lake over in Golden Gate Park. He told us that the hook ripped it clean off so that he was never able to close that eye again.

"How'd he sleep, Dad?" I asked.

"Didn't sleep. Never slept again. Couldn't close his eyes a wink."

"Can't he get a fake one?" By then we'd all stopped and were staring at him slack-jawed.

"Yes, I think they gave him a pig's eyelid, so that one eye had these long blond eyelashes and the other was just normal. He wouldn't eat bacon after that and we called him Pigskin."

Peter started to say "Oink, oink" and Dad laughed, and I got smart as only an eight-year-old can and went on and on instructing Peter about how you could be half pig and still speak just like a human, but it was Paul who said, "You're a pig, Neill—a fat pig; you ought to be slaughtered and sold as ham." His insults were always so shocking I'd just stop, and my father would laugh—they were so over the top from a kid—before gratuitously uttering, "Now let's not fight. Come on, Paul, we're having a good time here." But humiliating me seemed more often than not part of Paul's idea of a good time.

Not wanting to fight, but not wanting to run back up the stairs and miss out on the treasure hunt, I'd attempted a retort: "You're the pig, with your ugly nose." He'd been blessed, or cursed—depending on your aesthetic—with my father's Roman nose.

He glared, muttering, "Ham, bacon, pig's feet."

"Boys, knock it off," my father said halfheartedly.

Soon enough it blew over, and we were once again all lost in our various discoveries as we fanned out across the cellar, unearthing old books and dilapidated boxes full of trinkets and junk. I felt different about my father when I saw him reminiscing, as if he too had been a boy just like me, as frightened and sad and crazy in his imaginings and confusions. I'd think then that I loved him very much, and I would fill with an almost uncontrollable kind of joy and ecstasy, and I would want to scream out gleefully and sometimes did. And when I did, Paul thought me strange and girlish and irritating and would usually go after me for it. My father seemed perplexed when I yelped that day, but he'd smiled as he went on through other boxes, knowing he'd satisfied me somehow. I wanted to touch him then, but I knew I could not—that seemed very clear. Whether because of the dictates of my oh-so-boyish and manly brothers or my father's own reserve, or Irish Catholicism, or America, I couldn't say. It was all so complicated then. I knew only that I wanted to touch him in my glee, wanted to reach out and hold him. I wanted to tell him I was glad he, and not someone else, was my father.

And then, reaching up on my tiptoes through the bands of sepia dust-moted light slipping through the high basement window, a crate lurched above me as I pulled at it, and down it came, crashing to the floor, spilling the milk tops at my feet. I squealed shrilly and kneeled, running my hands all through them—a pot of gold at the end of a rainbow, my brothers jumping down to join me.

"The milk tops!" we screamed in unison. My father looked relieved and even a little sad, remembering, I suppose, one of those feelings or memories he never shared. He just stood and watched us, and when I looked his way and said, "You can come look too, Dad," he looked back at me with a face of such sweet sorrow that I felt for once he understood. He was like me; he was just like me.

After that, I'd decided I'd try to become his friend—his pal.

My father used to take the bus to work back then. We lived up a hill that he hiked up and down in his drab gray suits, passing the dozen or so faux-Colonial houses of Roble Place, a typical 1970s' cul-de-sac of suburban homes, across the bay and over the hills from San Francisco, where my father worked for an insurance company.

It was late summer, warm and balmy, when I began my trips to meet my father at the bus stop. I'd crouch there by the stop sign and wait. Then the bus would come, like a big orange and white dream of FATHER. He would smile a contrived smile when he got off the bus and saw me—surprised, even a little disturbed by the second or third day. It seemed he wanted to walk alone. He had things to think about, I supposed. It was probably the only time he had just to himself, walking up that hillside road that arced around the oak forest. Maybe he didn't necessarily want to be my friend. I wasn't particularly discouraged, as I was used to having a hard time making friends and could understand if he, like a lot of kids, didn't like me at first. Paul had taught me well that I was an undesirable choice for a friend. So we'd walk up the hill mostly not saying anything.

He might ask me what we were having for dinner. I usually knew and was proud of being a herald of important bourgeois news. "Chicken and rice." "Flank steak and potatoes." "Lamb." "You can put mint jelly on yours!" I'd exclaim as he smiled. The fact that I thought the stuff utterly disgusting should have helped him to see I was thinking of him, making an effort to show some interest and friendliness. He was also in the habit of eating the fat off meat—it made me gag to watch it, but I needed a friend—so I'd point out that this was a particularly bad cut of meat as well, chock full of fat.

About the fourth afternoon, I found a machete along the side of the road as we walked home. The public works crew had been cutting back the stickers that grew along that part of the street, where a ditch ran along next to the trees, and had probably left it there by accident. I saw it glimmering there and ran to fetch it, bringing it back to show my father. He told me it was a machete, and I asked him what that was. He told me a story of Japanese soldiers in World War II who cut off men's heads with them. He said it had probably been left there by the Japanese long ago when they tried to take over America. I was fascinated and excited as I listened to him go on and on. This is why I'd come to find him: to collect stories that only he and I would share, unlike the stories of lost treasures in Aunt Mary's basement that belonged to me and my brothers both. I knew most of his tales were quite tall. I was never surprised as I grew older and learned the truth. The truth, after all, was never what was important between us. There was a great light in his lies that was bigger and brighter than facts. He could have told me anything. I would have listened to him forever. If our friendship had been based solely on lies, that would have been good enough for me.

My father's job far off in the city always seemed to me like some curse he'd been sentenced to work off, like a kind of indentured servitude. I knew only that it had something vaguely to do with money and unfriendly people since he seemed to have no adult friends from there that I ever met, and he often complained about his co-workers, referring to them as "morons," "backstabbers," and "worthless slabs of meat." Few were "team players." He said it all with a smile of course, but his sort of philosophical contempt was obvious, and it colored his humor with a sadness that made him more the circus clown than the cheerful ham. And it was that heaviness in his heart that made me love him, probably more even than the constant humor ever did.

When we'd go to the annual company picnics, all the morons and backstabbers seemed to love my father, begging him to join their team at baseball. I didn't get it; my father was some kind of trickster—a mystery, elusive and impossible to pin down.

But I tried anyway. Though by the second week of my going down to meet him, he seemed bothered by my eagerness, and even a little concerned that maybe something was wrong with me. He started asking me why I wasn't at home playing or off with friends, instead of telling me more stories. I answered that I wanted to be with him, which made him smile in embarrassment. But I was probably crowding him. He got quieter, more monosyllabic, not taking me up on my invitations to stories when I'd find something in the ditch. I felt like some girl he didn't like too much who was maybe bugging him.

One day I just didn't go. I remember staring up at the clock: it was the kind that would buzz, like at school, then its minute hand would jump two minutes at a time, which always filled me with anxiety. It was so jarring in its reminder that time was slipping away with such heavy sure steps, such finality. I looked up at 5:10, my normal time to leave. And I watched it tick, two minutes at a time, all the way to 5:34, at which point in some very sad way in my boy's heart, I gave up on him. He never asked me why I'd stopped coming, which made me almost hate him, but you couldn't hate a clown.

"No one but you and Peter," is my answer to Vince when he asks me if I've told anyone else that I'm queer.

"Your parents haven't figured it out by now?"

"Well, let's say they're a bit distracted, if not clueless." I then asked him if his parents ever suspected he was gay, or if he'd ever told them.

"Yeah! When I was fourteen, when I went back home from the group home." He laughed then, rolling up a cigarette. We were sitting on the floor as there were no chairs, just the lumpy bed which was fine for sleeping but not for sitting. There was of course no smoking in the hotel, so he walked over to sit on the windowsill to prevent stinking up the room, which he knew could get him kicked out.

"I decided that I'd just totally try to be myself and take no shit," he began, as he lit up. He tossed the match out the window and, turning back to me, added, "A mistake of course." He laughed again. "I pierced both ears, dyed my hair—which was still a queer thing to do back then. Now every little straightboy's doing it—they always follow us. They'll be sucking dick in five years." He chuckled. "Anyway, I digress . . ." And he said it slowly and sarcastically, as if to relish his story and the joke both. "My mother got suspicious eventually, looked at me with her shitty look and asked me what the fuck I was doing. I always muttered "nothing," or something stupid like that. I didn't speak to her unless I had to. And it was driving her crazy. She just had to know," and he rolled his eyes. "Suddenly she's interested in my life," he said bitterly, "only when it might reflect badly on her, of course. As if anyone cared or had any respect for her." He nodded his head then and I thought he might stop, but he was only warming up.

"She even followed me once to a gay bar, this one I'd started hanging out at. Can you believe it?"

"Were you having sex with guys?" I asked curiously.

"Yeah, all the time now—tons."

"Did you have a boyfriend or anything?"

He looked at me as if to ask "are you naive or what?" before answering slowly, "No, I didn't want a boyfriend." And then he added flatly, "I still don't, so don't get any ideas." I was a bit taken aback at how he'd thrown in that warning as he rambled on with his story. By then, even though it had been only a few weeks, I'd thought we were boyfriends. Whatever that might be. We certainly weren't heading toward any kind of domesticity. Everything about Vince had a passing-through quality to it. Even then I must have been steeling myself for the day he'd go, while at the same time I built brick by brick a fantasy that we'd wander the world together forever. I knew we were fellow travelers; we weren't ever going to end up settled together somewhere—that always seemed obvious. But to me, that seemed an even closer bond, more than being boyfriends. Of course, I wanted to reassure him that I had no such notions. But that seemed pathetic on my part and maybe even insulting toward him. And besides, it would have been a lie. So I said nothing. *Whatever you want, Vince,* I thought, *just don't go, and don't send me away.*

"I can still see her," he shook his head back and forth, lost again in his story, "the dumb bitch. She rolled down her window and started screaming at me from across the street as I stood there talking to the doorman."

Her voice was high-pitched and almost frantic. The content of her speech hasn't mattered for years. It was all just venom dressed up in words anyway. She was forever trying to get a foothold in the total chaos she experiences as her life. If she could just hit one pin with this bowling ball we call the human personality, she would be on her way. But it was one gutter ball after the other. She threw them harder, faster, but it was always the same. The pins mocked her, standing still, gathering dust.

"Don't you go in there, Vincent Malone. You come here!" He only stared, amazed she'd pursued him this far into town. "You better not be gay!" she shouted.

He started to laugh at her, then he yelled: "Get the fuck away from me, you crazy bitch! Get the fuck out of here!" And he was suddenly furious at being embarrassed in front of the doorman and worried that other friends and acquaintances might see this shameful ruin that bore him. He picked up a bottle and bounced it off the roof of her car. He crouched down and picked up pebbles, a pizza crust, a spark plug—anything he could get his hands on—and flung them in succession at her car and its open window, which she was now desperately rolling up, ducking as she did so. Momentarily, she gunned it, skidding and heading down the street. He is his mother's son; she's trained him well. "You fuckin' whore!" he screamed at her, running out to throw a final stone.

Vince ran away again after that. He'd only been able to hold out a total of about four months. Actually, he didn't really run away this time so much as get kicked out for good. He knew better than to go home that night after the shouting incident in front of the bar, figuring he'd need to let her cool down. Instead he went home drunk with yet another nameless boy who he spent his anger with through furious all-night sex.

She wouldn't let him in the house the next morning. She'd opened the door a crack, not removing the chain, as he crossed the lawn—the frozen, parched, dead lawn of Buffalo winter. Pressed down by the freeze of snow, mildewed by slush, it was a brown, smashed thing in the first clear days of March.

She told him she had called the police and to get off her property. He stopped, wondered whether she was bluffing. Was she capable of this? Would she really do that? It would be a final insult, but not terribly surprising, considering. He stood there, still, as she slammed the door. He stood for five minutes, not moving an inch, seeing if she'd really do this, waiting for the "alleged" cop. Did she think she could scare him off by threatening him with the police? Did she think he was afraid of the police? "Dumb, game-playing bitch," he muttered to himself, kicking at the lawn.

Just then a police cruiser pulled up. It was the same old thing, the cowboy cop walk of controlling the situation, the set jaw, the "I'm a reasonable man; I expect you to be too," smirk on his face. Vince turned and saw his mother staring out of the kitchen window from behind the curtains.

The cop said, "How ya doin'?" or something faux-friendly like that, and Vince answered: "I live here." It was overcast and very cold in East Buffalo; the street was replete with expired lawns, cyclone fences, poorly kept one-story homes, no sidewalks or curbs. Vince stood in the middle of the dead grass in his ragged punk outfit—the long, tattered black overcoat and combat boots; his pink and platinum messy spiked hair. He was pointing, gesticulating, explaining to the cop that this was where he lived; he's not doing anything wrong.

His mother stared out the kitchen window and the cop turned to look in that direction as she guiltily pulled the drapes closed. The cop went to the door, knocked, did his cop thing, peering in the side window. She opened it a crack and he asked her if this was her son, pointing to Vince in the middle of the lawn, wholly exposed to the elements.

"Yes, he's my son, and he's not welcome here anymore. He's been kicked out, so he's trespassing. I'd like him arrested, please," she said with uncharacteristic poise.

"Ma'am, I can't arrest your son for trespassing on his own property."

"It's not his property. He doesn't pay the mortgage on this house." Vince wanted to yell: "No, I don't; your cunt does!" but was biding his time to watch her sweat.

The cop explained to her that Vince was a minor, but what could be the point of talking legalities to this crazed woman, so full of hatred and ruin she would bar her own son entrance to his house? "Ma'am, would you like to step out here and talk to your son? You must have a reason to have kicked him out. Perhaps you two can talk this out."

"There's nothing left to say. I don't consider him my child. I don't want to speak to him again ever. Let him go to his father's."

"Ma'am, do you and your—I assume—ex-husband have joint custody?"

"Of course not, he's a child molester." She was coming apart as she always did—it didn't take more than a small breeze or a couple of innocent questions. By this time, Vince had turned to go, and had proceeded across the lawn, past the police car and onto the potholed street. He felt a sudden enormous need to cry, pushing up through the ever-present hate and anger. He felt it in his throat, like a flood or a wave pushing up. He didn't want them to see it.

But he heard the cop's voice. "Mr. Malone—excuse me, Mr. Malone, can you come back here for a minute?"

He turned to see the cop and his mother, huddled in her pink bathrobe, standing together now on the walkway. The weather was awful; this whole street was hell, the entire scene irrevocably sad. He couldn't bear another minute of it, but he couldn't let her see him cry, so he screamed it out: "You fucking bitch, whore, cunt!" ad infinitum.

She turned, throwing her hands up, and marched back toward the door. The cop was left holding the bag, losing control of a situation he obviously would rather not have been in at all.

"Ma'am, you need to tell your son why you won't speak to him or let him into your house, which is rightfully his residence."

She stopped, and leaned forward, pathetic looking in her curlers, her faded bathrobe. "Isn't it obvious? Besides, he's a faggot, Officer—a homosexual, a pansy, a sissy, a poof!" and she ended her litany of insults with a crescendo of exclamation aimed at Vince whom she was now glaring at maliciously. The cop turned to Vince, having become a spectator.

Calmly, Vince responded, "She's right, Officer. And she's just jealous that I'm getting more dick than she is." Infuriated, she ran at him, but the policeman intercepted her, her fists flailing on his shoulders. She pushed at him and screamed, "Let me go!" which he eventually did, after she'd spent her anger. She pushed him away ungratefully and walked into the house, not looking back, slamming the door loudly behind her. A dried-out, emaciated wreath bounced on the door as it slammed. *Home sweet home,* Vince thought cynically.

The cop turned to Vince: "I can give you a ride to your father's, if you'd like."

"Fuck you," Vince snapped, irritated by this stranger, sitting smack-dab in the middle of his exposed and shamefully ugly life.

"What did you say?"

"I told you to get the fuck out of here. We don't need you."

"Yes, I can see you're handling things very well. Now you listen, punk," and the cop was moving toward him now, hands like parentheses to his hips, poised, speaking slowly, "You want me to take you in? Huh? Is that it? Because I can and I will." Vince realized the cop had to at least deflate the situation if not solve it, and he was nowhere standing here outside his mother's house and unable to gain entrance, so he agreed to take the ride to his father's. He hadn't seen the old kidfucker in close to five years, but he knew where he lived.

The cop asked him questions on the ride: "How old are you? What school do you go to? What's the problem between you and your mother?" Vince answered only that she was a bitch.

"You're gay?" the cop eventually inquired.

"Didn't you believe my mother?" he answered. The cop snorted derisively and turned to look out his window before continuing his casual interrogation.

"Are you aware that if you are gay and are having sex with men, that statutory rape is a crime punishable by prison?"

"Only for the men, though, right?" Vince answered tiredly.

"Regardless, you shouldn't be encouraging criminal behavior. We can nail you for that. It's called contributing to the delinquency of a minor."

"Who better to contribute?" Vince knew he was a wiseass, but he couldn't help himself. There was too much built up behind the dam of his life to even attempt any kind of real conversation with this policeman.

"Listen, kid, I'm only putting up with your bullshit because I feel sorry for you."

"Don't feel sorry for me—you're the cop."

"And you're the smart-aleck kid."

"The smart-aleck faggot, actually."

They made the final turn in silence. Vince saw the big faux-Tudor house at the end of the block that looked to Vince like a sick Polish castle full of Nazis who were likely torturing Jews down in the cellar .

As he pulled to a stop, the cop looked Vince in the eye. "Now tell me the truth. Your mother called your father a child molester. Is that true? Because if it is, I can't leave you here if there's any injunction against him seeing you."

"He doesn't have a record and I have hair on my dick now, so you don't have to worry," Vince replied sarcastically, opening the door. "I'd worry about his two sons who live in there. But it's probably too late. Thanks for the ride." Vince hopped out, having delivered his final cocky remark.

The cop was leaning across the seat as Vince grabbed the door to slam it closed. "One word, kid: AIDS. Be care—" But Vince didn't hesitate and the door clipped off anything else the officer had to say. The police car pulled away, and as Vince crossed his father's lawn he carried on the conversation with himself as if there was someone listening in his head. "Actually, that would be *four* words made into an acronym," he said snippily, shaking his finger out in front of him.

He took a deep breath, riding completely on momentum now, knowing that if he stopped to think everything would quickly implode and swallow him whole. So he rapped hard and confidently on the door three times, which was soon afterward answered by the new wife he'd never actually met, but who must know who he is. She looked suspicious; he just smiled.

"Can I help you with something?"

Vince walked past her. "I'm here to see the kidfucker."

She had a horrified and frightened, worried look on her face, but she attempted to stay calm, albeit with great effort. "Excuse me?—Jim!" she yelled out. And then to Vince, with just a hint of relief, and maybe even some concern, "Are you his son?"

"Yes, I'm the boy he molested." Vince heard himself saying these things and couldn't believe it was actually him speaking. The words were simply blossoming off his tongue. He felt giddy and out of control.

"Jim!" She didn't know what else to do but yell for him into the vast thirty-foot ceiling of the living room. He momentarily appeared at the top of the stairs, looking down over the railing. Vince's father had done surprisingly well as a college math professor, now tenured with his new, younger, mellower wife and two small children. His short auburn hair was graying above his ice blue eyes; he had thickened considerably and wore reading glasses, which made him look intelligent and cruelly distant, both of which he was. He went to church now too, Vince had heard, but he knew he likely hadn't changed.

"Vince." He said it like a statement of recognition, like an acknowledgment of a chronic foot fungus that has once again returned—a bother. "What are you doing here?" He was obviously surprised, but stone-faced about it.

"Looking for a place to stay, I guess." But he reconsidered, knowing his plan to run away was not up for review and this would be an insane idea. It was all happening too fast, and he didn't seem to be directing it anymore. "Maybe I just came to take one last look at you."

"Why?" his father asked indifferently.

That hurt; he felt it pierce right through him. If you have to ask . . . Surprised and unable to come up with a comeback, Vince answered dryly, "Why not?"

"You're not staying here," his father commanded.

Vince feigned being relaxed and in good humor, and mockingly replies, "Ah, come on, Dad, it'll be just like old times . . ." He wanted to say it, but he wouldn't; it stuck in his throat. He was still intimidated by this man and he was back now in the shower, helpless. It had been so easy to say it just now to the new wife and to the cop, but to look into the eyes of the beast itself and tell that truth seemed terrifying and near impossible. Why did he come here? He felt an awful panic in his chest. "Are you gonna come down and give me a hug?" Where did that come from? He felt tears again.

"I think it's best you go, Vince."

"You can't do this," Vince blubbered as he started to cry. "You can't kick me out." He raised his voice as the tears pushed to get out. "You can't kick me out of your fucking house!" He looked around frantically then and grabbed a large vase, flinging it hard onto the tiled entryway floor where it shattered violently. The wife threw up her hands hysterically and ran into the dining room. Calmly, James Malone came down the stairs, his jaw set firmly. He ordered his wife to please go upstairs—she readily complied—and grabbed Vince hard by the arm.

"Listen, you little punk, you get the fuck out of here or I'm calling the police."

"Mom already did. It doesn't work. I'm your kid. Besides, that's who brought me here." He was still blubbering, but breaking the vase broke something else in him and he was shaky now. But his father's firm hand helped him regain his composure, his sense of humor even.

His father forced Vince's arm away. "What the fuck do you want—money? What can I give you that will make you go away?"

Vince thought of something corny and pathos laden. He thought to answer, "How about my childhood or my virginity?" but he would never allow those words to cross his lips. "Give me two hundred dollars," he said with desperation.

His father grabbed his wallet and, in one motion, quickly peeled two hundred-dollar bills out of it. Vince thought then that he should have asked for more. "Here," and he shoved the money into Vince's open hand—a boy's hand, a faggot's hand, a hand of shame because he greedily took the bills. His father went to the door and opened it. "Now go!"

Vince approached the doorway, and out of the corner of his eyes saw the two young boys at the rail at the top of the stairway. "Are you fucking them too?" he asked point blank with those cruel black eyes he had learned to use so well to inflict pain when necessary.

It must have been like looking into a mirror for his father, who compulsively cuffed Vince hard on the back of the neck, sending him through the door, and slamming it behind him.

Vince was amazed he had even been able to say it. Or that *it* was able to speak through him. He was still sniffling a bit as he walked across the lawn, but he felt a renewed strength and approached the living room window. He stopped momentarily and then kicked his boot through the glass. Then he ran down the street. He looked back once to see if his father had come out, but the door was still closed, the windows empty, and the curtains drawn—all was silent as if he had never been there at all. Or if he had been, he was already long forgotten, as dismissed as the Avon lady or a Fuller Brush man, or some embarrassing, maybe even hideous, thing you did a long time ago when you drank too much at some insignificant and not-very-good party.

"And that's the last I saw of them," he said without emotion, looking at the ceiling. "What a fuckin' day, got rid of them both. Good fuckin' riddance," he added with a cold finality.

When he was angry like that, I didn't feel as tender toward him. I just felt lucky that my life was vanilla compared. I had a renewed regard and acceptance of my family. I was through with whining, but of course he wanted to find things out about me too.

"It was just a typical suburban upbringing, Vince. Nothing very eventful ever happened. My parents are actually pretty cool. There was no violence. I never ran away. But I should have." This last comment surprised him.

"Why?" he looked at me.

"Well, it was so normal, it was insipid. And I had a shitty older brother to deal with," I tiredly recounted. "I don't mean I would have never gone back, but I should have done something to get my parents to see something was wrong. I just kind of avoided dealing with everything, hid out in my room."

"You're lucky you had one. I didn't even tell you about my sisters."

"No, you didn't," I said, displaying a marked curiosity and jumping at the chance to shift things his way, fearing I'd bore him with my own dull family life. "How many sisters did you have?"

"Two. And there's not much to say. One's born-again and the other's a bull dyke."

"Are you still in touch with either of them?" I should have known not to ask.

"Fuck no," he snapped. And then he grinned widely. "What's great is that none of us will ever reproduce. The born-again had an abortion in high school and now she can't have kids. And the bulldyke and me, well, we're not the turkey-baster types. So fucking James and Sylvia Malone's genes have been stopped dead in their tracks. Good fucking riddance. Their only progeny is a dead fetus. Ain't that fitting." What could I say to that? "But fuck them, tell me about your brother."

I was still digesting the shocking vitriol of this last comment, and it took me a moment to recover myself. "Wow. Well, he was just a little fascist, Vince. He was always telling me how I should be, and if I wasn't like that, that there was something wrong with me. He was just a jock conformist little Nazi," I said bitterly but, remembering my contemplations from when he'd last visited, I reconsidered, wanting to be rid of the bitterness and feeling that I was backsliding, indulging once again in things that didn't matter so much anymore. "I feel sorry for him, Vince. He's fucked up. I shouldn't have believed him, but I was a kid."

"Well, families are pathetic, aren't they?"

"I don't know, Vince. I guess I was pretty lucky." I felt like a chump, like he might even hold it against me that I'd had it easy compared to him. But he seemed to be feeling good, well into his second cigarette.

"So, your brother, Peter, what was he like?"

"Peter's always been just, I don't know, kind of like self-contained. He didn't cause any trouble for anybody."

"You never fought with him?"

"Oh, yeah, a little. But mostly because Paul would provoke it by praising Peter for being good at sports or stronger than me, or whatever. He'd load all this shit on me about not holding up my end of things, like I was really pathetic and couldn't even beat up my little brother."

"That sucks," Vince remarked.

"Yeah, I'd go into his room— he wouldn't even know that Paul and I had been at it. I'd go find him and punch him in the gut or something. It was really ludicrous; he had no idea why I was doing it. I feel pretty bad about that, especially now."

"Yeah, I guess. Whatever—you didn't know he'd end up with cancer."

"Yeah, it's all a long time ago." Then I nervously added, since he'd brought it up, "So, Vince, how's your treatments and stuff? Are you still going?"

"Why? Is Peter telling you he hasn't seen me?" He looked at me defensively.

"No, Vince, we don't talk about you."

"Good!" he snapped. Then begrudgingly he added, "I go now and again."

"Well, isn't it like a schedule you gotta follow?"

"What are you, my mother?" he said angrily.

"Well, I just care about you."

"Really? You don't even fucking know me," he said disgustedly, blowing a big puff of smoke out the window. He chucked the cigarette out soon after and hopped to his feet, announcing cheerfully, "Let's go take a walk."

Vince seemed to repel my curiosity this way whenever I got too close. It made me tentative and fearful of prying, and it gave me the feeling that he told me only what he wanted to tell me just then—nothing more, nothing less. I could accept that, I suppose, whether I liked it or not. But it wasn't like his cancer was some secret—he'd elucidated profusely in the clinic waiting room. Why was he being so dodgy now?

Walking around the neighborhood, Vince pointed out various characters from his hotel. He motioned his head toward a towering black woman who must have been well over six feet.

"That's Candy, there; she's a tranny. Very fucked up on speed. And over there, on the bus stop bench, that's Henry." On the bench sat a skinny little guy, perhaps thirty, hunched in a gray overcoat.

"What's his story?" I asked.

"Oh, he's this whiny little poet dude. But he's seriously bipolar so he can't get his shit together, and his relationship to his meds is like all caught up with his ball buster of a mother, so he doesn't take them—pathetic," he concluded, tossing his third cigarette into the gutter.

Vince could be so harsh. I certainly didn't get what he saw in me if he was so eager to write off most of humanity. What was I to him—some middle-class kid with all the fixins? Whatever would he want with that? Certainly, he found me physically attractive, but he was usually commenting on how ugly people were, if anything, so he didn't seem like someone in pursuit of beauty or aesthetics. His only interest seemed to be books, and cigarettes of course, and alcohol. Or that's what I'd noticed so far anyway.

"I'm gonna make you dinner," he announced.

I was perplexed. "Where?"

"In my room," he answered, as if to say, "What's so strange about that?"

"You don't have a kitchen."

"Wait and see," he said coyly, grabbing my arm to cross the street. "We need to go up to the Castro," he said then, as we arrived at the bus stop, now vacated by Henry.

"Why we do we need to go up there?" I knew he hated it there; he'd told me so when I'd asked him to take me there one night. Because to Vince, the gay ghetto was just another shopping mall with slightly better taste and more sex—"But I'm not impressed by 'slightly'; I hate shopping; and I don't want to have sex with any of them," he had said in disgust.

"What about, like—just like, they're your people?" I had countered.

He'd lowered his forehead so his brows nearly covered his eyes as he glowered at me. "Are you fucking high?" I'd just shrugged, letting it pass. It was all new to me, and he was my guide.

The reason we were going there now was because there was a large Safeway market up there and Vince wanted to get us food for dinner. But when we got to the door, he told me to wait outside.

"Why?"

"Because dinner's on me," he said cryptically.

I didn't get his meaning, but I waited for him there, next to a yellow coin-operated Dumbo elephant kid's ride.

He came out ten minutes later, moving quickly. "Come on," he said without smiling.

Back on the bus, he showed me the booty, which he now pulled from his deep trenchcoat pockets.

"It's gonna be a vegan feast," he announced smiling, pulling forth tofu, snow peas, minute rice, a bottle of Beau Tour wine and another bottle of Glenlivet scotch.

My mouth was agape. "You ripped all that shit off?" But I was also thinking, *What big pockets you have.*

"I'm out of food stamps, Neill," he said cheerfully by way of explanation.

"Vince, I got money. I coulda bought all that."

He looked back at me coldly. "I said dinner's on me, Neill. Don't argue with me."

I'd obviously hurt his pride, but I was uneasy again. I hadn't figured him for a thief, or a habitual one anyway, naïf that I was. I said nothing more.

"Come on, I'm gonna make a vegan of you," he said next, a satisfied smile on his face. And he winked.

↷ XII

I'd cooked for Peter those months of his convalescence. My mother claimed she was too distracted, though every meal I prepared was done so in her company, since she sat drinking tea, unwilling to assist me but very proactive about advising my every move. She drank a lot of tea and talked a lot all those months—to me, and on the phone. Otherwise she read self-help books or kept busy sewing, trying as hard as she could not to dote on him, since that drove him crazy.

She rarely left the house and my father was rarely in it. Since Peter had been home, my father had been spending most of his time gardening. Even though it was winter, he found things to do. Each Saturday and Sunday morning we'd awaken to the sound of his busyness, the squeaky wheelbarrow full of last year's refuse trundling back and forth all day—and sometimes even at night—across the lawn from the vegetable garden to the hillside, where he'd dump it to compost at the foot of the big oak tree outside my window.

Peter and I had laughed at him out there, at yet another example of his comic eccentricity.

"Your father," my mother would shake her head in disapproval.

And we'd laugh because he'd wear these old brown, shiny slippers, made out of some kind of ugly fake leather that looked like shiny burnt Velveeta cheese. My mother hated those slippers—as she did the majority of his gardening gear, as she called it—and would occasionally throw them away. A week ago, I found him in the garage digging through the garbage and pulling them out from under a bag of rotting vegetables. He seemed only mildly irritated, whereas in the past he would have hollered at her. But much of their bickering was simply like a cartoon nowadays. Maybe it was his way of giving her a little leeway, considering.

Because it wasn't just about taking care of ourselves, or even Peter. We had to take care of one another. I'd become like a good waiter or bartender—I kept my problems to myself and kept Peter served and occupied so my mother could play hostess and Dad could do the books. Chez Cancer, the restaurant.

I'd go out early to shop for food or run whatever errands were necessary, before he was awake. Sometimes I'd miscalculate and he'd already be up when I returned.

"Peter, what's up?" I called out, entering the kitchen with a bag of groceries, seeing him from behind, bent over at the table in his pajamas, sipping from a cup of tea.

"Not much," he grunted, turning and smiling, trying to be cheerful. Not enough was going on, after three weeks. I could see he was getting antsy.

"You wanna do something?"

"Yeah, I guess," he said dispiritedly. He was obviously out of ideas. Each morning it was the newspaper, followed by *Divorce Court* and *Leave It to Beaver*. Then it was on to a shower, which could be harrowing. He had patches of healing, raw skin from the skin grafts they took from his legs and shoulders to use in refitting the sausage to his chest. His face was incredibly sensitive from stitches and the graft, and his neck muscles were all bunched up from having his head cocked to one side for so long. At first, I had bathed him in the tub with a sponge, but he was impatient now, so we'd moved up to showering. He tried to do as much of it himself as he could, but he cursed when he bent too far in one direction, or when the water or soap burned one of his wounds.

"Let me do it, Peter," and I reached in the open shower door and soaped up his back; carefully washed his hair from behind so the shampoo wouldn't run down his face. He tried not to curse when I hit one of those tender spots, asking me patiently to be careful. I apologized, he smiled, and I moved on with my little sponge, cleaning him and, in a sense, worshiping him for his fortitude, humility, and cheerfulness—his perseverance that seemed to speak of the same persistent will to live as that of all those struggling people I'd known about only through reading books. He yanked it all off the page and out of my imagination and put it in my hands; he made it all real to me.

"So, what shall we do, Peter?" I'd ask him, as he sat vacantly watching reruns, slouched upon the sofa. "Take a walk?"

"Nah, I can't today. I'm just not up for it," he said, his face almost begging for a second choice, fearing he was disappointing me and sincerely wanting to do anything but watch more TV. At times, he seemed so overwhelmed by his boredom that he looked almost hopeless.

"OK, another time. How about a game?" my brows arched up because we hadn't—he and I—played one together since he came home from the hospital, though he'd been playing cards with my mother, along with a vast array of board games.

"Like what?" he asked skeptically. I took too long to come up with a sellable option and he vented his frustration because the walk was what he really wanted. "Damn, I'd like to walk, go running, lift weights, jump over the—"

"Honey, you can't do that yet," my mother called out from the dining room where she was sewing a pair of pants, the needle and thread in her mouth slurring her speech. She was always listening. But she was cheerful of late. I thought it was because she had always been more comfortable with small children, and that was what she'd decided he was for now. Not a good long-term strategy, but whatever helped us find our way. If today she needed it to be 1975, so be it.

"I know, Mom. I was kidding," he said, and he rolled his eyes at me.

"Come on, let's play a game, Peter," I insisted.

"I can't play another game. Me and Mom have played Scrabble, fuckin' Yahtzee, Chutes and Ladders, Monopoly—what else? . . ."

"UNO, honey, and gin rummy. You want to play again?" The thread was out of her mouth then and she was back to full, clear volume.

"*No!*"

"Peter, you haven't played Risk or LIFE, right?" I resumed.

"No, she doesn't like those."

"Yeah, but I do," I beseeched him.

"I know, Neill, but I'm bored with games."

"How about if we remake them?" He lit up a wee bit, but I could see he was still skeptical.

"Come on, hear me out. Remember how we customized Monopoly once?" I implored, trying to encourage him.

"Oh, geez," and he was grinning as wide a grin as he was capable of.

"What did you do to Monopoly, honey?" my mother called out, apparently still listening in on our conversation. I was slightly annoyed, but I knew how happy it made her just to be having a normal suburban conversation again.

"You better not tell her," Peter warned.

"Mom, we changed all the properties," I called out defiantly, smiling at him. "Each one became a house on our street and all the little green houses and red hotels became furniture."

She was likely smiling too by now as she asked the inevitable question. "Which property was our house?"

"Baltic Avenue," I responded, looking directly at Peter who knew what was coming next.

"Gee, honey, it's not that bad."

"Well, I know, Ma. We were trying to have some fun; that's all."

So that Wednesday afternoon we did the same thing to The Game of LIFE. There were only a handful of job possibilities on the board, so we got out a deck of cards and increased that to more than fifty occupations, ranging from real estate broker to hired assassin. There was also the problem of fertility in that particular board game and it breeds children like lice. It's difficult to navigate one round of the game, let alone several rounds, as Peter and I liked to play, without ending up with not one or two, but literally a fleet of minivans to house the sniveling lot of them. We were progressive, even cutting edge, we told ourselves, and boldly rewrote whole swaths of squares with the aid of masking tape, penciling in, "Choose Abortion, lose $5,000" and "Miscarriage: lose turn and go back to bed and try again." You could buy birth control pills like stocks and bonds that would cover you for whole rounds. We also added divorce, stock market crashes, failing S and Ls, both white- and blue-collar crime, alcoholism, and drug use. To top it off, we had a square for affairs. (I hadn't the courage yet to suggest a gay affair or a coming-out episode, nor the caprice to add public indecency in a men's bathroom as part of our crime grab bag.) We had other squares for job terminations, moves to other cities, heart attacks, car accidents, and—of course—cancer.

We laughed out loud as the game played out, and Peter had to get up and leave on occasion as his scars would pull and ache from the laughing jags. He ended up a pornographer, ex-rock star with ten children, while having two affairs, each of the "other women" having had not one but several abortions. All ten of his children had various kinds of cancer and his wife was a cop who'd had three heart attacks and four head-on collisions that had resulted in fatalities for the other parties. We considered creating some kind of judiciary system, or at least some kind of police oversight board, but the game was becoming a bureaucratic nightmare as we attempted to keep track of who'd fathered whose child, whether our birth control had run out, and how to explain the inevitable inconsistencies, such as convicted felons embarking on political careers and players moving to Chad to open ski resorts. When Peter's wife's eleventh child was aborted midcollision, he had to get up and leave, holding his mouth.

"Honey, maybe you should stop. Neill, it's too much. Do something else," I heard her voice from the next room.

"Laughter heals!" I called out.

"All things in moderation!" she yelled back.

"Get back in here, Peter, I'm in the middle of an abortion and I need the forceps!" I barked, which sent him into further squalls of laughter. I heard my mother laugh too, even though I knew she was shocked at our sacrilege and sarcasm regarding abortion, marital infidelity, cancer, etc. It was in poor taste, but comedy often is, and it was all we had left in many ways. Hell, they'd turned my brother into Frankenstein—who's accusing whom of poor taste?

Besides, this was our paternal legacy. Though we'd never get him to play, he always smiled to see Peter smile and I knew he must have felt some self-satisfaction to know he'd raised sons who could somehow keep laughing if nothing else. He'd arrive home and always say the same thing: "How you doing today, Peter, feelin' better?" answering his own question in the affirmative because he had no idea what to do about the negative response to such an inquiry. It was as if he were telling Peter he'd love to talk to him, but could it wait until he got better and there was no more danger of him dying? Peter would smile and answer "Feeling fine," letting him off easy. Peter was happy with everyone just staying the same. Which in the end, considering what was happening, was a far taller order than it seemed then.

☙ XIII

It turned out that Vince had a hot plate in his room. He hid it under his bed and although it was obviously against the rules, what with it being a fire hazard and all, he'd been getting away with it for a while, he told me.

"Why'd we never use it before?" I inquired.

"No reason; we went out." I'd paid for all our Chinese meals, which was fine by me as I had a student loan to eat up since I'd dropped out of school.

Vince turned out to be a good cook, as I half-expected considering his knowledge of macrobiotics and that story about the deli. He turned to preparing dinner now on the little bedside table that he'd pulled over to the window. He was tossing the vegetable cuttings and trash out the window. When he noticed me watching him do so, he said simply, "If they see this shit in my garbage can, they'll flip." It's not like the Baldwin had maid service, but the management used their master key whenever they suspected anything, and they might come in while he was out.

"So, hey Neill, guess what?"

"Huh?"

"My herpes is gone," he grinned.

"Cool," I smiled.

"But don't get any ideas," he added as a disclaimer. "I might not be into it." I was mystified by the comment, and of course he'd rapidly changed the subject to bamboo shoots and curry paste. It was always best not to second-guess Vince, I was learning slowly but surely, so I let it go. I reminded myself that I really didn't care that much. I just liked being with him and listening to him.

He began ranting about San Francisco politics as he poured me red wine into an old peanut butter jar, serving the meal on paper plates from a bag under the bed.

"In San Francisco, it's always the same, Neill. It's all left-wing rhetoric, and even the business community has learned how to speak it. I've never seen developers so gaga over low-cost housing. But, you see, it's all a scam, and city hall is in their backpocket the whole time. They build these big apartment towers, hold a press conference to lament the cost overruns, claim they'll have to pull out, and the next thing you know a compromise deal's been worked out, and when the units hit the market, they're seventeen-hundred-dollar studios. But who cares. I'll never live in one of them, nor would I want to. This city's days are as numbered as mine."

"Ah, don't say that, Vince."

"It's a yuppie hellhole, and it's getting worse all the time." There was no point in arguing, of course; it simply brought up again the fact that he was only passing through anyway.

He was on to the next thing by then besides, insulting the mayor and bemoaning the idiocy of politicians in general. He'd move on to national and international stories—wars and political hypocrisies, right-wing machinations and maneuvers—talking animatedly, burning up the excited adrenaline that I suddenly wished he'd turn instead on me. He was up and running. He'd get to me in time, but first there was the news and his long grocery list of grievances.

"This stupid bitch at the market followed me around today like I was a thief." I wanted to say "You are," but that was pointless, of course, and redundant. "I'm definitely gonna have to rip that place off," he concluded, as if he'd show them. I guess now that I'd seen him in action, he was comfortable talking about his burgling woes, which he'd never mentioned before.

He continued then to recount each incident wherein he'd been insulted since I'd last seen him. "Henry tried to read me a poem today. These fucking people think I'm one of them."

There was as well the usual drama of the Baldwin Arms, which included at least one paramedic call a week, and a dozen or so altercations of one kind or another, whether verbal or physical it was never quite clear, nor whether, or in what way, they involved Vince himself. Then there were the injustices rendered by the system (he was on food stamps, general assistance, and Medicaid), and complaints about the worthless bureaucrats "whom they paid to get in my fucking way, just so that I earn every fucking dollar they dole out to me. So much for welfare." He'd end his litany so pissed off and disgusted that I'd lose my desire to share any of my news, and I'd just lean over to kiss him instead, often as not inspiring a surprised scowl, before he collected himself enough to realize I didn't work for SSI, at which point he'd give in and lean over and kiss me back and smile.

I wasn't coming to see Vince looking for attention anyway. I came to him in order to listen to him, so I didn't find his self-involvement unattractive. Not in the beginning anyway. Besides, he was brilliant, and seemed to understand everything, tearing away layer after layer of bullshit, and then when he got to whatever nugget of truth remained, he'd toss it to me like a peanut, no longer interested. If I didn't want it, out the window it would go.

"Let's go," he said now, tossing the used plates out the window and stashing the hot plate, cups, and silverware back under the bed with the scotch and wine.

We liked to walk, so we rarely went anywhere specific. We'd sort of wander. Maybe we'd walk as far as the Haight or down to the Mission. We tended to avoid the hip places, although that was never easy in San Francisco. But we'd always end up finding new streets and neighborhoods we never before knew existed. We'd end up tired and in some corner bar, drinking beer and wondering who they all were, what their lives were like. Like my father used to do, he'd make up stories about people, but Vince's were never in jest.

"She's slumming," Vince would say about some punkish-looking girl who looked a little bit too cleaned up. "She's probably a poet or a prostitute though, thinks it's real cool and edgy. San Francisco's full of 'em." I was beginning to think he hated San Francisco, but then Vince probably hated every city.

That night we went up to North Beach because he was looking for some book he claimed he'd only find at City Lights. He stole it, of course, and we made our way up Powell Street, which ran over the hill among all the big hotels before descending steeply down to Union Square with its department stores and theaters. From there, it was just a short walk down Market Street to skid row and the Baldwin Arms. The cable car ran up and down Powell Street, clanging by as we hiked up the sidewalk, and I had to laugh when that song occurred to me. I mocked it for Vince, "I left my heart . . ."

"Oh geez, Neill. Well, ain't that nice? I left my fucking testicle in San Francisco, and your brother left half his face here."

"And some teeth," I chortled; I was in a good mood.

"Yeah, and you're about to leave your virginity here," he bumped me playfully with his shoulder, working his eyebrows in a sort of mock-sinister Bela Lugosi. I blushed, unable to come up with a rejoinder as my heart began to beat more rapidly.

We reached the crest of the hill where we entered the milling crowds of what everyone always referred to as "Midwestern tourists" waiting for the cable car (could they really all be from that one region of the country?). Whoever they were, they were likely paying a hundred or more a night in these four- and five-star hotels.

"Mammon-worshiping morons. What they really need is a vacation from money—and they come here!" he joked angrily.

But I was just suddenly overcome with the joy of being with my gay boyfriend in what seemed the heart of suburban normalcy, so I put my arm around him then. And the families began to ogle us. The kids especially. They were curious at least; I'll give them that. They looked at Vince more than they did me, with his punk getup and his orange hair. I wasn't much to look at—not much different from them really.

"Cattle," he said with disgust.

But I was still beaming. "Does anybody know where the Baldwin Arms Hotel is?" I called out just for fun. No one answered until I fixed my eyes on them. Then they just shook their heads "no" and moved out of our way. Indeed, they were like cattle.

Vince laughed at my joke, and then said in a voice loud enough for them to hear, "Are you kidding? These people use San Francisco like they use their brains—about ten percent of it, max! They never venture south of here, at least not beyond the theaters."

Down the other side of the hill we went, which proved to be a sort of bell curve of socioeconomics. We were happy to leave its apex. There were only stragglers who'd missed the cable cars climbing opposite us now as we descended. But near the bottom, where the shopping was, they swelled again, like mosquitoes in a spring pond. We cut off Powell Street and took the back way, where the loitering strangers were less clueless and certainly more interesting to look at, but also generally more suspicious looking, begging the question in my mind: *Is nothing in this world interesting that doesn't carry some kind of danger or risk?*

When we got to the fluorescent-lit lobby of the Baldwin, the Arab man at the desk waved us by with a clipped smile, before looking quickly away. Vince smiled at me as we rode the rickety elevator up to Floor 6.

Pulling back the clunky door of the lift, he grabbed my hand to urge me out into the hallway, nearly breaking into a run as we headed to his room. "Come on!" he shouted gleefully, in an uncharacteristic outburst of joy. He opened the door quickly, pushing me in and slamming it, all in one motion, then he turned, grabbed my cheeks in his hands, and kissed me. He breathed a sigh of relief as if that were enough, and I smiled at him, finding it comic and endearing.

We took off our shoes and jumped onto the concave single bed that creaked and squealed under the load. Kissing passionately, I watched the neon reflection that lit up his cheeks a pinkish-yellow, and its rhythm made me feel as if I was inside some song, between the notes or bars, and all I had to do was follow along with the music. I started to pull at his clothes, but he stopped me again, reminding me that he'd take off his pants but the shirt would have to remain. I once again tried to convince him otherwise, careful not to push him too hard and thus ruin the moment, but it was no use. I yanked off my own shirt then, hoping I might prove a role model in this tiny comic drama. But he was unconvinceable.

So the shirt remained, a sort of bulletproof vest of chain mail issued by his father, as the buckles came unclasped, and the seductive black hair of his thighs and knee was revealed. I was almost overcome by the electric excitement of my own skin as it pressed and brushed against his, I felt no shame or guilt as I'd feared I might; in fact, my mind chattered an inner commentary—*how beautiful, how perfect and good this is.* But it was sad to keep running into his shirt and knowing what it symbolized each time I did. He let me run my hands up inside it at least, so I was satisfied, feeling the smooth, cool skin; its creases; his clavicles and taut little nipples. There was something almost dear about the shirt after a while, like a third party we wrestled around.

He pulled at the elastic band of my boxer shorts and down they went, as I fumbled and did the same to his, our cocks together finally, so full of eagerness to meet as we pressed them together and moaned a sort of gratitude for this joy we could so easily share. Mostly we kissed and rubbed ourselves together, but he seemed disturbingly concerned, frightened, even timid at times. At once passionate and then weirdly lonely and at a loss, he was like an abandoned, disoriented kid in a grocery store, full of anxiety and an inward angst that included no one but himself. All of it was erased in our final assault on each other as we consummated for the first time what was deep inside us—the seed of our genes, the history of our being through ancestors and immemorial time—all that we were and all that we could become. An image of him remains from that first orgasm together: his head back, the furrowed, almost frightened brow—his spine arched, the semen shooting from his long, crooked stem, and the T-shirt: Boycott Table Grapes.

∾ XIV

They released Peter and then they brought him back a month later.
The doctor'd been grave. The latest CAT scan had revealed yet
more cancer growing back in his cheek, under the graft.

"Fuck," Peter had yelled after the phone call.

My mother's hands were in the air, her face collapsing into a tragic
frown. "Oh, Lord."

"Not now, Mom," I quickly ran to the rescue.

Peter was in a fury, and I knew if he stopped, he would break down
and cry and I was so afraid of that. Not so much for him, but I was terrified that somehow my mother would one day just disappear into her
sorrow and never come back.

"And guess what," he half-hollered, "he thinks he might have to
take my eye."

That did it. She was gone then, actually on the floor, on her knees.

"Peter, man, I'm sorry," and then I was starting to tear up, hoping
he would help me with Mom.

"Don't start, you guys; don't fucking start!" He stormed out of the
room.

I felt terrible suddenly, like I'd forced him to leave, as if this were
about him helping me deal with Mom and not about his own feelings.
But it was all the same really. Our emotions had become collective.
I'd get her calmed down, and then I could go to him.

"Might, Mom," I raised my voice. "*Might!* Everything's gonna be
OK. Round whatever in a fucking fight." I got it all wrong.

She stopped crying then, but she just sat there on the floor, dejected
looking. "Come on, Mom," but she looked at me so hollowly it scared
me. I half wanted to say, "I can't help you; just don't leave us now.
Please." But I knew where that would take us. I kissed her forehead

and left her there on the floor, hurrying off to see Peter, who'd seques-
tered himself for privacy in the bathroom. There wasn't a sound. *We're
fucked,* was all I could think then. But what was I going to do? I
couldn't think of a thing, so I just kept going.

"You OK in there, Peter?" He didn't answer.

"I'm gonna make you some tea," I offered, having no other ideas.
It's what we always fell back on. While I made it, my mother, now sitting up against the wall (*This is not a person who sits on floors,* I reminded
myself, worried), looked into the middle distance—which in this case,
would be what? the garden? the big oak tree?

Of course Dad would be home soon, which would either help or
bring yet more drama. I was confident of the former and he suddenly
seemed to be exactly what we needed. I was in way over my head, and
though I'd thought that of him, maybe he really wasn't. You never
knew with him; he had reserves. He was just careful to keep them until absolutely necessary.

Within an hour, we heard the garage door opening. By then I'd
gotten my mother up to the table and Peter had returned, composed.
She was still distant, but she was there, offering a small smile to Peter.
But we were all oddly silent, saying only such things as "Pass the
sugar," or "This is good tea."

How could he know what he was walking into? And who was going to tell him? We just looked at him as he entered the kitchen and
then watched it dawn on him that something was obviously wrong,
considering the silence and all of us gathered there with no light on as
the dusk receded to dark. Of course he knew the results of the CAT
scan were imminent, so he obviously figured it out.

"Hey, Dad," Peter said, in his best jock tone, "CAT scan was no
good." He glanced quickly at my mother who showed no sign of hearing, staring now at her teacup. "So we're going back in," Peter added
mock-triumphantly.

"OK," my father hesitated. "What exactly did they tell you, Peter?" But Peter gestured his eyes toward my mother, indicating, *better
not get into it right now.*

But she spoke next. "Well, Frank, they found a little more and they have to do some more cutting." She said it slowly and we all watched her, transfixed and nervous. "The doctor says he might lose the eye, but we won't know until he goes in."

He nodded his head reassuringly, pausing as he picked up on her sudden solemnity.

"OK. I think our man can handle that, eh, Peter?"

"Yeah, sure."

"Fourth and long, Peter. You've done it a thousand times."

"No punting for me." It was between *them* now and my mother and I sat in rapt silence as they proceeded to discuss some former football game Peter'd been in. How do they do it? I got up and stood behind my mom, with my hands on her shoulders, and just listened.

He took us out to dinner that night, acted uncharacteristically cheerful, flirting with the waitresses and smiling "thank yous" at the busboy. He'd provided a fulcrum after all. I really wanted to thank him, but I couldn't risk it. We had to keep moving.

"It's all in the research," he said at one point. "This cancer, a fibro-sarcoma, often comes back. It's got like these tendrils and they don't always get them all. It's like a root system; no big deal." He waved his hands around for emphasis, but my mother kept hers in close, picking slowly and carefully at her food, as Peter and I communicated with our eyes for him to please spare the gory details for her sake.

Ꮽ XV

"Should I go, Vince?"

He seemed to have folded inward the minute our sex was over. He was already fully dressed again in T-shirt and long johns—and not because it was cold—and sitting on the windowsill smoking, looking outward, but in a tense and distracted way.

"That was fun," I offered. "I like to be with you, Vince," I volunteered unimaginatively, hoping to draw him out.

"Well, don't expect me to want to do it all the time," he warned me, still not looking at me.

"You don't like it?"

"No, not really. Someday I'll be old and won't want to have sex anymore. I can't wait."

I remembered then all that he'd told me, and again I had that guilty feeling of being the lucky one as I had when Peter first got sick. Whatever I said now, I didn't want it to be trite or selfish.

I tried to be reassuring. "Vince, I just like to touch you; that's all. I don't care what we do, really."

"No, I know what you want," he said cynically.

"Hey, Vince, you know I like you." But there was no bluffing Vince. He always read my mind. He looked at me then as if to say, "Really? Prove it." I became silent and figured it was probably better not to talk about sex at all with him. Just do it and say nothing would probably be the wiser tack, though I wanted to talk about everything with him. I'd just made love to a man for the first time and it felt like a great weight had fallen from me, like a window had opened.

He flicked the cigarette out the window and ambled back over to the bed, hopping spryly over me to the wall side and turning his back to me.

"Go to sleep," he softly commanded.

I slept deeply, dreaming of Vince playing guitar on a stage I was unable to climb up on.

I awoke to shouts from down on the street. The alarm of these frequent shrieks wore off in time as I learned that for the most part they either regarded nothing or were just part of how people communicated in this, Vince's neighborhood.

I gazed then upon Vince, his heavy, pouting lip hanging now precipitously from his mouth, framing the big Chiclets of his front teeth. His inch-long hair was a random mess, crossing every which way, and his skin had that olive green pallor I found so attractive against the black roots of his scalp and his dark, full eyebrows. His eyes were moving under the lids, and it made me wonder what he dreamed of. Good things, I hoped—reaching down to pull me up onstage with him, perhaps.

I got up and went down the hall to the bathroom. We used the sink to piss, but if you really needed a toilet, you had to go down the hall to the common bathroom. It was relatively clean—too clean really. The ammonia cleared your sinuses. There was a urinal and a couple of toilet stalls as well as two showers. A tattooed old sailor, or merchant marine, was in one of the showers singing "Unchained Melody" at top volume, his voice terrible but very sincere and soulful.

When I returned to Vince's room, he was already up and dressed, fumbling through a pile of books, muttering he needed coffee and a cigarette. He brushed by me without making eye contact, I assumed to go to the bathroom. But in no time, he was back at the door.

"You ready?"

"Yeah," I answered, shoving yesterday's socks and underwear into my old gym bag, which I always brought with me when I came to see him.

"I'm starved," he said dispiritedly. He seemed oddly put out, not just by me but by everything.

We wandered down to the coffee shop we'd first met at, where we ordered coffee and bagels, and Vince disappeared into the newspaper. I was beginning to get impatient, feeling ignored and even a bit angered by his distance as he sat there like some unaffectionate sitcom husband thumbing through the paper.

"So, what do you want to do, Vince?"

He peered momentarily over the newspaper. "I don't know yet." So he was lacking his usual decisiveness as well, it seemed. I wasn't re-assured. I'd need to leave today eventually, and right now I was think-ing maybe it was time.

"Well, I have some stuff to do with Peter this afternoon, so I guess I better go."

I saw him peer over the paper again, his brows rolling in over his eyes as if he was getting increasingly pissed off as well.

"No, you don't," he snapped.

"How do you know?" I asked defensively.

"I just do. Come on, let's get out of here." He then commenced to get up and collect together the paper, which he tossed in a heap onto a nearby table. I wolfed down my bagel to join him, chugging the last half of my coffee along with it, and noticing as I did that he'd barely touched his bagel and had only drunk half his coffee.

"I'm a little fucked up, OK?" he offered, raising his eyebrows, with just a hint of being put out in having to say it at all.

"Yeah, OK, that's cool," I lamely answered, seeing in his expression that he wanted me to try to ignore it, and that he definitely did not want to discuss it.

We spent the day in bookstores, saying little, but being together all the same, which was enough for him and me both, I suppose. When I had to go I told him I'd had a great time, but he only looked down, al-most whispering, "Come back next week, OK?"

"Yeah, I will. Friday night." He gave me a peck on the cheek and ambled off as I hopped in my car and headed back across the bridge to home, perturbed at his sudden silence but also giddy with having had for-real sex. It was like he'd filled me and left a hole both.

When I got home, I felt like I'd felt in high school when I'd been doing illicit drugs. But more so than any drug could ever be, gay sex was definitely a contraband in the world I'd grown up in, far more abominable than any narcotic. I felt that I'd be telling my parents *I* was losing an eye now. (But the proper analogy would be that I never actually had one; it had been glass all along.) I was more afraid, in some ways, than ever after I saw what happened to my mother that night eight months ago. So I kept it to myself.

But it was still disorienting, because it really wasn't that big a deal suddenly. Well, not for me. I felt I'd been a fool all these years to have tortured myself so, ruminating on this innocent animal truth. I felt I'd been stingy with life, like I'd carried it around all this time, holding onto it in my clenched fist. Peter never had a choice. They pried *his* hand open. And when they did, my fingers lost all their strength. It felt good that way, what I'd done with Vince, like my hands being opened. But that didn't reassure me about my parents.

My mother took notice that night of my thinly veiled elation and seemed suddenly curious about these "friends" I hung out with on weekends in San Francisco, and "Was there a girl?"

She oughtta do game shows, I thought; *she's good.* I wouldn't lie to her, nor would I tell her. "No, it's not a girl," I said impatiently, the tone of my voice hinting for her to drop it.

"Aren't your friends in Berkeley?" she persisted.

"I have friends everywhere," was all I said, a tad dismissively, but if she'd asked me point blank, I think I'd have told her. I never lied when people wanted the truth—I lied only when they didn't. I'd come to believe cynically that this was one of those truths she didn't want. As intuitive as she was, she'd never suspected I was gay, to my knowledge. But then she hadn't figured on cancer either. She saved her intuition for good things, I suppose.

But this *was* a good thing! Yet it was all so complicated. It saddened me to feel the distance it created between us, especially now. We'd all grown so much closer in the past year—and yet this part of me was far outside it all, and maybe even pushing me farther and farther away.

I told myself I wasn't ready yet; I told myself *they* weren't ready. I told myself I was protecting them, making a necessary sacrifice for the good of all. And when I lay down to sleep at night, I told myself I was full of shit and grandiosity. After all, I'd told Peter outside the Baldwin that day that I felt like I only needed him to hold the secret until he was well. And he'd have his last radiation treatment this very

week. Now what was my excuse? I didn't want to rain on their pa-
rade?

Well, it could wait. We'd all grown so used to waiting as it
was—for CAT scans and biopsies, through the long hours of surgery
and convalescence. And *this* waiting wasn't about life and death besides, so what was the rush?

So I lied, or "didn't tell" since they "didn't ask," making me the
good son and a coward both, my heart full to bursting but not yet really free, as I fucked Vincent James Malone every weekend in a flea-
bag hotel.

"See ya Sunday," I'd call out each Friday evening, as casually as I
could, not wanting to let on. I still felt guilty for leaving them at all,
and here I was taking off and more or less lying to boot. A sin of omis-
sion, my mother would call it.

Peter would be goofing in the kitchen with Dad, pretending tur-
nips were tumors he'd found growing under his armpits—trying to
keep my father laughing and loose—while my mother, who'd returned to cooking (a good sign), distractedly assembled dinner. Or
else he'd be complaining to my mother that his "vagina ached" which,
odd as it sounds, made a twisted kind of sense because he'd been pre-
scribed vaginal suppositories to ease the pain of ongoing oral infection
from the radiation. She'd laugh then, seeing as it was so absurd for her
little jock stud high school boy to be complaining in earnest about fe-
male trouble, and pleading for relief to the only woman in the house.
Little did they know their other son was off to suck dick.

"Have fun!" my mother would shout out to me from the range. If
she only knew. Peter'd snap a perfunctory "Later," and my father
would chime in with "Drive safely" or "Don't run anyone over" or
some such nonsense, and off I'd go.

℞ XVI

He was his old eager self again when I stepped out of the rattling cage of that elevator, his silhouette leaning out of the doorway into the milling dust motes and backlit by the flashing neon at the far end of the hall.

He was handsome when I reached the door and hugged and kissed him, missing him. He was lucky it was dark as it made it easier for him to hide his grin that gave it away that he was happy to see me. Forever the poker-faced bluffer and tough, he masked his adrenaline and his joy by lighting up a cigarette and turning to gather up some books he wanted to show me. It was as if he wanted to move directly into the mind, avoiding the muddy ground of emotion, as he handed me his latest discovery: Evans-Wentz's translation of *The Tibetan Book of the Dead*.

He pointed to it after depositing it into my hands, speaking through his cigarette as it bobbed and fumed, "Now *that* is some intense shit."

"Yeah?" I said, acknowledging his fascination and thus encouraging him to say more.

"It's fucking mad," he went on, taking it back out of my hands, and quickly paging through it as he motioned me to sit with him on the floor by the window so he could smoke.

"Look at this," and he started to read excerpts. "'Then the Lord of Death will place round thy neck a rope and drag thee along' . . . It's really cool; it's like this whole fucking detailed explanation of dying and what happens and how you get reincarnated and shit. I've never seen anything like it. You gotta read it."

"Sure, as soon as you finish it, I'll take it."

"I already finished it. I fuckin' read it all the other night. What I really love about it is that everyone has to go through hell—there's no back door for goody-goods." And he pushed it at me. I was vaguely frightened by what he'd read, but also grinning empathetically at his satisfaction that he wasn't the only one headed for the inferno. All the same, I didn't want to read about death and deities. I was sick of religion with all its threats and spooky prophecies. I'd had my dose being raised Catholic; I didn't need any more of it. And I certainly didn't want to be considering any novel grim eventualities for Peter, who I felt had suffered enough already, embodied or otherwise. But one didn't hand a book back to Vince, so I chucked it on top of my bag and accepted the glass of cheap red wine he now offered me.

"I got you a bunch of stuff too," and he nodded his head toward the table where he'd arrayed my gifts. I walked over and there was a bottle of organic multivitamins (easily twenty-five dollars), an orange knit ski cap (so my head would match his?), and a necklace of tiny hematites. I realized right off that he'd stolen it all.

Something in me wouldn't thank him for stealing things for me, so instead I asked him where he got it all.

"Rainbow Market," he said, with slight defensiveness.

"You don't have to steal shit for me, Vince. I don't need anything." I knew I shouldn't have said it the minute the words left my mouth.

"I know I don't *have* to steal things for you, Neill. Do you not want them?"

I hesitated, and he marched over and snatched them off the table. "Jesus Christ, what bullshit. What bourgeois, fucking bullshit!" He went to the window then, forced it up, and tossed the stuff out the window, before turning back to me angrily. "I could have been fucking arrested stealing that shit for you, you ungrateful fuck!"

"Vince, man, all I said . . ." I attempted to defend myself.

"Don't say anything else," he snapped, before pulling out the hot plate from under the bed. He put his finger to his mouth and I thought I detected a slight smile even.

"I don't want to have to throw all this food out the window too, OK?" What was I going to say? "Will you eat it?"

"Yes, Vince, I'll eat the food." I thought of going downstairs to retrieve the "gifts," but I didn't know whether that would prove my contriteness or just anger him all the more. I did nothing—always the safest bet with Vince.

He was making soup tonight and already drinking directly from the wine bottle. He seemed superenergized, in fact, and I wondered where all this was headed.

He started chopping up carrots and celery sticks and tossed me an onion. "Cut that up, will ya?"

I looked around for something to cut it on, but soon enough he was handing me a hardback book and a knife. "Books are great cutting boards," he said, flashing a smile.

I raised my eyebrows momentarily, and then hunkered down and set to work.

"You like coke?" he asked.

"Nah, wine is good," I answered not looking up. He stopped his chopping then and I raised my eyes.

"I mean cocaine, not cola. I got some if you want some." He turned and went back to work on a head of cabbage.

Before I could decide whether I wanted the cocaine I was wondering where he'd gotten it. He refilled my wine glass, wary of my sudden silence.

"I didn't steal the coke; it's perfectly legal," he quipped, sarcastically.

"How the fuck did you come into it then, Vince?"

"General assistance," he said gleefully. "I got my check today."

I rolled my eyes. "Great," and added, "sure, I guess I'll have some."

"No moral dilemmas sucking on Uncle Sam's big titties, eh, Neill?" he chided me, pinching my cheek. I brushed him away.

We got royally fucked up that night. We drank two bottles of wine with the soup, snorted several lines of coke, and then smoked a joint before he hustled me up off the floor and marched me down the street for coffee.

Then he dragged me home for more cocaine and book talk. All I wanted was to kiss him at that point, but he was on a run, so I ran along with him as he laid out the Tibetan cosmology before my eyes, gesticulating with his hands and cigarette *one sorry little Buddhist, I* giggled ironically to myself, *expounding on all color of lights emanating from primordial voids. And he's one of them,* I felt like proclaiming. But I also felt sad, sensing that he loved every world but the one he was in. I'd heard it all in only a few short weeks: Ramana Maharshi and all that emptiness and nothingness; the Kabbalah and its mystical map of the universe that made of America the grossest kind of sham; Gurdjieff, gnosticism, Aleister Crowley. I felt grateful for how he fed me—I was starved for anything that cut away at the mask of the world I'd felt betrayed by. We had that in common, I suppose. But what good was any of it *really* doing Vince?

When he pulled out the Glenlivet from under the bed I pleaded, "No more." So he swigged on it himself for a while as he drew my picture on the back of a paper bag with a set of pastels he'd lifted.

I was dozing off by the time he decided he'd drawn me long enough. Now he pulled me up and began to undress me while I giggled out a drunken laugh. But this is what I'd been waiting for, so I found my second wind and wrestled with him.

After that, it was a free-for-all as we went at it, though at times it became tentative (and he'd look at me almost frightened). We'd stop and lay off a spell until he was ready to go again, and then he was all over me once more, dragging me around that little room like a drunken rag doll.

He'd playfully slap me whenever I tried to yank at his T-shirt, but I was no match for him. I was blitzed and along for the ride and he seemed amazingly sober all of a sudden. It was all a blur until the final moment when he grabbed me by the back of the neck and looked hard into my eyes with his own—those drill-bit black eyes—and I felt him shoot on me, before he fell backward, as if dead, expelling a huge breath and exclaiming, "Fuck!"

We woke up all knotted together. One of his hands was laying in front of my mouth and I nibbled at it, and began licking his palm and up across his wrist and right down the long pink scars that led toward his elbow. He turned toward me then.

"So what about *these,* Vince?"

"I thought you'd never ask," he said with affection. How could he be so inviting when talking of his self-destructiveness, and yet if I mentioned his radiation treatments—which were after all about his survival—he'd give only brief or vague answers?

"I didn't want to be rude."

"You've had your tongue in my ass, Neill; I think we're beyond rude. I don't recall you even saying *please may I?*"

I smiled.

He held up his wrists then, studying each scar. "These are old," he said, disinterested, "three years at least." That didn't sound old to me. But as always, while I reflected and mused on his utterances, he was on to the next thing. "I tried to OD once too, but people always find me when I want to kill myself. I'm totally alone all the time, and then the minute I go for it, someone walks in." He talked of it so matter of factly and even with disappointment. Then he was up on his elbow again. "Did you ever try it?"

He looked suddenly like he so wanted me to say "Yes, I have." If I could have lied to him then, I would have, but in addition to me being a bad liar and that he was impossible to lie to, there was the fact that this was just not a subject about which you could ever possibly lie—not to someone who's been there. I felt so inexperienced again, wondering why he'd hang with me when I was so innocent and boring.

"I only thought about it," I said sheepishly, not adding, "sorry," which I almost felt I should tack on.

"Well, something to look forward to," he joked. "It's a boring story anyway. I need more sleep." And he rolled over.

I tugged at his shoulder, "Ah, Vince, come on, tell me the story."

"It's depressing." I couldn't argue with that. But he turned around anyway, sighing heavily. "I was living in Miami. I took a handful of pills and downed them with bourbon. I fell asleep but woke up puking and coughing them up. So I stumbled into the bathroom and slit both wrists. I kept coughing. One of my roommates came in cuz he heard the racket. A fucking mess. Blood all over the place cuz I was staggering around, drunken and dosed. They were all pissed off at me for the mess and called nine-one-one. I think they'd been watching a movie. If they'd been true friends they would have let me die. But they all hated me. And like most people, they watch out for themselves when the chips are down," he added, bitterly. "They didn't want my dead body ruining their movie or hassling them with the cops. To them, I'd just messed up the bathroom and they were gonna have to clean it up." He scooted himself up on both elbows then. "That was in fucking Florida where the cops by law have to put you in a psych ward for a month if you attempt suicide. Nobody can get you out like here." I muttered such inane things as "uh huh," and "wow" as he continued on with a litany of insults for the doctors and nurses in the mental health wing of the county hospital. "At least I didn't have to clean up the bathroom. That was my going-away present to those fucks. But it was hell in that psych ward. I refused the drugs they pushed at me and I abused the therapists, so they sedated me. It pissed me off. Those fuckers. The only ones who talked to me talked down to me and I wouldn't tell them shit. Besides, I had nothing to say. I don't buy the psychobabble bullshit about a call for help and all that. I didn't feel anything. I wouldn't even know who to call for help, for Chrissakes; it was a completely practical decision. I wasn't crying; I wasn't even sad. I just didn't care. I was a bother to myself. I wanted Vince out of the way. I was just doing what seemed necessary." He let his head fall back and he stared at the ceiling.

I was getting frightened again to hear him talk this coldly about himself and his life, but I persisted. "So, how the hell did you deal with that hospital for a month?" I asked by way of bringing him back.

"I didn't. I escaped," he said flatly. Then turning suddenly to me, he smiled. "I climbed out a window in my gown. I doubt they ever even noticed. I'm sure they can't have cared. I was a pain in the ass; they were probably glad. Once I got down the wall, I even walked past security guards. They're used to people wandering the gardens in pajamas, I guess. I took the bus home." I could see Vince then—the furrowed brow, broadcasting *fuck you* to anyone who stared at his humiliation in that hospital gown, the thick white bandages wrapped like mummy tape up both forearms, the plastic admittance tag still clipped around one wrist—exposed in that city bus fluorescent light like some specimen in the formaldehyde of night.

Nonchalantly, almost as an afterthought, Vince contributed his follow-up suicide tale. "The other time I shot a huge load of heroin. It should have killed me, but it didn't, and then I was out of money *and* junk, so I had to go on living." He shrugged his shoulders. "I'm tired," he said, and he rolled over toward the wall and went back to sleep.

It went on like that for the next few weeks, with the booze and the drugs and the sex and the philosophy and the stories next morning. One night he'd have acid, the next mushrooms. And always there was twelve-year-old scotch for when we returned from one of our meandering walks. He had expensive and excessive tastes for a hobo.

Then one day it all stopped. He never would say why. We returned to coffee and long silences, each reading our own books for hours in some café or on the floor of his room. He cooked and we slept together, but always with that inward expression etched on his face which said, "Stay back; no sex." I didn't mind his quietude so much, but I missed the sex; I was young and hungry for that. But I loved Vince for all the windows he opened for me, and for what I saw as his bravery—the decisive knifelike way he had about him.

I knew sex was messy for him. Accepting that was the one thing I knew he needed from me, if anything. It was never something we talked about. When he'd see me look at him a certain way, he'd offer up his, "I'm fucked up, OK?" or he'd say, "What the fuck are you looking at?" Either way, I'd reassure him in the only way I knew how that it wasn't a problem and that I wasn't disappointed. I'd suggest we go out.

So sex either happened or it didn't, a wholly unspoken thing. We relied solely on body language and plenty of booze. We would touch, and I could sense where it was moving by how he responded. When we went to that magic land of sex together, he would always hesitate. I'd have to coax him along now and again—he came along, slowly, like a person groping in the dark, unsure and tentative. As I came to know him better, I'd find ways to be reassuring and pull him along, but not with words. In his eyes, he always answered *I know, but—*. And we talked only with our eyes, only with our hands, only with our bodies' touch and our tongues. We always began this way, slowly and tentatively, but once we set our bodies free they wrestled what they wanted from each other fast and violently, until we fell exhausted, sighing and heaving our breath, looking at each other as if to say, "What the fuck just happened?" He'd even smile sometimes then, but usually he became distant again. Sometimes I thought our bodies had a different relationship than our minds. Sometimes I thought he was two people. Sometimes I felt my body could show me where the other of him was hiding, and sometimes it felt I didn't even have to look very hard. In the end, I knew only that there was a light there, and so perhaps our place of sexual communion—that part of our friendship—was where the little flickering light of him lived, uncynical, hopeful, vulnerable, and without anger; deep down, far below the seemingly endless layers of night that enshrouded him, quivered a tiny flame I'd cup my hands around to protect from the howling wind of the world and the black wrath of his tortured, wandering mind.

One night some guy in a bar asked me if Vince was a hustler. Callow youth that I was, I'd never even thought of it. But considering his sexual reluctance in general I dismissed the notion, as I couldn't fathom how he'd manage prostitution. It was, of course, logical to assume he was a hustler. Many guys probably thought he was, as that was the assumed, and even natural trade of cute, young desperate boys with no money, prison records, or drug problems. It was easy money and obvious. But Vince couldn't have done it. If not for his sexual hang-ups, his pride and misanthropy would have prevented him: he'd likely insult his johns and lecture them on how pathetic they were—hardly a good marketing strategy. He certainly would have had an easier time making money if he'd hustled, and he wouldn't have wanted for clients. But he wouldn't have been Vince, and so it was useless conjecture. *Vince is no hustler,* I thought to myself; *he's just a thief, plain and simple.*

The world knew it and looked askance at Vince. An old queen at a bookstore we frequented once quipped, while Vince was outside smoking: "Oh yes, he's handsome, but I wouldn't trust him alone with *my* silver." But the suspicious and the naysayers only strengthened my love for him. Who were they but the silly, outside, middle-class insipid world that had attempted to destroy us both? They made me feel brave right along with him. They hadn't been let in on the secret, or couldn't see it, and that was their loss.

Off we'd go to the next bookstore, "free from their provincial squea-
mishness forever," engrossed in a conversation about neurolinguistic
programming or the origins of the tarot deck. We'd find what we were
looking for after rooting about on Valencia or Church Streets; or we'd
find something completely different that would end up captivating us
even more. That night it was the Mayan codices, *Popul Vuh,* their
book of the dead. Things were winding down according to their
prophecies and Vince hoped they were right.

One afternoon, we'd wandered down once more to the derelict
warehouses and crumbling factories among the rail yards far south of
Market Street and, lonesome, sat on some old freight dock in the waning sunset hours, swinging our feet like kids at a lakeshore, dreaming
of anything or nothing in particular. When he was quiet and by my
side, I always wanted to kiss him. Of course I had to be careful. But
that time I did, perhaps out of nostalgia (how quickly it emanates
from the void) for our walk here all those weeks past.

We wandered back to the Baldwin and I was figuring he was ready
to have sex again, so I was feeling giddy but being careful too.

Once in the room, he didn't jump me as he normally would when
he was horny. He just stood there and let me undress him. When I
had him down to his shirt, I lifted his chin to look at him and he lifted
his arms for me.

He stood there almost shivering as I tossed his shirt aside, and he
looked like a small child, staring downward at his chest and belly, his
biceps tight and flexed, his arms held against his body as his shoulders
hunched in and forward. He looked as if he'd just been rescued from a
frozen sea, in fact. His body seemed tinier to me when he was fully undressed, pale and thin, full of shadows where the bones stuck out or
where the muscles curved deeply at his flanks. He had a sort of lanky,
thin, saintly body that looked like he'd been painted by El Greco,
with his mother's pale olive Sicilian skin—and though his thighs were
smooth and almost hairless, his shins were a dirty mess of black hair as
if leading down to the dark soil of the earth. I undressed myself with
my eyes upon him then, as he stood immovable, and then I reached
tentatively toward his shoulder as if approaching a timid dog. When I

saw he wasn't going to stop me, I touched his shoulder and slowly pulled him to me. Holding his chest against mine, for the first time, all skin to skin, we clung to each other, immobile and vaguely sad. We clung together for a long time and said nothing. He seemed so nervous that I feared to let him go, to expose him without his armor. *I'll be his shirt,* I romantically asserted to myself, knowing that if he could read my mind he'd have pushed me across the room in disgust. But everything about him was so sweet and fragile in that moment. He was such a tough, little fragile weed: his bony shoulders and dark nipples, the way his hipbones stuck out; the hunger of his mouth when he gave into this change that had come upon him and kissed me hungrily, with a kind of devotion I'd never seen in him before.

That night at least I felt he trusted me and he'd taken a chance. I don't think I ever appreciated how difficult it was for him, and he never told me either—not in so many words. Fortunate in my own sexual history—at least physically, anyway—I naively told him after we'd made love that I liked skinny boys best. Tracing circles on his chest and around his dark nipples, I thoughtlessly drew far too much attention to something so precarious and new, and confirmed the very aspect of himself he was so hung up on not showing, and that had in fact kept his shirt on all these weeks. He pulled away and grabbed for his shirt, putting it on again before climbing back into bed and going to sleep with his back to me.

"Are you OK, Vince?" I whispered guiltily.

"Leave me alone. Go to sleep." I had forgotten again to be careful with him, to be careful with steel, with iron—iron when clothed and on the street, that is. I forget that when we are naked, he can be as glass, or the thinnest of papers. He has all the power on the street— he's a giant Don Quixote, and I'm a clumsy Sancho Panza. But here, in this lumpy little bed, he is an infant and I am his protector. I should not ask anything of him here, I think to myself now. Why do I ask so much from him? What do I give him in return? Who is the thief really?

"Bring it on," said Peter, and in he went.

They didn't take his eye.

"Oh, thank God," my mother said, deflating visibly when she got the news.

She'd remained distant that whole week after the bad CAT scan, hadn't cooked once. We'd run out of local restaurants and were starting to repeat.

Now she was coming to: sitting in the corner of Peter's room, awaiting his imminent arrival. Something about that eye had been her limit. Before I had a chance to welcome her back, whatever she'd been obsessing on all week finally came forth in a torrent.

"Did I do something wrong, you think?" she asked, with quiet desperation in her panicky eyes. I knew where she was going with this because I'd seen it before: she thought that she caused the cancer; it was all her fault.

"Of course not, Mom." But she was too quick in accepting my answer. Her mind was running through the Rolodex of possible causes and she was not so much ruling out the possibility as simply checking in on it as she reviewed the myriad explanations that haunted her.

"It was a tough pregnancy. Premature. . . ."

"Mom, that's not your fault. Besides, that has nothing to do with cancer. Don't torture yourself."

"How do I know that he wasn't born weak?"

"Mom, he's the best athlete in the family." I looked at her incredulously.

"But somewhere inside that we can't see—maybe he was damaged. He was born jaundiced, you know—orange."

I was getting frustrated, but what could I do? She was back and I had to keep her there. "Mom? Stop."

But she wasn't listening. "There was that basketball game where that boy elbowed him in the nose. Lord, the blood." And so she continued on, looking for answers. "And that shelf that fell on his head when he was small . . .the jungle gym . . . the baseball . . . the bat . . . the tree branch . . ."

My father arrived while she was in midspeculation, and since I wasn't agreeing with her, she started on him. "Frank, do you suppose Peter's just fragile? I mean the incubator, being orange, all that."

He hesitated, noticing what I'd noticed—that she'd returned to normal cognizance.

"No, Grace, I think he's tough as nails. As are you." And he walked over and kissed her. That shut her up for a while.

But five minutes later, she was at it again. "Maybe he wasn't supposed to survive," she stated blankly, staring into the distance.

"I'll go unplug him," my father jibed, getting up and walking out.

"Come on, Ma, time for a walk." But she wouldn't budge; she didn't want to miss him, as his return from the recovery room was imminent. "Mom, we'll just walk up and back. We can watch the door."

So we strolled through the ward, and I reassured her: "There've never been any studies to prove that premature birth, or birth color, or any of that is a factor in cancer. Put it out of your mind. It just happens; we don't always know why." Was I going to use on her what she always used on us as kids when faced with the mysteries of life?—"Sometimes it's not our place to ask why"? Whatever works had turned out to be the best strategy.

"It's God's will," she said, defeated, beating me to the punch. "God has chosen him," she sighed, and her expression of relief—so distinctly Catholic in its frown of resignation—erased the anxiety from her visage as her facial muscles went slack. "Or maybe he's chosen you or even me?" I wanted to answer.

"Maybe he's chosen us all," I offered diplomatically.

"Oh, Lord," she whimpered.

She wasn't quite ready for that one. "We're all in it together, Ma; that's all I meant." I had to hug her to hold her up. I held her firmly and thought to myself, *we should just shut up and do* this *more often.*

Peter came rolling in then and we heard my Dad yell out, "He's here," as we hurried back toward his room. It had to be the biggest nonevent of this whole experience—the return—since Peter was always completely stoned and immediately went to sleep on us.

But she was giddy, of course, tucking him in, thanking the orderlies and nurses who nearly ran out to escape her smothering attentions. *They better take what they can get,* I thought to myself, *I doubt she'll be baking cookies this time through.*

That was when *she* started staying the night. Susan got a cot for her. My mother had always been someone who wore makeup and fashionable outfits. I'd never seen her in anything remotely unpressed. Now here she was three days running in the same beige skirt, with big creases across the back, and a green silk plaid blouse that was getting uncharacteristically disheveled. Her hair was looking lifeless and her face was pale and without makeup.

I'd gone home with my Dad the last two nights, worried to leave him alone on that long drive and through the night in that big empty house. My mother was acting distinctly religious now, so I felt secure in leaving her in the custody of Anita, who worked nights.

But I'd be worried when I arrived mornings. The floor bustled again and she'd wander out to make friends and chitchat. Fortunately, Peter had to be in there for only five days this time, but that didn't reassure me about my mother. That was a long time to sit in the corner while Peter slept it off.

On the third morning as I arrived, I saw her alone down the corridor as I exited the elevator. She was moving slowly, as if holding herself together with effort, like she'd been shot or something. Peter was obviously asleep, and she was wandering the corridors of the hospital in search of someone to talk to. But the hall was deserted. She had that false but inviting smile on her face, but it had all come to naught this morning. As I approached her, I wondered just how long she'd been out here looking.

Her eyes were like thick, clear glass when I reached her, as if her tears had set up permanent residence atop her irises, refusing to recede or to fall. She saw me approach and she knew what I saw and she came toward me. And we didn't run to embrace. We walked toward each other self-consciously, as if one of the longed-for friends might appear and discover us, blowing our cover. What was our cover? That we could take it? Remain standing? When I reached her, I hugged her with everything I had. "I love you, Mom. It'll be all right."

"Do you think so?" she feebly entreated me.

"What do I know?" would have been the honest answer, but what good was that kind of truth at a moment like this? Our roles had reversed and I remembered then as a boy how she'd always knelt down with me on the living room floor and made me pray when all seemed lost. That was the part of religion I was OK with, I realized in that moment.

So I took her hand and led her down to the little hospital chapel where I instructed her to pray, and heard once again the rustling of her stockings, combed slowly and silently the curls of that same long-ago hair, gazed upon the woman who was my mother and who had taught me all those sorrowful mantras: "Hail Mary, full of grace," and "Remember O Most Gracious Virgin Mary . . ." We both cried, certainly in part for Peter, but I think the greater part of our tears ran for ourselves and the things we'd lost.

Some part of her died with the cancer; some part of all of us. I learned to smile in the same way she did when she looked upon her scarred child—with a pregnant sort of tearfulness, bent into a smile by way of a sigh. It was rather humiliating to realize that all we could often do for one another was say "Hang in there," and then just hope for the best. Well, if life weren't pathetic, whatever would we do with these burdensome hearts? It wasn't even about fearing his death so much now as going on from here—the scars, the explanations, the long haul. There were scars across us all that we could no longer hide. Maybe those tears tore things away from us like a flood. Maybe we had lost too much too fast. Maybe we were free or maybe we were lost for good. Maybe that's the choice we'd all been left with.

CR XVIII

There was a hole in Vince's story. He never said anything about what he did, who he'd known, or where he'd been since Florida.

"Where did you last live, Vince?" I asked him out on the street one day.

"Everywhere, nowhere. I told you; I rode trains." He was rushing around, crossing streets in front of speeding taxis and buses, talking too loudly. I was barely keeping up with him, but I knew he needed cigarettes and he wouldn't stop until he got to a Walgreens because that was where he stole all his tobacco, since cigarettes were kept behind the counter everywhere else; for some strange reason Walgreens left its Drum cigarette tobacco out on the floor with the pipe tobacco and cigars.

"Why don't you just let me buy you cigarettes?" I asked, exasperated, feeling the first drops of rain come down and tired of always going ten blocks out of our way just for his cigarette habit.

"Shut the fuck up, Neill. I can't listen to your bourgeois whining right now." It was hard to feel too offended at these names he called me since I realized that anyone who actually paid for things was considered hopelessly middle class in Vince's view. His exclusive club apparently was made up only of thieves.

He looked back at me now, as we reached the other side of the street, surprised I hadn't said anything in response. I just looked at him, expressionless, not wanting to smile and let him off, but not wanting to start arguing either. This actually drove him crazy, I'd begun to notice. He had to have a response from the world—he didn't necessarily care if it was positive or negative.

I stood outside while he lifted the Drum, my constitution too nervous to risk being found an accomplice. I marveled that he was never caught or arrested, considering how he pilfered his way through San Francisco all those months, and looking almost embarrassingly suspicious the entire time, in that ratty overcoat with the dark wild eyes and satanic goatee. Watching the flow of pedestrians, and seeing a mother and child, I remembered the time in a coffee shop when a little boy, who couldn't have been more than five, announced too loudly, "Mommy, is that man the devil?" I'd laughed, but Vince had just glared at the mother who was visibly mortified. "Yes, and your mother can't protect you from me either," he'd snapped, scowling. The kid didn't really pick it up, but the mother was up and out of there with him faster than you could bless yourself.

"Let's get some scotch," he suggested as he strolled out, his pockets well stocked, though they were so voluminous I could never tell from the outside. So we went home with a bottle. He'd even let me buy it, which in his case was a kind of apology. I'd gotten used to this backward logic—not so backward in the clumsy commerce of power. And I knew he felt he still owed me because alcohol led to sex and sex was how he apologized.

Halfway into the bottle he was on me. And while the rain pelted the chipped little windowsill—the glass propped open with a dog-eared copy of *Moby Dick*—he cleared our little slate of discord (if for but an hour) with our bumbling attempts at sex, which had the quality of traffic, starting and stopping, and moving always around the jack-knifed presence of his father.

"Vince, we don't have to have sex at all, if you don't want to."

That made him defensive, of course, but his brows soon relaxed as he climbed into his long johns and pants. "Sure we do, Neill, we're fags. We have to have sex." And he leaned his face toward mine, bugging out his eyes. I knew better than to discuss sex, but it had never seemed so transactionary as it did today. A lovely system, I thought: the worse things get, the better the sex will be. Well, that was nothing new in the world, even if it was new to me.

The next time he insulted me, I wasn't as composed. I suppose because he was stealing in my presence. I'd asked him to please only do it when I was outside, but he was ashamed to have to warn me all the time and, besides, he never knew when something would cross his line of sight that he wanted. And what he wanted, he stole.

"Limit one per customer," I'd joked as I'd seen him put not one but an entire Penguin series of some author en masse into his coat.

"Well, I don't see you volunteering any cash," he snapped. But before I could offer, as he knew I would, he added, "And why should we pay when we can just as easily get it for free? And don't—" his voice raised threateningly, "—lecture me on right and wrong, white boy."

"So I'm white now, and you're not?"

"My skin may be white, but I'm not white," he clarified. I knew what he meant, but it occurred to me that he was actually light green and I was more of a pink shade, which made him wrong twice. "You're a middle-class white boy, Neill, don't fuck with my world," he finished, drawing a final and uncrossable line between us that made me wonder yet again just why he hung out with me at all. When he got this irascible, it made me want to just leave and go home to the 'burbs, which would of course just play into all his theories about my bourgeois wimpiness. Not to mention my own fears that he was right. And I didn't want to be what he hated. I felt lost between two worlds, which was nothing new, and I was even complacent somewhat in my indecisiveness. But I admired him because he'd chosen, even if he'd chosen wrong. I admired his irreverence and his balls, if you could call it that. He was my dark angel, and I felt I had no choice but to accept him on his terms because he actually *had* terms. He couldn't really accept me on mine because mine were muddy and ill defined at best.

I was outside by then, waiting.

He exited the buzzing doorway with a fury and quickly lost himself in the Union Square shopping crowd before they could find him.

I caught up with him around the corner. He'd told me once, "Always just keep veering right and you'll eventually find me; cops will follow to the right, but they like a straightaway and they never veer right again fast enough. Besides, like anyone else, they like variety, right-left, right-left kinda thing." I'd laughed when he'd related that little theory.

Today he wasn't so collected, snapping at me as I reached out to tug at his shoulder in the crosswalk.

"My father liked to hassle me all the time just like you do," he snapped. I must have really pissed him off this time. He'd never called me his father and I knew that had to be a new low.

"Vince, man, don't say that. I'm not like him; it's not fair."

"You kinda look like him actually," he said cruelly, and I thought I saw my brother's ten-year-old face in his then. "The whole tired, middle-class moralistic trip—that's so James Malone. You'll probably end up a child molester too, you know that?"

"Jesus, Vince, I'm sorry."

"You like skinny, hairless guys. You know that's fucking code for little boys, you fucking pervert!"

"Vince, knock it off," and I was furrowing my brow now, not so much because he was pushing any real buttons but because he was yelling it out in the middle of a crowded downtown sidewalk. And he knew that's why I was getting upset too.

"You're a fucking philistine; why do I waste my time with you?"

I can't remember now whether I really felt the sadness well up, but that's what I showed him. I must have pouted and looked hurt then as I said, "Fuck it," and crossed the street, half-running. He followed, of course, and I just kept walking as he yelled behind me, "Neill, come on. Wait up!"

I knew by then I was playing a game, even though I sniffled tears. I wasn't hurt so much as sad. I knew the only way to reach him now was to fuck him. And he'd shown me how to get him to that place.

So he followed me back down to the Baldwin, where on the corner I sheepishly told him in the waning light that I thought maybe it was time for me to go. For someone as ungullible as Vince, I still wonder how he ever bought it. Perhaps he never did, but what was the compelling need in him that was so much greater that it made him let me get away with it then?

I'd wondered if he were playing me somehow at times. I knew he'd been a junkie and I'd seen he was a thief. I'd witnessed his desperation and I feared sometimes that he could be one of those people who had been reduced by his tragic past into complete disingenuousness. But I didn't know any career criminals—where would I have met them? In the end, I'd always conclude the same: I was a poor choice for seduction from the junkie's or the thief's standpoint and, besides, whether he realized it or not, he was giving me far more than he was taking. And right then, on that corner, I had the empty realization that I was playing him.

Well, I can't justify it now. But then, I figured I was playing for his heart; I was playing for keeps. And that's how romantics hurt people and make a mess of things, I suppose.

Up the elevator we went, lurching to our stop at the sixth floor, the cagelike door rattling open as Vince threw his body into it. We both must have looked like silhouettes then, I thought. Vince smiled when he reached the door, the sad sigh of a smile I've seen on my mother's face so many times as they carted her son away for more surgery. Vince still looked like a lit match to me, the orange of his hair (but how long and dark now have grown the roots), the shine in his obsidian eyes, and whatever comes from far, far away through them and burns always bright.

His tongue and mouth were so familiar to me, like a body of water I entered into, abandoning myself. It was like we swam in each other. He tore his shirt right off. I was glad I at least gave him that for all I felt that I suddenly was taking.

I thought of the hospital as we made love. The ritual of it, putting this here and that there and doing things to each other, so like surgery. Would we surface horribly scarred, I wondered, or healed? Or was it a little or a lot of both?

We were silent, sheltered under the blinking neon, which I thought just then was like some mother's amber heart beating for two dark twins in the uterus of the city, as yet unborn. I knew I was his only friend, though he'd talked of friends from all across the country. He'd lost touch with most (they too were moving and wouldn't be traceable anyway) or had final arguments that left them estranged. He told me then, out of nowhere, that many accused him of stealing things from them, as if it were the most outrageous and unlikely of suspicions to have toward him.

"Did they steal from you too?"

He looked at me like I was being ridiculous. "I don't have anything. What the fuck would someone steal from me?" I thought of his ideas, his energy and brilliance, his unique physical beauty—they'd likely fed off that as I had. But he gave himself no credit. I was beginning to think that his whole life was an ugly barter with the world—he stole and was stolen from.

I looked over at his slouched little boxes that held all his possesions. I'd never really looked at them before, but suddenly I noticed addresses written on them. I hopped out of bed and read them, pausing as the light came and went. All of them read the same: Denver.

"The boxes are from Denver, Vince!" I said triumphantly. "That's where you were."

"I've been there a thousand times, Neill."

"Well, that's where you got the boxes," I said, smiling.

"You're a real fucking Columbo, or whoever."

"Come on, Vince, what happened there?"

"Nothing happened there, Neill, fucking nothing." And he said it firmly so I wouldn't ask again.

"I've never been to Denver."

"It's a shitty place," he said apathetically. "Only the mountains are cool, you can see 'em out there on a clear day—these big, fucking rocks covered in snow. That's all that's good about Denver."

"Did you ever go out to them? The mountains I mean."

"No, I just looked at 'em, Neill."

I had a sudden idea. "You wanna go to the mountains?"

"What?" He looked surprised. "Don't tell me you're a fucking Boy Scout too?"

"Hey, man, all us child molesters are Boy Scouts."

He looked at me then, taking it as an acknowledgment that I'd let that slight go. Of course. That was the game: Insult → sex → forgiveness → fresh slate. I felt guilty actually, knowing that formula probably cost him more than it did me.

"Let's go to the mountains, Vince," I said with enthusiasm then. He didn't match my exuberance as he answered indifferently, "Sure, whatever," so I didn't consider it necessarily something that would happen. It involved a lot of planning after all; it wasn't something you just did. But I thought then I wanted to share that with him. I thought that was something I could give him.

He was thinking of those other mountains still. "I was in Denver for two years, Neill, and I was a junkie the whole time. Nothing happened," he said bitterly. "You fucking happy now?" It came out angrily, as if I'd pulled it out of him. He even pushed me, so I got up from the bed. Even *I* had an urge for a cigarette then. The claustrophobia of that tiny little room and the shifting weather of it was almost unbearable at times.

I yanked up the window and sat on the sill. "How can I love you if you don't tell me your story, Vince?" I chanced, knowing it might fall flat, as it did.

"What the fuck does that mean, Neill? In fact, all that proves is how incapable of love you are." And he was once again off. "You gotta know everything to try to convince yourself that I'm lovable. Well, I'm not, asshole!" He looked directly at me. "My parents supposedly loved me, so I'm not interested in your fucking love either. You can dig me all up, spread me all over the fucking street—you won't find what you're looking for, Neill."

"Your parents didn't love you, Vince."

"What the fuck do you know?" he snapped angrily.

"I love you already, that's why I want to know everything. I want to get closer to you."

"Well, don't; you're way too fucking close as it is. Quit while you're ahead." He got up now and violently yanked up his pants and put on his clothes.

"I don't want to talk about me or 'love' or any of this shit anymore," he commanded. "You fucking hear me? Quit asking me to spill all this shit! I don't like it, Neill; I don't like to fucking remember it! I hate my fucking life!" He was yelling at top volume now, and I was just sitting there half in shock and half in awe. "And if you're a fucking part of it, I hate you too!" He was about to start bawling, but he sucked it up and went to the sink and splashed cold water on his face, breathing heavily to calm his nerves.

"Let's go; let's get the fuck out of this fucking room!" he exclaimed. I did what he said, stood up and put on my jacket. He slammed the door behind us. I knew better than to offer an apology. Too bad the old geezer coming toward us in the hall couldn't read Vince's mood. He was muttering, and it rose to an audible level as we drew nearer.

"Know ye the wages of Sodom . . ."

"Oh fuck you, you Christian pile of shit; a lot of good Jesus has done you!" Vince barked at him, scooping up a discarded shoe from the floor and firing it at him at high speed. I'd never seen this guy before and almost wanted to warn him, but he only shielded his face and smiled as the shoe ricocheted off his shoulder, probably comforting himself with the satisfying martyrdom of the attack on his "walk with God," or whatever he called his rotten, judgmental way of greeting so-called "sinners." *Who's the pervert?* I wondered to myself.

Vince pushed the down elevator button and told the geezer, "The booze will wait, old man; you take a step closer to me and I'll fucking rip your heart out and feed it to Satan!" The guy stood back, needless to say. Vince explained on the trip down that the man was a hopeless alcoholic who spent most of his time at a bar two doors down. "He's usually too drunk to proselytize, but I guess after a nap or whatever he feels guilty and wants to dump all his shit on someone else, the motherfucker." I noticed Vince was pale and shaking, but I didn't dare mention it.

The old geezer wasn't alone, of course, in having problems with Vince. He never complained at the desk, though, as he likely didn't want lost souls getting away before he converted them. But other people complained. It wasn't like the hotel would investigate any claims as most of them were of the "He's an asshole, that guy in Room six-forty-five. You oughtta kick him out of here" variety. He said, she said, blah, blah, blah. Vince was not in the minority thinking that everyone here was crazy.

"What did he do?" the Arab would tiredly ask, when a complaint against Vince or anyone else was lodged.

"He called me a bitch!" would be the reply, or some other such infraction.

The Arab would nod, unimpressed. "OK, I'll ask him about it." The Arab liked Vince more or less, but he didn't want to deal with these people any more than Vince did, and Vince was making his difficult job more so. He told him one afternoon before we went up, "Vince, don't argue with people so much. I'll kick you the fuck out." "Yeah, yeah," Vince would reply flippantly.

"I'm serious," and he ran his index finger across his throat. He gave Vince more leeway than others only because he wasn't as crazy or fucked up as the other residents, and he paid on time. Sane people were attractive tenants in such a setting, no matter how rudely or arrogantly they behaved.

Vince stopped once outside the big glass doors and he looked almost disoriented. I wondered where we were going, but suddenly it seemed he was at a complete loss. I didn't know what made me do it, but I just grabbed him and held him hard to myself and he squeezed back with even more gusto.

He released me and shook his head hard, like a dog after rain, and then growled out a deep roar, before blinking his eyes and saying, composed again, "I shouldn't have done that."

I just looked at him as he became his old self again, full of ideas and places and things to show me. "Come on, you need to come to this Tibetan place with me, man." *Oh that,* I thought. I hadn't read the book he'd given me and wasn't terribly enthused about visiting whatever place he had in mind, but I wasn't going to be contrary just now. A little jaunt would do us both some good, I figured. We'll let the world absorb and neutralize our pain, dissipate it, blow it away like unlucky blossoms or dead leaves in the wind.

"Did you read the book?" he asked me.

"Some of it," I bluffed. I'd actually only looked at the pictures, one of which, I thought now, Vince had assumed the character of for the past ten minutes.

"You need this shit if anyone does," he said arrogantly, though I felt suddenly very together, considering. "This shit" was apparently Buddhism, a Zen assessment if there ever was one. "It's up near the park."

"What is? Where are we going?"

"Something 'gotso' or some name like that. I don't fucking know Tibetan," he answered impatiently. "Anyway, you'll see. There's a lama there; he's kinda cool. I met him a few days ago."

"At the Zen Center?" I queried.

"Fuck no, not at the Zen Center. You know I don't go there any-more. This guy's Tibetan anyway."

Vince had once taken me to the Zen Center on one of our daylong excursions around town, but of course that was Japanese Buddhism, not Tibetan, as he'd just now reminded me. We'd gone looking for the Zen Center after he'd read *Zen and the Art of Motorcycle Mainte-nance*—though it was probably the author's nervous breakdown more than the book's Buddhist philosophy that had first inspired Vince to seek it out. A sprawling brick renovated girls' school from eighty or 100 years ago, the Zen Center was surrounded by trees and always looked to me like the kind of place you'd want to go inside of and look around. It didn't disappoint. It was replete with stairways and little arched windows, courtyards full of plants, and old relics and bells from the mysterious faraway worlds of the Buddhas. We went to the zendo and did the meditation, after which I remember walking down Haight Street while Vince enthusiastically and maniacally went on and on about his newfound desire to go live in a cave or mountain meditation center where he'd heal all his wounds and leave this wretched and impure world behind forever. I was surprised he'd be in-terested in anything so structured, or with any kind of rules other than his own for that matter. Vince always seemed an unlikely candi-date for Buddhism. Wasn't it about patience and peace of mind? But I figured it was just another of his momentary enthusiasms, like film school and all the rest.

Sure enough, a few weeks later, his Zen plan and its promise of en-lightenment self-destructed. He'd had a run-in with another "practi-tioner" on one of his visits there who'd made the mistake—the "zealous little by-the-book new-age creep" Vince later called him— of grab-bing Vince's shoulder and gently turning him since he'd accidentally faced the wrong way in the zendo. But no one touched Vince without permission, gently or otherwise. "I don't like those people," he'd de-cided after that, and I assumed that was the end for Buddhism.

But just as one book had led him to the Zen Center, it was yet again this *Tibetan Book of the Dead* of his—with the aid of an old junkie ac-quaintance—that had brought him propitiously into contact with the lama. Vince had met the lama while foraging with his drug connection, Hal, through Golden Gate Park, on his way to score some acid or whatever else might be available up on hippie hill.

"I met this guy in the park," Vince continued as we hopped on the streetcar, paid our fare, and plopped down. "He was sitting on a bench, and Hal dragged me over to meet him. You know, I'd fuckin' read that book, so I wanted to ask him some shit. I never even got the acid," he laughed. "Tibetan Buddhism *is* acid," Vince beamed. "It's nothing like that Zen crap."

"So what's this place we're going to, then?" I asked him, curious but also skeptical. I'd noticed that he was careful to point out that Tibetan Buddhism was altogether different from Zen, thus preventing me from possibly protesting that he was being inconsistent.

"Shangri-la," Vince joked, answering me sarcastically, before telling me. "It's like a house they've turned into a Tibetan shrine. There aren't loads of people like at the Zen Center; that's what Hal says anyway." The less people the better was a general rule with Vince, of course. He was always more drawn to ideas: the ideas pulled him in and the people drove him away. What an indictment of religion, I thought. One of his many ratty old T-shirts—erotic memories: how many had he worn, and had he worn this one when aroused and refusing to remove his shirt?—said, God, Save Me From Your Followers. Soon he'd make his own, with a black felt marker, a variation on a theme: If you see a Buddhist in the zendo, kill him.

"You haven't been there?" I asked, slightly vexed.

"No, I told you I just met him," he looked at me as if I were stupid.

Cho Phel Gyatso Center of Tibetan Buddhism was out near Golden Gate Park, within view of the hospital on the hill where Peter had been cut up. *How strange,* I thought briefly to myself, before dismissing it: *yet another new and mysterious thing, like Vince, loitering around ground zero and close to the knives.* Maybe I wasn't living in two different worlds after all.

We crossed the Panhandle, a long narrow section of the park that ran out between two boulevards near its eastern entrance. It was a blustery day, as this was summer in San Francisco, and the high branches of the giant eucalyptus trees whipped about, looking furious and put-upon. We reached the opposite side and, crossing the street, saw before us the red and gold painted Victorian which was our destination.

We climbed up the house's steep wooden steps and knocked. A middle-aged woman opened the door for us, smiling and saying hello softly. Vince told her we were there to see Lama Tenzin, and she asked us if we had an appointment.

"No, I just met him in the park and wanted to see if he was around, and for him to meet my friend," Vince said with uncharacteristic politeness, offering a thumb in my direction. She looked a little perplexed or unsure what to do, but he kept talking. "He said come by anytime. We were talking in the park about *The Tibetan Book of the Dead*." She relented finally and invited us in, after which we removed our shoes and followed her up the stairs.

When we reached the upstairs landing, we were in what I supposed was once a living room. It had since been converted into their meditation hall, an elaborately decorated shrine room that reminded me of a Catholic church, what with all the candles burning, incense wafting, and its endless array of saints, or what they called incarnated emanations of the Buddha, lining the walls. Opposite us was a huge bookshelflike structure filled with literally thousands of small golden Buddhas. The rest of the room was hung with numerous silk Tibetan tanka paintings of various other Buddhas. A large gold-trimmed wooden altar and throne sat at the head of the room, in a garden of statues and flowers, burning candles, incense, and offering bowls of rice and fruit. Before us, all across the floor, like waves in a sea, were rows and rows of red and gold cushions for meditators. I'd assumed that all Buddhism was simple and unadorned as Zen was, but this was like the Catholic church all over again and then some. There was something both comforting to me and vaguely threatening in that fact. I thought it rich and pretty, peaceful and warm—a sanctuary. But I remained wary of whatever belief system propped up all this beauty.

"Wait here," the woman softly instructed us. We looked at the square cushions—the Tibetan version of a zafu, I assumed—but not knowing how long we'd wait, and being in new surroundings besides, we remained standing, a little restless in the almost oppressive silence of the place, gawking at the decorations that Vince was now exclaiming as "fucking dope!"

Momentarily, the lama appeared, smiling. He was a diminutive Tibetan man, only around thirty or so years old, with a shaved head and robes of magenta and gold. He softly said hello and bowed his head quickly, before motioning us to follow him into what was ostensibly the center's library.

The lama gathered up his robes to carefully seat himself in a chair, and motioned us with a nod to sit in those opposite him, which Vince and I quickly plopped into.

Vince introduced me as "his homosexual lover." I was mortified, having been thus outed against my will, and for the first time—and in front of a religious man, no less. But I was also strangely flattered to have finally heard Vince refer to me as any kind of lover or boyfriend, though I realized he was probably only using it to discomfit the lama, which seemed, considering the circumstances and Vince's assessment of him, even more disrespectful than usual. I blushed.

But the lama just laughed, a sort of jubilant open-mouthed bark almost, which relieved me somewhat, but also made me more vexed as to how to act in front of him. He reached out to shake my hand heartily and I managed a tentative smile.

He liked Vince, he told me, and proceeded to ask him all sorts of personal questions about his money and job woes, his feelings about society and his family. He seemed to know a lot about Vince, but I thought they'd only met briefly. I was still recovering from Vince's introduction, but now I was beginning to wonder about just how long they'd actually talked that day in the park. They were going on and on about all sorts of things, like old friends. What would Vince steal from *him?* I wondered absently.

With no other recourse, I just listened. The lama, whose English was impeccable, displayed a combination of patience and lightness in talking to Vince, which was wholly unlike anyone else's reaction to him. I could see he took Vince seriously, but not what was happening to him, whereas Vince himself as well as everyone else seemed to do just the opposite. The lama didn't mock him or trivialize him, but he laughed at Vince's dramatic reports of injustice and paranoia. When Vince looked hurt, the lama would simply smile briefly and kindly, and then he'd get serious and say something like: "The activity of the world is empty and pointless. None of it matters, Vince. None of it is what's in your heart. Your heart is the world that matters and that is real."

Vince would accept such answers, but I'm not so sure he'd agree. He didn't have that opinion of his heart or the world. He went on and on instead with his litany: he'd had it with the welfare office; they were worthless, having no desire to help anyone. Smiling again, Lama Tenzin agreed. "And that is the nature of the civil service. They are not the people who decided this generosity they dispense. They are only the administrators of it, and as such are more interested in keeping it all in order than in helping anyone. You must understand intention, Vince. You see, they aren't there to help you; that is not their intention, though there may be individuals who are there for that reason. But ultimately, they are there to execute certain duties; that's all. You shouldn't expect otherwise, although sometimes you may benefit from a kind person who works there."

"I disagree," Vince snapped.

"Please explain your position, Vincent," the lama calmly replied.

"They are paid to help me, to serve me. They don't do either of those things."

I remembered then one of his nuggets regarding me and the middle class: "The worst thing about the middle class is that they not only want, but expect, something for nothing." I thought at that moment that every insult he'd ever hurled at me was really aimed at himself.

The lama continued: "Ask them next time you are there what they are paid for, Vincent. Ask them how they get promotions. I think you will find that it has little or nothing to do with love, which seems to be what you want from them."

"I want their money; I don't want their love," Vince said defensively, looking almost shocked at how the lama had called his bluff.

"You don't need either, Vincent, but you do seek their love in your odd way. That is wholly natural; we all seek love. Good for you."

Vince bristled and then looked confused, his brows scrunched up in frustration as if to say, "What the fuck are you talking about?" But the lama was so disarming, it threw Vince off. *My God, he's met his match,* I thought to myself, watching them spar back and forth as if they were playing Ping-Pong or tennis. "You tell me you want them to help you," the lama continued articulately, "and maybe they are helping you. I think they are. Vincent, remember what I said about nothing is as it seems. You are too suspicious of everything when you try too hard to understand it."

Vince just sighed. "Who fucking cares?" he said dolefully. I winced at his language, but the lama didn't. He seemed to find it almost endearing, smiling whenever I thought he should look offended or shocked.

"Exactly!" the lama now announced, grinning broadly and with complete self-assurance, sitting back as if to signal the lesson for today was over.

It was unbelievable to me. The lama had silenced Vincent Malone. And yet you couldn't say he'd beat him. He just kept kneading the dough of whatever it was until they reached a sort of stalemate where they agreed—or the source of Vince's trouble was once again laid bare. I suppose what the lama did that the rest of us never could, was to stay with Vince, keep up with him and not react. It was all really just patience. Vince could be worn down too, it appeared, or exhausted as the case might be. Or perhaps he really had met his match. Either way, I figured, this exchange was doomed. I looked at the lama then, almost as if to warn him that Vince would turn on him too, but the lama only put his hand on my back as he led us out, patting me softly as if for encouragement.

"It was nice to meet you, Neill. Do come again," he said. Then to Vince, he added curtly but kindly: "Pay attention, Vincent; pay close attention."

We ended up arguing on the way home. We were so close to the hospital, nearly in its shadow—how could I not ask?

"When's your next radiation appointment?"

He glared at me and answered sarcastically. "Well, as you can see, Neill, with all my metaphysical dilettantism and such, that I'm big into death, so why would I seek out hospitals?" I rolled my eyes, but he wasn't going to let me off. He put his face in mine, "Huh, Neill, why would I fucking care about you and your little brother and all your cute little cancer adventures with your fucking family? Huh?"

"Leave them out of this, Vince."

"Out of what, Neill? Our fucked-up relationship? I thought we were supposed to share everything, tell all our stories . . ." He was gesticulating like a cheerful lecturer now, while the bus crowd watched from downturned faces and I kept my gaze averted, out the window. "In fact, why haven't you invited me home for dinner?" I looked at him then. "Huh?" he snapped. "Huh, what's the deal, Neill; don't I rate?" I didn't want to get into it there on the bus, but I was trapped.

"Vince," and I looked at him as he looked smugly back at me. "Vince, you would never come if I invited you. You know that."

"You couldn't do it anyway. You're a little closet case." Then he shouted. "Hey, everybody, look at the fuckin' faggot!" *Who's like whose Dad?* I thought then.

"You are a total asshole," I stated then righteously and pulled hard on the stop-request cable. And I *was* near tears this time, as I got up and brushed by him. He followed me off the bus, of course, and we took the long walk home, all the time his half-contrite barking from behind filling my ears, while I contemplated whether I really wanted to have sex with him ever again.

When he caught up to me, he had that look on his face. "Neill, I went on the wrong day, and all hell broke loose, and I called the receptionist a fuck wad and that pretty much got me kicked out of there."

"You're a real charmer, Vince," I answered him, but I felt I no longer cared.

"I'm effective. I love mistreating heterosexual women who think they can flirt their way through life. I'm their worst fucking nightmare."

"And their cutest nightmare," I added cynically.

"I'm not cute," he stated matter of factly then.

I shook my head. "No, of course not." But by then he was already in the corner liquor store and I was stranded, resigned to wait outside. He was back in a jiffy, opening a package of gum with his teeth, a bottle visible in his pocket. Those places weren't easy to steal from, but he'd managed it with the time-worn and as such bold deception of buying some trivial little item such as gum.

Back to the Baldwin we went to spackle over the cracks. I truly wasn't that into it, and maybe he sensed that as we rolled and roiled on the lumpy little bed. With one great shove, he pushed me off and out of him, then climbed out of bed and got dressed.

He'd never done that before. I'd always been careful with Vince. He was like a whirling dervish of boldness and fear both, and no place more so than when we were having sex. There were never words between us then, and so I learned to read the warnings that flashed across his eyes, cautioning me that any wrong move could turn me into his father, at which point he'd repel me then embrace me desperately in rapid succession.

But the embrace did not come this time.

I knew it was his father. I'd waited for him. Now something had brought him back or triggered the domino effect of it. I hadn't been paying attention or I hadn't cared enough to keep track. Without looking at me now, he quickly grabbed his pack of Drum tobacco and matches and went out into the hall and on down to the fire escape to smoke.

I don't know what made me do it. I knew better than to confront him when he was in that dark mood. Maybe I just felt guilty and responsible for it having gone wrong. I followed after him, hoping against all evidence that this time it would be different—that something would finally change. He glared at me when I approached him, and his furrowed brow said clearly, "Stay away." I reached out for him anyway, as if to break his fall from the fire escape and hold him here, help him push through whatever had once again risen up to cut him off from me. But this wasn't about a T-shirt, and an embrace was not what would bring him out of it. How could I really know what twisted like a snake through his mind at those times? I'd been arrogant to think I could.

He barked at me, and slapped my hand away, "How dare you touch me!" And then he reached out with both of his hands in front of him, dropping the cigarette that sparked momentarily at his feet before descending six floors, and he pushed me hard against the door-frame.

I was momentarily shocked—even terrified, and every part of me felt it was suddenly folding in, or as if the iron of the fire escape had fallen prey to metal fatigue and was now collapsing under us, from where we'd freefall down, down, ending up in the refuse pile of his stolen booty, cigarettes and paper plates far below in the alley. Vince was enormous then—enormous in his anger and in his raw animal fury. I saw fire all over him as the neon flashed and raging dragons in his eyes. I stood there, every muscle in my body clenched, wholly paralyzed. I knew if I attempted any move he might send me away once and for all, if not attack me outright and throw me off the fire escape. And yet holding him was all I wanted to do or could think to do. I couldn't very well walk away now. I felt, in fact, that if I turned from him now, he would not be there when I looked back for him. I felt stuck, and my eyes filled with tears for him, one little boy for another, reaching out for him and calling him toward me all at once, but only with my eyes. My body had lost its voice in the one place that belonged to it. And so I spoke words, chancing it all, in a place where no words had ever been uttered.

"Fuck me, Vince," I begged through my tears. He pushed me indoors and did just that. He was like a wrathful god then, one of those crazy tanka pictures from that disturbing Tibetan book of his I'd never read, with flames in his eyes and blood in his mouth—his cock like a reptile, its heartless tongue flipping in and out. He simply crushed me and I bled. He purposely hurt me. When he was through, he was pale and shaking as he'd been earlier that day. Then he got dressed and left.

I laid there ruminating, dreading that something had changed and that perhaps he would be a violent maniac from here on out. I told myself that I should get out while I still could. But I couldn't turn from him. I looked at the ceiling and its stains, making shapes now of them, remembering the old forgotten Virgin Marys I'd found in such places in my youth, and wondered as the tears came again: Where is all this going? How did I get here? And why? But I had a vague idea, even if I didn't understand it completely. It was as if some part of me that had been lost had been found when I first saw him that day in the clinic waiting room. I knew if I left, I wouldn't just be leaving him; I'd be leaving something of myself—something of my better self.

I dozed off and fell into a vivid and disturbing dream where I found myself in court, being grilled by some prosecutor who looked uncannily like Paul. Peter was in a cage, hanging from the ceiling, whimpering, and I knew his fate rested somehow on my testimony. The scene shifted and then it was an enormous cathedral, the walls dark and shadowed behind vast buttresses and columns, a smoke of incense obscuring the teeming congregation. My mother and father, dressed in white, were carrying forward the gifts, but when I looked upon the chalice in my mother's hands, in it I saw Peter's eyeball and Vince's testicle both. My father, walking next to her, carried on the golden plate not the host, but Peter's prosthetic palate. I had a sense that I was the priest as I watched them come forward. Peter still hung in his cage, higher up now in the vast reaches of the cathedral's vault. Suddenly a great moan rose from the crowd and then the great steel doors of the cathedral were flung open: Vince in black armor upon a furious steed galloped down the aisle in painfully slow motion toward me as my parents fled into the pews. There was a restrained fury about him, like those eucalyptus trees whipping their branches about in the park the other day. The crowd, in the pews, gasped fearfully as he rode—nuns, clerics, and altar boys fled from him. I could not stand the slowness of him—out of sync with the rest of the dream—and I stepped down from the altar and moved toward him, even though I knew the sword that flashed above him was meant for me. There was a horrible sound then of chains being hoisted, like the sound of an anchor being raised, and I looked up to see the cage Peter was squatting in pulled furiously upward, through a hole in the ceiling and far up, up the church's steeple, until he burst through the roof and the entire steeple began to collapse inward toward us, into the church, which now, as I looked around me, I saw was consumed suddenly in flames. Giant wooden beams were falling all around the panicked congregation. I was on my knees now and Vince, having reached me, reared up on his steed, the faceplate jarring loose and falling forward to reveal within not his face but a furnace of flames.

That woke me with a start. And I knew then, if I didn't before, that I was not living in two worlds. I tried to sort it out in my mind, breathing heavily, but all I really knew was I missed Peter and I wanted to go home. So I got up then and packed my little gym bag, thinking of how we laughed, and how even when my mother was falling apart things never got as twisted as they did here with Vince.

And then he returned, and I saw his eyes, calm again. And in them I saw the part of me that had fought to save itself from that bourgeois sleep of a world that had never been my own, even though it was the only one I knew. I belonged here in the Baldwin with Vince, come what may. I put my bag back down and sat on the floor.

He went to the window to smoke and we sat there together in silence in that sad little room in that run-down residential hotel, watching the sky as the light of dawn slowly muted the neon's flash; and I understood suddenly that *this is it*—this is home. Because what was true and what was a lie was always very clear in Vince's eyes—you could see it there, almost yelling from beyond his pupils: truth, with a "goddammit" tagged on for emphasis. His truth at least, but often mine too. Whoever he was, and for all his many flaws and poor technique, what looked out from deep within him always relentlessly, vigilantly challenged me to cut to the painful, raw core. I loved him for that. If for nothing else, I loved him for that because no one else had ever demanded the truth, and that was what I'd longed for. I knew now why I'd felt some satisfaction at Peter's scars, my mother's tears—it was the rawness of the love and honesty they demanded. It had taken an actual knife to cut to the core of what mattered between us. I'd needed to bleed too, and Vince was the knife, and I would take the scar.

"Gonna go home, Neill?" A part of me still wanted to, but I said nothing. "None of that should have happened, Neill. You shouldn't have come out there on the fire escape. You gotta give me some space." I just sat there and listened, feeling he was a blessing and a curse both and I had to take one with the other. "Sit down, here,

Neill. I'm not gonna hurt you. Let me show you something." And out came his books.

We sat there on the floor, the sun finally streaming through the window during the one hour of morning that the sun reached his room. I watched those ever-present dust motes that always haunted this place or blessed it—or both, or neither. He sat Indian style, with a big copy of Jung's *Man and His Symbols* opened to a beautiful picture of a Tibetan mandala, and he started exclaiming on it, sharing his insight and relating it to all the millions of other occult or metaphysical books he'd read. I didn't follow his reasoning nor see the parallels, but I didn't need to—I was too distracted in fact with the real thing.

I just watched him, and I could see he was hounded by some nagging anxiety, among those countless thousands he rarely shared that clawed at him from below—dragging him back to hell?—and he was doing what he did to stay above it, or elude its grasp. He was building a tower. All the time, brick by brick, it grew like a big mental edifice—a spiraling, dizzying minaret doomed to fall, with no foundation really but the chaos of his subconscious and the world around him where he gathered his bricks. Inside it, like magma, the pain was rising just as fast, so there was no time to waste. *He must have built it a thousand times by now,* I thought, *those suicide attempts being the most deafening collapses, the farthest falls.*

My eyes teared up because I couldn't seem to look at him then without feeling the full weight of him and everything that has made him this little bricklayer of ideas and theories, hopes and dreams, conflicts and despairs. He would build it around himself and he would build it around me too, I supposed. Which makes of it a tomb. I loved him surely, but that didn't mean I believed in what he was doing. I didn't.

He stopped midsentence when he looked up and saw my tears. "What the fuck? Don't suck me into that!" I've angered him, of course, and though it smarts, how could I have expected otherwise? I've interrupted the construction. He would smooth it all over by changing the subject, but he wouldn't cry. Vince never cried—the tower would cave in. He believed in the psychologists' assessment that depression is anger unexpressed, and he was happy to cut it off at the pass with his fury and rage. But I wasn't crying tears of depression. Albeit, they were sad tears, they were tears of love. You couldn't expect those from Vince either. He couldn't take that chance.

"Don't fucking whine to me," he said with disgust. "I don't pity anyone." I thought then how he sounded like all the right-wing politicos he was forever condemning, but why remind Vince of his inconsistencies and contradictions? Such a criticism would be just another wrecking ball to his tower and he'd have none of it. I realized then that he had a lot more to lose than I'd ever thought he had—which only made me more tearful. And so I excused myself and went away.

"Where the fuck are you going?" he called down the hall.

"I'll be back," I managed to say. He believed me, knowing that I knew better than to lie to him by now.

"You have nowhere else to go!" he shouted as I entered the elevator. I thought to myself, *True,* and *shame on you, Vince, for saying it.*

As I rode the rickety elevator down, I thought sadly that another moment of connection had been lost. Oh, and how many there have been. I think to get in the car and go, but where to? I would wander in limbo. What better place to fill the role than this skid row? I opt for silent self-pity, walking the streets in the hope that I can spend my tears and thus save him the bother of them. I stand and watch the passed-out drunks; the muttering schizophrenics; the scamming immigrant kids and runaways, forever scheming how next to score; the tired-looking prostitutes and their heartless pimps. And I don't feel lucky this time.

I knew only one way. The body was the way to reach him. So after wandering the streets all day, I went to the corner liquor store and I bought a bottle of scotch and up I went, back to the sixth floor.

I knocked at his door. He opened it a crack and then completely, looking contrite and pulling me in. He was all over me and we made love again quickly and fell off to sleep.

And then late he woke me up, shaking me by the shoulder like a kid, like there's an earthquake or a fire or something, like it couldn't possibly wait.

Blurry eyed, I muttered: "What?"

His eyes had a weird young and innocent light to them, and he said: "I love you, you know. I really love you." I squinted and pushed myself up on one elbow, just as he rolled over away from me and closed his eyes again. Had he been dreaming? Had I? I nudged him, but there was no response. I knew he'd never cop to it. But he had. And in the deepest dark of night—he'd copped to love.

CR XIX

My father vanished into his garden again—a sure sign of emotional crisis. It had been quite a summer for his garden and he had produced a bumper crop of tomatoes, green beans, artichokes, and several varieties of squash. At night he prepared platters of them for Peter: great pinwheels of sliced beefsteak tomatoes, zucchinis sliced and slathered in butter and pepper, buckets of artichokes.

It irritated my mother, who would comment, "He can't eat all that" or "You know that those artichokes are difficult to eat with his retainer."

"It's good for him, Mom," I halfheartedly defended my father. My mood wasn't as cheerful nowadays what with how preoccupied I was with Vince, but I did my job.

"Thanks, Neill," he said defensively, looking not at me but at my mother. I knew it was all he could do, and like a child presenting a hideous drawing, it was cold to do anything but smile and say it was wonderful. She knew it too—why did she pick at him? Perhaps simply because he was doing far more cooking and food preparation than she was by now.

"Bring 'em on," Peter joked. "I can eat whatever you throw at me." My father smiled, exonerated.

Peter had completed radiation now, so he wasn't a patient anymore. He was a student again, though it was just summer school and he was still constantly going back and forth to the hospital for refittings of the problematic palate prosthesis (scar tissue kept crowding it out) and his ongoing hassles with gaposis on his chest. (Believe it or not, the hospital staff used such a word to describe a suture that pulled apart, leaving large, shiny red gaps where the skin had separated between stitches.) We always laughed at that comically literal term, and when we first heard Susan use it we accused her of making it up. After all, she had her own lexicon for everything else: Peter's postsurgical catheters were often referred to by her as "old ironsides," and the bed-pan was "the sacristy." As for "gaposis," she swore by the sausage that it was the truth.

"So, what you been up to out there in the city?" my father asked me. It wasn't a real question he'd care to know anything about so I knew something else was coming

I answered accordingly, vaguely. "Oh, you know, wandering around," I said casually, spearing a slice of tomato the size of a compact disc. "Bookstores, coffee shops, you know, the bohemian life," I smiled toward him, and turned and smiled at Peter as he sipped from a glass of milk.

"How you feeling, Peter?" I asked him, hoping to elude my father's interrogation. Before he could answer, my father interrupted.

"No money in Bohemia, Neill. And no universities either," he retorted in a kind of mock finality. I knew what he was thinking: Peter was getting back into the swing of things and so should I. But the fact was, I had just missed the last registration deadline for school and my temp job expired last month.

I attempted to dodge him with humor. "Actually, Dad, they've got an extension program. One of those exchange things, study overseas, you know? And they're handing out scholarships, like, well—like zucchini." But he just looked at me, unamused. I wasn't about to get into any of it for real with him—that school seemed irrelevant after what had happened this year, and that I was in a master's program at Baldwin U besides.

My mother joined in then, saving me the trouble. "Oh, Frank, he'll go back to school when he's good and ready," she said, as she wiped her hands on a cloth napkin. "I need him here," she said with finality, muttering, "I need *someone* to talk to." He immediately got up then. "There he goes off to the garden—we've already eaten, dear; we don't need any vegetables," she raised her voice after him. But he closed the door without responding and I could see him then, cutting flowers—marigolds and roses. He was cutting them for her.

"I'm not allowed to run," Peter stated flatly, obviously annoyed. I looked at my mother for an explanation, guessing he would only get pissed off explaining it.

"The doctor called. He doesn't want him running—it's too much for the scarring. It's too much stress and jarring and everything." Having supplied me with the answer, she began to edify: "He's been through so much." She was doing her usual collapse into woe is me and woe is he and woe is the whole fucking bunch of us. It made me angry and I knew it made Peter angry because she didn't get angry so much as she surrendered. I wanted to say: we don't need the Catholic Church's bad advice right now, or warn her that limping horses get shot for less. But I also knew I wasn't really angry at *her*. We were all angry at cancer, at the situation. We could blame one another, the doctors, God, and fate—even the Catholic Church. But it was that snake, that indifferent reptile of disease—wholly without malice and thus all the more infuriating—that dogged us and wouldn't let us rest. Even after it was gone. Now we were all trying to tread water in its enormous wake, the ten-foot swells of it.

"Can he do something else?" I offered, searching for solutions. I knew Peter wanted to get back in shape so he could play football in the fall, which was why he'd begun running again and even lifting weights in the garage. My mother was probably thinking what I was thinking: We couldn't imagine ever seeing him get tackled again. I wondered if he was in denial about all this, and yet it seemed so healthy to us that he wanted to get back into the swing of things, we didn't dare share our reservations and fears. I had even been encouraging him, thinking it was the right thing to do. But I wasn't about to sign anything.

"He says I can swim!" Peter quipped disgustedly. "It's that or I can sit home and watch fucking TV for the rest of my life. I'm never gonna make the fucking team now," and he threw his napkin on the table.

"I'll swim with you," I said. It was the best I could do.

He slightly loosened the angry grip he had on his brows, glancing at me momentarily. I understood from this that he appreciated the thought, but no thanks. It left me but one option.

"Well, you can still walk. How about we go backpacking, Peter?"

That got the desired smile, but not without a sigh, as he answered: "No, it'll have to wait. The doctor doesn't want me to do anything too stressful. I can't carry all that weight, Neill, that's just like running. He says I gotta lay low until the reconstruction."

"Which is when?"

"He wants to start in about six weeks," he said tiredly.

"So, what's the plan?" and I looked at my mother and Peter both because his body was like the royal "we" when we talked about his illness; we discussed it as if we were national security advisors and his body was our country.

She explained it to me. "Well, first a CAT scan, just to be sure," and she held up both her hands with fingers crossed. "And then they start reducing some of the graft and fine-tuning the scars, that kind of thing. There will have to be several surgeries." She sighed as she finished.

"Looks like I'll be lettering in plastic surgery this fall instead of football," Peter cynically remarked, before downing his glass of milk and getting up.

My mother looked suddenly worn out, frayed like a rope about to snap. When he left the room, she was likely to unleash her despair. But I had gotten good at intercepting it, cutting it off at the pass, soothing her fears.

"Hey, Mom, he's a good sport. I know he'll swim with me." My mother eyed me sympathetically—she knew I didn't like going back to the swim center. But her mind undoubtedly was filling with stories of fairy-tale brothers who deeply loved one another and would make any sacrifice. Which wasn't that far from the mark, so why deny her the pleasure of it by looking back at her with my usual embarrassed annoyance? I got up then and went down the hall after him, leaving her smiling, which was how I liked to leave her.

The next afternoon, Peter and I were standing like a couple of geeks in our Speedos, with our goggles around our necks, and a kickboard, paddles, and buoys in our hands, eyeing which lane to choose and stalling the inevitable shock of cold that would greet us when we got up the courage to finally jump in.

"When's the last time you swam, Peter?"

"Laps?" he looked at me. "I don't know. Years." He shrugged his shoulders. I knew exactly how many it had been for me: 2.8. I'd swam at this pool daily for four years when I'd been a member of the AAU team, before abruptly quitting. I'd been as reticent as Peter'd been to return to this pool. I hoped I wouldn't run into anybody I knew, especially Max, my coach, whom I'd disappointed, and who'd disappointed me.

I'd been one of Max's accomplishments, actually—not a great one, not one of the Olympic hopefuls or the national level kids. But he was proud of how he'd guided me from the ranks of the hopeless, uncoordinated dorks to a boy to be reckoned with, at least on the high school level of competition. He was very good at what he did, and I benefitted from and was grateful for his expertise. But he was also a bit of a Nazi, and watching him berate some errant ten- or twelve-year-old, let alone the older kids, with his substantial temper, calling them good-for-nothing lazy losers and quitters, was always disturbing and often unnerving. But most of these kids could take it, and their parents would likely approve of these dressings-down anyway. AAU was for overachievers—straight-A students with pushy parents who expected them to be nuclear scientists and Olympic swimmers both and who never blinked at the demanding requirements of year-round double workouts, endless trips to other parts of the state for important meets, and whatever else might give their child the edge over his or her competition.

I was there for different reasons, which were all wrapped up with proving myself to Paul, or beating him at his own game, or maybe just trying to become that lifeguard from long ago. Whatever the case, I became a good swimmer in time. Max liked me because I was driven. He had us all fill out goal sheets, lift weights, meditate, the whole nine yards—or in this case, the whole twenty-five yards. I faked my way through the goal sheets, claiming I wanted to make nationals, not knowing how to express in a four-inch blank space that I wanted my brother's love, peer popularity, and to be a normal, heterosexual male who stopped getting hard-ons in the changing room next door. I knew by then that as long as you filled out the forms completely with *something*, no one asked any questions.

At some point, I guess I felt I'd put in enough time proving myself and then there seemed no reason to keep swimming. I went to Max and told him I was quitting. I claimed it was about a job opportunity. He was furious; his voice rose; he pulled open his drawer and shook my goal sheet at me.

"What the hell is this?" he had bellowed. I said nothing, since that's in effect what it was. "You're giving up on your dreams?" he asked incredulously. *What did he know about my dreams?* I thought bitterly, knowing he'd probably laugh at them if he knew what they really were. But they filled my heart and mind with longing all the same. "Is this about your parents?" he went on. "Are they making you get a job? Do you want me to call them?"

"I have to pay for my own college, Max," I said sheepishly, which was true, and at least a part of the decision, if not all of it.

"You can get a scholarship!"

"Maybe," I said doubtfully.

"No, not maybe!" and he leaned into my face. "If you want it, you can get it."

"I don't want to just go to any school. I want to go to Berkeley, and I'd never get a scholarship there."

He didn't want to agree with me, but he knew I was right all the same. Berkeley's swim program, unlike its notoriously bad football team, was stellar. With nothing left to say, he gave up on me. "So be a quitter," he said, and he threw the goal sheet down on the desk. Then he thought better of it, picked it up, and crumpled it in his hands, looking directly into my eyes as he did so. I nearly burst into tears, which I'm sure was his hoped-for effect. He tossed my goals into the trash, never taking his eyes off of me. It struck me then that he was Paul in another form and always had been.

"Thank you for everything," I managed in a low voice, holding back tears and trying to remain in control. I meant it. He'd helped me.

"Don't thank me," he snapped with disgust. "You gave up on me and yourself both." Then he held open the door for me, kicking me out. He never let up, but that was all part of his tough-love Nazi technique, taken once again too far. He probably thought he could bully me into reconsidering and figured I'd show up tomorrow with my tail between my legs. I must have really pissed him off because he was using his time-honored method of breaking me or whomever was "slipping"—leaving the cult—in order to find out what the real problem was, and I wasn't telling. I didn't dare. But as I scanned the pool deck now, nearly three years later, some part of me wished he were milling about. I felt suddenly that I did owe him the truth after all he'd done and was finally ready to tell him. I wondered suddenly how long he must have waited for that inevitable follow-up, apologetic, groveling phone call from me like those he'd get from other kids in crisis who'd eventually come around and see "reason." He never called my parents, knowing they weren't the pushy kind. He'd likely never even met them, come to think of it. They were a wave from the car, an infrequent spectator at meets. They weren't lobbyists like the others, and so he probably dismissed them as expendable. He knew which families kept him in business.

I didn't see him, not surprisingly—he was an ambitious fellow and had likely moved on to a more important team. Peter and I were both beginning to shiver by now, so in we went. I was once again greeted by my past with the taste of the chlorine, the feel of the pool's tiles under my hands, the turquoise blue gutter I reached for at the end of my first lap, the rough texture of the cement wall against my feet as I planted them there to push off and swim back. My ears filled up, and I stopped and banged my head for that special release of unplugging an ear. How could I not think of them all: Max; his assistant Judy; the other loners—Tony and Stan (they too were elated to just get those third-place ribbons, their parents never anywhere in sight); Angela, who liked me and made me wish I were normal. And of course Lars, the lanky Norwegian boy I had a mean crush on. He went all the way to the Pan-American Games. He was one of the stars. He was the lifeguard of my boyhood realized, and the final evidence that I would never become one. It broke my heart to gaze upon him, and I hated myself for my attraction to him, yet never failed to watch him at workout's end pulling himself up out of the pool, water glistening on his long tan back, his suit clinging to his buttocks and balls, the golden hairs of his legs caught in the sunset's amber rays. Eve may have picked the apple and Adam may have eaten it, but I just sat there and looked at the tree, drooling. What a fuckin' tree!

I watched Peter now in my peripheral vision, his vague outline through the bubbles and waves and the misted filter of my goggles. I thought how vital Peter looked then, kicking and pulling his arms through the water. I half-expected a shark with CANCER tattooed on its side would come up and pull him down in one terrible thrashing capture. Or maybe that tattoo wouldn't say CANCER at all—maybe it would be the same as Vince's: enigmatic and illegible, a mystery full of sound and fury, signifying nothing.

I considered then that it might be time to tell Peter about Vince, but it had gotten so complicated and twisted. It felt heavy, like I couldn't pull it up out of myself to share. It felt it would take forever to explain, or that it was in some way inexplicable. I'd have to take Peter over there with me for the weekend to show him how it was. And yet Peter already knew, really. I could explain Vince's hold on me to him in just a few words, all of which he'd understand without elaboration: surgery and cancer and a scar that won't close.

Later, in the locker room, I watched Peter pull on his shirt over the massive scar across his chest, its three sides outlining a sort of open-ended rectangle—the flap that had been rolled into what we'd called the sausage. I had to catch my breath when I noticed for the first time how it looked like someone had literally pushed a shovel into his chest, aiming straight for his heart.

"How's that gaposis?" I inquired.

"It's OK, but it's not quite right," he replied. "I'll probably have to go back in. Chlorine always dries my skin. It'll probably rupture the whole fuckin' thing." He rolled his eyes.

"Make sure you put some lotion on it when we get home," I encouraged him, patting him on the back as we exited.

On the ride home, he told me he felt good about his swim and wanted to go back in a day or two. I supposed I'd join him, though I'd really only volunteered to get him started. Besides, there was still that nagging desire to discourage him from getting in shape for football and thus risking some horrible wreck on the field this fall. I had to at least pose the question, just to check that he wasn't completely delusional or overly invested in it.

"You're really gonna play football?"

"Yeah, why not?"

"Well, you know why . . . I mean—maybe run cross-country or something for a change this year."

"Geez, you sound just like Mom."

"Look, Peter, do it if you want to do it, but at least consider the fact that everyone's gonna think you're crazy, and maybe they're right. And besides, if you're going in for reconstruction every few weeks, you'll have to sit out all the games." He looked at me tiredly, and I suddenly regretted having even brought it up. I backpedaled, resorting to humor. "Well, who knows, maybe they can give you some kind of special faceguard. Maybe you could wear one of those hockey masks like that psycho guy Jason in *Friday the 13th*."

He rolled his eyes, but he laughed. "Yeah, I'd be the freak of the league. Phantom of the Gridiron—no one would know who I was." And then he launched into an imitation of some creepy English scientist. "They say he was a boy once, prince of the sophomore class, and then a strange thing happened—no one really knows what. It came out of the night. We don't know if he has a face behind that mask, or if it's only a scream of terror frozen for eternity . . ." And he crowded me with a spooky little scream.

That did spook me, in fact, but I kept with him. "Yeah, and then one game, you'd get really knocked on your ass and the mask would fall off and you'd have no head at all. The cheerleaders would scream."

"The refs would call penalties—'laying without a head!' Whistles and mass pandemonium." He laughed, but then he paused and his smile vanished as he barked, "Fuck it! Maybe I can't play football." He turned to me then, almost pleadingly. "I gotta stay in shape, Neill, just in case, and because I gotta leave the chance open, you know? Otherwise . . ." I knew he was about to cry, but I also knew he didn't cry. He looked out the window. He's like my mother the way he does that. They both contemplated following my father out that window for good, I guessed, but they held their ground, standing in the difficult but necessary place between worlds.

"We'll swim then," I said jokingly. "We'll play goddamn croquet and badminton; we'll bowl . . ."

He smiled then from under his hooded sweatshirt, appreciating my solidarity with him but still not wholly reconciled with the situation.

"We'll always be able to hike, Peter, remember that. Even if we gotta wait until next summer. We'll go packin', way the heck out there."

"Yeah," he said resignedly, but somehow consoled, "we'll go packin'."

⚘ XX

Only Vince was cheerful when he got a herpes outbreak. It meant he was off the hook. And yet, he told me it made him horny, explaining to me that it wasn't him though, it was the disease's lust to spread: "It makes even me a whore." He laughed heartily to himself then, thrilled somehow by the self-abnegation, as he cut up onions for a miso soup he was busy assembling on the hot plate.

I was just glad to see he was cheerful after last week. "Yeah, the hospital made me horny sometimes," I chimed in. "Sex and death, I guess."

"Well, I don't know about that. Herpes isn't going to kill anyone."

"Yeah, I know, but disease, decrepification, all that. It makes you want to fuck."

"To bring it all back, eh? Reproduction? Keep the fucking horror show alive and kicking; feed the fire. How does that work for fags?" While I pondered that, he answered for me. "I'll tell ya. It has nothing to do with reproduction, all that sex and death bullshit. It's just poison that you've got to get out of your system. Kids are just a by-product. This whole world is the price you pay for spilling your diseased self into it."

I almost laughed but I couldn't deny it made me feel sad too, whether I agreed with his premise or not. "The Buddhists call it samsara, right?" I was looking at the side table, the one that he always displayed his stolen booty on. He'd converted it into a Buddhist altar of sorts. It was decorated with pretty postcard Buddhas, stolen candles, incense, feathers, and stones. He had to put something there, I figured, since he'd stopped bringing me stolen gifts. I'd been replaced as something to provide offerings to, and it touched me more than insulted me to see him make that table into a sort of altar, realizing that was what it had always been to him and I'd only now come to appreciate that fact. All at once, I wanted to apologize to him and plead with him to please steal things for me again.

"So are you meditating?" I asked instead, nodding toward the altar.

"I've tried it a few times, but I need to go back to the lama to find out how to do it. I don't know what the fuck I'm doing. I just get bored or think of stabbing my father or something that makes me stop and do something else." I admired him for trying, imagining what solitude and quiet might allow to rise up from his psyche. It didn't seem particularly promising as a strategy for Vince.

But although he failed at meditation, our tantric sex practice thrived, though we didn't know it as that. The Buddha manifesting as herpes? That night was like our first night that we'd made love—the ridiculous, frustrated groping; the impossible logistics; the sad little comedy of inconvenient sex, with Vince in his long johns and me in my boxer shorts. At least we were both shirtless as we tumbled and wrestled around for hours, looking into each other's eyes, the energy forever unspent between us.

There was no tentativeness on Vince's part tonight—I guess he felt in control knowing that nothing was really expected and he wasn't completely exposed. I was glad he seemed more comfortable with it. With all that time—an eternity really in the surreal timelessness of intercourse—we explored each other's beauty in a deeper way; a more goalless and thus a more sustained and attentive way. I think back now and remember that our best sexual experiences were those few times when he had his outbreaks. The good luck and blessings of the Buddha of Herpes.

The next morning we were both full of the same jolt we'd had the last time we'd been through this. In my exuberance, and seeing that the summer was waning and Peter was not going to be able to go—and because I was full of wanting to love him; full of wanting to give something to him—I asked him again. "Let's go to the mountains, Vince, wanna?"

"Sure," he responded, raising his shoulders. "But coffee first."

The next week, I showed up with all my gear, and we hustled down Market Street to the mountaineering store and gathered up supplies: rope to hang our food in the trees and so keep it from bears; plastic bottles for water; candles and matches; freeze-dried food; fuel for the stove and batteries for the flashlights. We had to rent him a pack and sleeping bag, as he had no possessions save his stack of collapsed boxes full of clothes and his ever-evolving pile of books back at the hotel. For once, he followed my lead.

It was the same at the auto parts store, buying oil and making sure the old chipped green VW was up to snuff. Vince had never even bothered to get a driver's license and in fact despised automobiles, so he stood there watching me, following me about with his furrowed brow as I readied the old heap in the store's parking lot. *A good thing Vince doesn't drive,* I thought, *as that would have led him quite likely to grand theft auto by now.* Prophetic thoughts. As if he'd have needed a license for it.

We set off early the next morning, rolling over the Bay Bridge and out past Oakland and Berkeley, and then through the tunnel under the Oakland Hills, and beyond to the suburbs where I pointed out to Vince the direction of my parents' house. He only shrugged, uninterested and still drowsy, nursing his coffee. When I pointed out the exit a few moments later, he rolled his eyes as if to say "Enough. Do you really think I care?" He wiped the sleep out of his eyes then, stretched, and seemed to come to somewhat—showing now that intent and furrowed brow that so characterized his visage—as we passed beyond the final hills and made our way into the hot, dry Central Valley, heading east toward Yosemite.

He wouldn't go into the convenience stores or markets when I stopped to get gas or something to drink, but he needed caffeine all the same, so he'd sit brooding in the car while I bought us coffee and donuts. Though he'd traveled all over the place, he seemed markedly uncomfortable outside the city. He did get stares, with the black eyes and orange hair, the tattoo and stubbled goatee, the ratty clothes and provocative T-shirts. Today he was wearing his What Would Satan Do? black T-shirt. *Well, he'd probably pilfer all these 7-Elevens if he were to come in with me,* I thought, *so it's just as well. I won't have to worry about his thieving ways out here and all the trouble it brings between us.* But it was strange to see him act hemmed in, even though the world was opening up around us. I could see that my self-confidence and comfort level with all this generic Americana seemed to be getting on his nerves slowly but surely as I pointed out the sights, talking about the orchards lining both sides of the two-lane blacktop and guessing at their fruit; craning my neck to glimpse the snaking, slow rivers that lolled below us as we sped over bridges; remarking on places Peter and I had stopped to eat or had picked up supplies. He was a traveler, sure, but not this kind.

"So you're a mediocre, middle-class white person—I'm impressed," he'd cynically snap. "Do you fish and hunt too?"

"Shit, Vince, come on, man. *Try* to have fun." I was feeling bolder than usual as it seemed we were more on my turf out here than his. Besides, I wasn't going to buy beer and end up drinking and driving while he gave me a hand job just to calm him down.

"Fun?" he snapped. "I thought you said the mountains were 'sublime,' Neill. What's fun? Disneyland is fun. Fuck fun. I didn't come out here for fun. Where's your fucking sublime, Neill? I want to see a bear ripping apart a camper or something."

"Should I drive into oncoming traffic?"

He glared. "How about just slam on the brakes; I don't have my seat belt on. You can get rid of me that way and have your little trip."

"Nah, I'm only coming out here cuz I wanna show *you* this." That shut him up because he saw that I meant it, and on some level he appreciated the thought. But I was beginning to have doubts about the whole idea, even as I tried to hold to my conviction that the mountains were the last best chance for him and me, just as they'd been that for me years ago.

When we reached the foothills, where the copses of oak trees thickened and the rocky bones and reaching evergreens of the Sierras began to show themselves, I became more ecstatic with each new rise in elevation and each new cup of coffee. We'd stopped perhaps six times as Vince was insatiable. But he wasn't smoking. I knew I was talking too much, but I couldn't contain my exuberance, and I thought then, *why should I?* I started describing the various pines: red Jeffreys and

yellow ponderosas, towering lodgepoles and big-coned sugar pine. I
told him now about all my trips with Peter, the bear encounters, the
storms and river crossings. But when I looked at him, he turned away,
even appeared bored or mildly annoyed.

"How much longer?" he blandly asked.

I reconsidered. Maybe I should have concentrated on pointing out
roadkill instead of pine trees. While I felt I'd escaped from the city, he
seemed even more oppressed; if not that, then maybe he just felt exposed.

"About an hour or so," I answered. He said nothing, hunkered
down in his seat looking miserable.

I pulled over then. He sat up, with a questioning look on his face.
"We don't have to do this, Vince."

"What the fuck. You wanna turn back?"

"I don't, but if you don't want to go hiking, you should tell me. It's
kind of a commitment. You'll be stuck out here for three days."

"And what exactly would we be going back to, Neill?" I wasn't sure
if that was his despair or an insult—probably a little of both.

But I saw his point. "OK, well, trust me on this then. I guarantee
you that where I'm taking you is awesome. But you gotta be patient."

He smiled and nodded sardonically. I wondered then if he were just
so mental that nothing outside of the intellect meant that much to
him, and I'd been a fool to hope he'd be affected by a slope of pine
trees, a cottonwood-choked river, or a field of flowers climbing dizzily
up a hillside.

"It's pretty, Neill, OK?"

I pulled back onto the highway, struggling to get the car up to
speed on the slope. Well, if he lived in his mind, then I would let up on
the beauty around us. I brought up a film we'd seen recently, Tarkov-
sky's *Sacrifice*. I listened to him trash it, which surprised me as he'd
raved about it endlessly the day after we'd seen it. He'd pick apart
anything I said at this point, denying all his previous praise. I knew
better than to continue and got to wondering if he'd just keep getting
worse with every foot of altitude, while I got better, which wouldn't
be pretty since we aimed to climb over 10,000 feet by the end of the

day. Perhaps the thin air would mellow him—or knock him clean out, I joked to myself.

We drove on in silence, as the road wound snaking through the towering firs and on up into Yosemite National Park where we stopped briefly to pay a ranger our entrance fee. I braced myself for Vince's comment, which came as expected once we pulled away from the booth.

"Charging us to wander the fucking planet. Rangers are just fucking cops." I thought to defend them, but sometimes I could see the black-and-white argument we'd get embroiled in as it was coming, and that particular one was going to turn me into either a Nazi or a comrade in disinformation, so I let it slide. I always felt sorry for rangers; the forest service was so understaffed and people were so careless in the wild. He couldn't know that, of course. I was anxious at that point to just get him out of the car. Maybe the trees were making him nervous. We were headed up over the Tioga Pass, above the treeline, for that very reason, because it just seemed more Vincelike to be extreme. A forest wouldn't have done it; it had to be blasted granite, boulders, and a few sparsely scattered, gnarled little pines, high above it all.

The high country was ablaze with sun and flowers as we climbed toward the pass, winding up the smooth gray pavement, past enormous white granite chunks of rock jutting out over the road, their quartzite specs glimmering in the high altitude sunlight and vivid blue mountain sky. Big pines were scattered across the rocky meadows of open space, all littered with pinecones and little yellow flowers. It was a comforting disorder and randomness; an open endless spaciousness that made me suddenly think of sex—like Vince's semen splattering across my chest, creating its lovely, structureless chaos that was so like an echo of this place.

We parked at Tuolumne Meadows where there was a store and a ranger station. Winnebagos and pickups with shells lumbered by, full of campers who never hiked but simply parked and sat down in the trees for three days to drink beer or fish while their children ran among the wild things or experimented sexually off in the bushes. There were wiry, long-haired German climbers hoarding PowerBars and juice and Japanese groups of tourists buying postcards before driving on, never to set foot more than 100 yards beyond the parking lot. Vince was appalled and looked claustrophobic. I was still a little surprised he was taking it all so hard after all the rails he'd ridden, the hitchhiking and traveling. But hoboes didn't come through places such as Yosemite—people were lost in a wholly different way here, and I knew it was the bourgeois emptiness of the place that he objected to, that made him nervous. So we quickly got our permit and a few last-minute supplies and got out of there.

At the trailhead, we speedily packed up our gear and backpacks, and I hoisted Vince's onto his shoulders.

"Feel all right?" I asked, but not too cheerily, hoping to get an actual answer.

"It's heavy," he said drolly. I smiled at him and, grabbing his shoulders, shook him about, getting a little grin from his increasingly withdrawn visage. I pulled on my own pack and we headed up past the trailhead sign with its maps and warnings about bears, fire, litter, and snakes, and then on to the trail to our chosen destination, a smattering of lakes up a sparsely traveled watershed.

We walked in silence the first couple of miles, stopping now and again to help each other adjust our packs. He allowed me to yank his straps and pull at the buckles and guides until his pack sat more comfortably on him; his passivity reminded me of the night when I'd first taken off his shirt all those weeks ago. He was softening already, I could see, and I wanted to jump up and yell out: "It's working! Vince is being wildernessed!" But if there was one thing I knew Vince would scoff at, it was joyful exultation, so I kept my reserve. I was thrilled to have him out on the trail with me, such an unlikely place for one such as him. I couldn't help smiling any more than he could help scowling back at me. I was just excited to be out on the trail again, taking in the meadows and the dappled sunshine amid the big trees, absorbing the silence and endless space around us, thrilled to be here again and to share it with someone I loved.

I wished then that Peter was with us too. And Peter didn't even know I was here. I'd loaded the gear in my car covertly, feeling guilty, like I was betraying him, even though I knew he was incapable of such petty resentment. More likely it was my parents who'd inspired my secrecy. I couldn't bear my mother's frown or my father's pretended nonchalance if they had come upon me loading my backpack into the car to head off to the mountains without him. Then again, maybe it was just my fear of telling them about Vince. They all knew I'd only go to the mountains with someone I loved, and they'd want to know who it was.

In time, Vince got chatty, though it began with arguments. First it was books—Kerouac specifically, because I'd launched off on a glowing discourse about the mountain journey in *Dharma Bums*. Of course Vince hated Kerouac. "Sloppy tortured Catholic bullshit," he said dismissively, and changed the subject to Burroughs, whom he preferred among the Beats.

"I couldn't agree more," I concurred, smiling, which perplexed him and induced once again that characteristic furrowed brow. But I was thinking about how beautiful chaos was, looking out at the decaying collapsed logs strewn across the trail; the torn-apart pinecones and the scarred pines; the striated stone that told the long, sloppy, sweet, and sad story of creation.

Next, we argued about the food I'd brought.
"Why Top Ramen?"
"Because it's light."
"Why shrimp flavor, when we could have had chicken?"
"No reason."
"Why bagels?"
"Because they don't get smashed."
"Why cheese?"
"Because it's good for several days without refrigeration." We'd been through all this before in the supermarket, but I took it in stride, figuring he wanted either to learn or complain, both of which he did continually no matter where he was or what he was doing. I didn't mind now, as it felt nice for a change to have him accept my answers, instead of challenging them.

We stopped conversing eventually, content to watch the meadows and the streams emerge around us as we moved up the trail. In the early evening, we found an idyllic spot—a slab of granite hanging over a rushing river and next to it a cozy little dell of pines. I let him cook up the food he didn't like on the little camp stove he cursed at, while I hung up the rest of it in the trees to keep it away from bears who would otherwise come right into camp and eat everything in sight. I wanted Vince to see one, of course. Or did I just want him to be afraid enough to cling to me? Either way, I wasn't going to tempt fate and ruin the trip, so I'd never know my true intentions on that score.

Hanging up the food got him curious about wildlife though, and he began to ask questions about which animals I'd seen and what I'd done when bears had come around. The mountains were having their effect on him, I happily noted to myself, draining off his outer layers of anger and irritation like watershed, folding him up in the natural rhythms of wonder that could rejuvenate even the severest of misanthropes. The wilderness had done that for me. So, while we slurped our Top Ramen, I told him exaggerated tales about run-ins with bears since the real stories weren't all that exciting (I'd chased off a few with stones; a few others had stolen all my food, but I'd slept through it). He got quickly wise to my embellishments and began to feed me questions to trip me up.

"So, when you wrestle a bear to the ground, is it best to pin the front or the hind legs first?" and "If they're chasing you, is it better to climb a tree or find a river and dive in? Or do they swim?"

"They climb and swim both, Vince, that's why I carry my Swiss Army knife." We were having a good time, an almost innocent good time, and it sort of broke my heart because it was never this easy back home. I was glad things were turning out good, but I also knew that we wouldn't likely take this with us, and we couldn't very well stay.

His lips were so soft among all the stone; the tree bark; the coarse dirt and the almost steely hardness against your skin of the near-freezing water. We zipped together our sleeping bags up under the pine trees, and we made our hungry, abbreviated tantric love. I'd yearned for this—to be naked with him here—and even if the herpes precluded that, it was enough, and maybe even more considering I'd felt about it last time. Sex was a wilderness and always had been, always would be—even in the sad old Baldwin Arms on his rickety little bed. It had been a porthole to a place just like this, with the same silences and a river too—seasons even, constant and cyclic and yet always fresh, as if come upon for the first time. We went to that wilderness now from the wilderness we were in, so that we were a wilderness within and without. And the wind seemed to cheer for us through the trees.

After a while we just lay together, looking up at the stars and surrendering to the corny ingenuous conversations that emerge from that stunning view where no city lights, or hazes, or dust obscure the broad, thick bands of the Milky Way.

"We ain't shit in all this," Vince concluded.

"Nope. Ain't it grand?" I joked, believing in fact it was, and pulling him closer to me. So like the hospital that way, so like cancer. The wilderness brought out the best in us, and much of it was corny.

We fell asleep eventually, awoken every few hours by little sounds that could be small foraging animals, or even bears, or more often than not just the settling of trees—falling pinecones and needles, and the shedding of bark in little sections shaped like pieces of a puzzle.

In the morning, we waited for the sun to come up, nestling closer in the sleeping bag, sheltering ourselves from the cold night air. When a big band of light finally reached through the trees to touch us, it woke us and we emerged, climbing out and then jumping about as we dressed, rubbing together our cold red hands and yelping to keep back the cold. We cooked up oatmeal and coffee and held each other in big hugs for warmth as enormous tree shadows spread out leisurely around us in the rising sun.

We packed up and headed further up into the mountains, Vince mellowing with each step and looking all around him with great curiosity now. He started to ask more questions—the names of trees and flowers. I kissed him more, and he didn't turn away. It was odd, but what I'd hoped for; even more than I'd hoped for, as the mountains always are. I was so grateful to be there and grateful to whomever I was with. I'd get teary-eyed and overcome now and again, but I kept it to myself, which too was easier in the mountains, what with the single-file nature of the trail.

We stopped when he said he wanted to rest, and I took off my pack. When he took off his, he coyly motioned with his head away from the trail. Then he grabbed my hand and pulled me along through the towering trees, eventually pushing me against a rock where we stripped off our shirts and pressed our chests together, kissing passionately.

And then he just as suddenly jogged off back to the trail, leaving me to wonder: *Is he feeling playful and happy or is he just thanking me?* We hadn't been fighting after all and we had no liquor in our packs. Maybe it really was working after all.

Clouds gathered the afternoon of that second day. That night, as we rushed to set up camp on a lake, it began to rain. I wasn't worried, as I'd been through summer thunderstorms up here before—they rarely lasted more than an hour. Vince was a bit more concerned and didn't like hearing the thunder and seeing the flashes just over the peaks. It was a purple-pink dusk-time thunderstorm and it made the mountains across the high alpine lake look angry and magnificent. We were in a clump of trees to protect ourselves from lightning, and we hurried to cover our backpacks and sleeping bags with my tarp before we ran together and huddled in our jackets under a tree to watch the storm and wait for it to pass.

The forest got dark and everything became child-primal terrifying. The lake looked black in its gray granite bowl, and the trees were sinister shades. Vince had never been out in the mountains at all, and certainly not in such a storm, so he clung to me, asking me more questions about storms now, thunder and lightning and hypothermia.

I looked at him, surprised by his anxiety, but his fear was endearing. "What about all those railroad stories, Vince—those rainy flatcars and stuff?"

"Well, it's not like you're fucking stuck in the mountains. There's towns and stuff. You get off the train eventually and find a warm place, or at least a fucking drink, or some drugs."

"Well, you can always get high, Vince. What'd you bring?"

"This is your thing," he stated, looking away. "I let you decide what to bring, remember?"

"You didn't bring any?" I grinned, almost flabbergasted, visibly impressed. He'd done this a few times before—gone cold turkey— and it always amazed me. For someone so seemingly dependent on drugs in order to cope, he'd brought nothing: not a cigarette; no coke or speed; mushrooms or acid; not even booze. All we had was coffee.

"I don't suppose we brought any kind of a tent?" he then asked me.

"No, I hate tents," I answered confidently, not wanting him to think I'd forgotten it.

"Fuck, I could use a cigarette," he said now nervously, and his restlessness appeared to build.

I started to worry myself after an hour, since it looked like the storm wasn't waning at all. It was late summer, September, and there was always a chance that you'd run into an early fall storm instead of the usual summer thundershowers. We might be getting socked in, in which case it was a potentially dangerous situation. I never did bring a tent, foolishly—not in summer anyway, and I was confident it was still summer. I had a tarp, but it was small. If it got real cold we had our sleeping bags to keep us warm as long as we kept them dry by huddling under the tarp. Vince sensed my fear because he sensed everything, and so we were scared together then, and we clung ever closer.

It was holding him like that, both of us frightened and a little worried, that was wholly new. It occurred to me that we'd never both been in that state at the same time before. It was always one or the other of us who was happier or more in control, or more fucked up, or sorrier, or pissier, or scareder, or whatever. But now we were equal in it. Before we'd been magnets that pushed each other away. And now here they were miraculously clinking together, defying the laws of science. All the differences, the endless positioning and seesawing back and forth were absent, washed away. We were one thing now. A strange and tentative balance had come upon us—one that couldn't last. I looked at him to see if he felt it too, and I was startled when I looked into his eyes. I saw the boy I'd seen at night back in the city, who'd nudged me and told me he loved me—and who I'd wondered if I'd ever see again—some ghost of a long-ago child. We just looked at each other, saying nothing as all sorts of unspoken things flowed between us. And I felt he was showing me something precious—a jewel or keepsake—letting me fall further into him than I ever had before. Looking into his eyes then, it was as if his little boy's hands cupped around something he'd always held but never shown me. When he opened them, it was no jewel or memento, no rabbit's foot, coin, or shiny stone, but a brilliant-colored poison toad, bright orange and yellow and glistening black, breathing in its bubble-lunged way, and looking about frightened and tentative. A gift for me, poisonous and precious and rare, like something that could heal all your wounds if you knew how to use it, or kill you instantly if you didn't.

I felt my eyes might tear up, but I knew if I let them the frog would vanish and with it the little boy. He'd run off into this forest, never to be seen again. I had to respect Vince's hard-earned openness by being silent and not in any way emotional or cloying. I told myself I'd come here to give this all to Vince, not to take anything. For once, to just give. So instead of tears, I offered a very faint grin and then, with all the will I could muster, changed the subject.

"One more hour max, Vince." I let the frog and the boy vanish like a wisp of smoke into the air. I'll see them again, I reassured myself, and if not, that's OK too.

"That long?"

"I could be wrong, but that's my guess."

Forty minutes later, the thunder stopped, and ten minutes after that, the rain. We were relieved, and we hurried to set up camp as it was quickly getting dark, with the sun already gone, and the clouds planning on doing who knows what next. We set up the stove to cook, worrying that it might rain again. We had to at least eat something quickly and, the air being full of a damp chill, we needed to get some tea in us to warm up. I kept looking up from lighting the stove to see if any stars had appeared as the sky and forest went dark around us. Then I set a pot of water to boil and busied myself stringing the tarp up between two trees, figuring we'd need to sleep under it just in case.

"Hey, a star," I heard Vince's voice from a dozen feet away.

"Cool," I replied, hurrying over from the trees to see where he'd gotten a view near the lakeshore. It likely meant the clouds had begun to move on and the sky would soon be clear.

"I love you, Vince," I said.

"Yeah." Well, it was better than no answer, but I'd hoped suddenly that he'd be able to say it to me too then. Of course, I'd be greedy to expect or ask for that from him and the wilderness after what they'd given me just a moment ago. I could feel his comfort now, and that made me happy. He wasn't running away or pushing me away. And when we climbed into our big double sleeping bag, we snuggled close like that first nap, long ago. He didn't resist me and even pulled me closer, albeit with his eyes wholly closed.

I dreamt of Vince that night, and we were walking with our backpacks, but we were not in the mountains at all. We were in Iowa—in Council Bluffs. I knew because he had told me all about it, how it had this immense rail yard of derelict boxcars. It was like a huge graveyard, like the end of the line, like all the trains came to Council Bluffs to die, out there in the very smack-dab middle of America.

Vince wanted to sleep in one of them. "It's great," he said, "we've got a selection of thousands. Come on, let's go down there." And away from the highway and fast-food joints, we walked down this quiet potholed street with American Midwest houses of big lawns and flagpoles and mailboxes, all painted white. And then we had to climb a fence and hoist our packs over it, and trudge carefully down an overgrown, weedy hillside to the graveyard. All the boxcars were locked up, of course, with rusty old chains and padlocks. I felt discouraged, but Vince *knew,* he said: he knew.

He had a crowbar now and he was crawling up on top of the boxcars, hopping from one to the next, prying at them. I was standing down below among them, and their shadows were long and dark just like the shadows of pine trees in the mountains.

And then I saw his shadow on the dirt next to me, long, long—like fifty feet long, so it must have been late afternoon. And when I looked up to find him, it was just his silhouette, with the crowbar raised, the sun blinding my eyes, which shone at his back and made a kind of corona around his suddenly enormous image.

I awoke frightened; *he's too big,* I thought. I sat up, but Vince was unperturbed as the whole forest was unperturbed in its quiet little snappings and lake-lapping water sounds.

When I fell back to sleep, the dream continued. We were inside the boxcar now—and it was just like his room in San Francisco at the Baldwin—but it was not in Council Bluffs anymore, because I could see out the big open sliding doors and what was out there was not an old rail yard at all, but the purple clouds from the storm. And when I went to the edge to look, there was nothing, and I jumped back. We were floating in the sky in this railcar, and Vince was making oatmeal.

He looked happy and I hugged him from behind while he was bending over the little camp stove and I asked him if I can eat my oatmeal out of his asshole. Then we were naked and wrestling together and the railcar tipped suddenly and we were spilled out into the purple, thunderous clouds and I awoke with a start, breathing heavily with fright.

That startled Vince too, but only momentarily, and he adjusted himself and went back to sleep. I didn't know what time it was, but figured if I could get back to sleep, it would be morning next thing I knew. But it wasn't to be for a series of dreams followed, vivid and jarring, waking me over and over again: I was in some nightclub, coming back from the bathroom, and I saw his back to me on a stool at the bar. But when I got there, I turned his shoulder and it wasn't him, but someone who looked like him. I went home with the guy and ended up having sex with him, but I was frustrated the whole time, like I kept thinking I would find Vince in him; like he was hiding in the guy, and the only reason I was making him was because I kept thinking I would find Vince inside him somewhere. Then there followed a dream of helicopters that reminded me of mosquitoes, and I knew they were Vince, searching, but I didn't know what for. I dreamt after that of rocky islands; defunct, drifting spaceships; empty city streets with red flashing signal lights—down an alley, the hollow sound of angelic choirs, but no one was there. In the last of the dreams, Vince and I were in his hotel room, and I crossed the room to him and pulled off his shirt, but when I pulled it up and over his head, there was only outer space where his torso should have been, and his head disappeared then too, and he was just stars and Magellanic purple and orange clouds. And when I looked at the constellations I could see there, like Orion or the Big Dipper, I thought I could make out his image too—the Constellation Vince.

When I awoke, all the stars were gone and the moon too. The day was brilliant and crisp from yesterday's rain; the stone shimmering as it dried; and the wind rustling the trees that were like hair washed and shaken out. I felt a little desperate from the dreams and I kept wanting to make sure he was really there, worrying he'd suddenly vanish.

"Hey, good morning," he said, smiling, seeming so content, so present. I was a little off from my dreams, but I realized I'd done good bringing him here, and that cheered me. He was already collecting firewood and had the stove going. But I was shaky—maybe it was the dreams or maybe it was the electricity left over from the storm. I didn't want to think it was some new place we had reached because I didn't know how to hold onto it and I didn't want to fall.

We warmed ourselves up with tea and oatmeal (and I remembered my strange dream as I ate it, and smiled at him). We said little, but looked at each other in a funny way all morning, like we were both saying, "I know you from somewhere, but I can't remember where."

That day we made it to our final destination, Twin Lakes, which sat well over 11,000 feet, well above the tree line where there was just stone and stunted grasses. The two lakes sat in a bowl of orangeish granite, and the wind kept rippling the water hauntingly, one way and then the other. We spent a quiet day there, wandering around, just looking at things, growing calmer and saying little. There was no rain that night and the stars shone in thick bands again, so dense they looked like they'd fall under the weight.

We made a gentler love that night, in the dark. The words between us had been gone for hours now and we moved about quietly, communicating with our eyes and hands and mouths. I just wanted to tell him I loved him, but it seemed absurd to keep repeating such a phrase and I feared once I started I'd never be able to stop. But I didn't even begin as I remained terrified of breaking the peaceful spell—an enchantment—that lay now between us.

We awoke the next morning and quietly had our breakfast, huddled together for warmth. We'd risen early as we had a long hike back. It would be all downhill now, so we could cover the three days' travel it took to get here in just one. We climbed up the rocks to the sunlight spreading out from the first rays of the sun cresting the mountain, and we kissed there, his face burnished golden, his cheeks still cool from the morning, and rosy hued. *He's wholly fuji,* I thought to myself again.

"Wouldn't it be perfect to have sex right here, right now?" I ventured. Then we laughed; we laughed to echoing. I'd never seen him give into smiles like that—and regarding sex no less. We plopped down right there and, huddled together arm in arm, we watched the sun emerge over the peaks.

I felt so grateful then, for our trip and even all its difficulty, carved out of our common struggle, and vowed to ask for nothing more, suspecting somehow even then that this was a golden moment, even a final moment, a kind of climax to all we could achieve together, and the odds of it lasting were more or less impossible. My eyes filled from that thought, but I tried to hold it back, not wanting to upset Vince and ruin the moment.

"We ain't shit in all this," I shouted to get the tears out of me, lest they burst forth.

"Ain't it grand!" Vince shouted in response, and we laughed again, cuddling each other. *And ain't we lucky,* I thought.

"This place is beautiful, and we gotta go," I announced, squirming out of his embrace.

"Ain't it fuckin' grand!" Vince shouted again, getting up with me.

We hurried to get ourselves dressed and to pack for the long trip back. But before we set out on the long walk down, I looked at him one time and was overwhelmed by his beauty and his pain, and *the pain* (I couldn't separate him from his story: his mother and father; the group home and the suicides; the down-on-its-luck Baldwin, and I couldn't separate him from my own: my brother's scars and my mother's tears; that cold distance in Paul's eyes; the dodgy clipped ironies of my father). I felt suddenly weak in the knees, reeling from it. I grabbed Vince and held him to me and I couldn't help it—I began to weep.

He looked at me now, offended, and I knew I'd made a terrible mistake. He disengaged himself from me then as tactfully as he could. He just couldn't afford to break—I know this now; I knew it then. It was like Peter and all those times I'd held back so as not to upset or discourage him. I was able to do that once, twice, a thousand times then. But I couldn't do it for Vince now; I couldn't *keep on* doing it for Vince. He'd grown too big.

"I'm sorry, Vince," I blubbered, trying with all my might to stifle it. "Please, don't get mad." And I tried to walk away a short distance, hoping to contain myself as I had when stepping out while back in the city or at home with Peter. A whole wilderness lay before me, but there was nowhere to go; no escape; no place to hide myself from him.

"Don't do this, Neill, please," he tried to plead patiently, but I could see it angered him, put him out. I tried to stop, but there was something unbearable between us, so painful it made me melt. The joy had broken the skin of us, it seemed, and all the pain seemed suddenly exposed and pouring out like blood. I'd take the scar, but I thought then that I'd need to cry a lot to pull the tattered, gapped edges of that wound together again.

"I'm sorry, Vince. I'm so sorry. I tried; I've tried."

"Oh shit, fuckin' cork it, Neill."

I sat down then on a rock and began to cry in earnest. Maybe I should have done all this alone somewhere, but I knew these tears weren't just mine. Oh, how I longed that he could push through this once, let his skin break open and bleed, let it reach out to me across this distance—all the more unbearable because it just wasn't that far.

"I need your help," I beseeched him through my tears.

He might as well have said, "I stick my neck out for nobody," but instead he looked me right in the eye and said, "I can't help you, Neill; quit asking me to. I can't even fucking help myself." In that moment, as he began quickly packing up his backpack and zipping up its pockets angrily, I saw how defeated by his own cynicism he really was. He didn't believe in himself or anyone else, and he certainly didn't believe in life—he truly believed he was nothing and had nothing in a void of nothingness. But I knew, even if he didn't and never would, that, he was as vast and vital as this wilderness we stood in now.

I'd miscalculated badly from the start, or my heart had, or the stars. All along, I'd been looking for someone to grieve with, for what had happened to me and what had happened to them and all we'd lost. But he wasn't looking for that. Vince was through with grief or on the run from it. He'd wanted only someone to talk to, someone who accepted him. He didn't want to share "his pain"; he'd been overwhelmed by it a long time ago. And it was a whole lot bigger than mine. Best to keep what he could sealed over in concrete. He was probably right—I shouldn't have asked. But it was too late for my guilt now.

Vince pulled on his pack then and began to walk down the trail, and all I wished for then was that somehow he would keep on going and surviving and trying and striving to make his life work. Nothing more. I didn't even want him to look back. I let him go and it dried my tears.

He kept walking away down the trail and, as I had wished, he didn't look back. And I loved him for that too—for not giving me what I wanted but rather what I ultimately needed. Vince always gave me what I needed when all was said and done—the good and the bad of it. He just always did so in a rather blunt and harsh way.

After some time, I packed up my gear and followed. I remember the wind in my wet eyes, and how tiny he was 100 yards down the trail ahead of me. And how glad I was, even in my disappointment, that we'd come this far, this high. We'd had a good time despite how I'd fucked it up or we'd fallen short. Like always, it would blow over in time. Vince was a jerk in many ways, but I couldn't blame him considering who he was—and he was a forgiving jerk besides.

I thought then about where I'd hike with Peter next year, knowing that I'd never return here with Vince. We were going back to the world where he was strong—strong in an insect survival way. There'd be no storms to huddle in that he didn't have some safety valve for. He was going back to the world he knew, and I'd likely never see him as vulnerable and unchained as he'd been here. People lost their identities in the wilderness—or nearly—and that's what was so profound about it. Well, for what it's worth, Vince, I gave you this.

It was a long, lonely hike out and he was sitting on the hood of the car when I got there. We made the long drive home, and our silence waned before long. We were still boyfriends, I realized. He'd forget the whole thing in time, I figured, just as he had the incident on the fire escape. And so would I. It wasn't really forgiveness, but we could go on like this forever, sharing meals, arguing about books, drinking coffee and booze. We'd become habits of each other.

We stopped at dozens of produce stands as we headed back across the valley, gorging ourselves on cherries, peaches, apricots, and kiwis. Vince bought corn and pistachios and asparagus, and began to plan out a meal for tonight and the nights that followed. I smiled at his plans, but he wouldn't look me in the eye although we talked plenty. I tried to say sorry a couple of times, but the part of me that was bleeding wouldn't let me. Because I didn't want to be his habit; I wanted his love. Which made of me a thief.

ᘓ XXI

He didn't seduce me when we got back to San Francisco, so I guess he wasn't really sorry either. Otherwise things went on as before more or less, though when I came up the elevator and pulled back the clanging, rickety door, his silhouette did not await me anymore. The dust motes floated like old bunting hanging from the ceiling now, and I had to knock before Vince tiredly opened the door for me.

"Hey, Vince."

"Hey," and he'd turn the minute he saw me, returning to whatever he was doing, be it a book, cooking, or the production of cigarettes. He hadn't just forgotten it all as I'd seen him do before. He still cooked expertly; we still walked and talked. But he smoked more, and I'd catch him staring off into space or out the window, and when he'd meet my glance he'd shift himself and get up, closed for business as it were, whatever ghost I'd seen in his eyes having disappeared back into him from where it came, just like I'd feared. *Even his own best chances abandon him,* I thought cynically.

But I also felt it was all my fault. Of course. Wasn't it always so when it came to Vince? I'd taken him to myself out there in the wilderness, and he'd done the same for me, but he wasn't going to bleed. I could bleed to death for all he cared. *So what are we now, Vince?* I thought. *What are we now, hunkered down in this hotel, once again in hiding, having botched another heist, which is the best this love affair of thieves can ever hope to be—what are we, Vince, but the scar of that wound now?*

"I gotta get outta this fucking dump," he said one night.

"Where will you go?" He only glared at me.

"Where did you live when you were in Berkeley?"

"Dorms," I stated expressionlessly.

"That won't do; maybe we could get a place."

"You and me?" I asked, surprised.

"Yeah, why not?"

I didn't want to hurt his feelings, but he was hurting mine in saying it. I knew he hadn't brought it up out of some sudden desire to be with me all the time. It must have to do with expediency, I figured.

"Why the sudden desire to leave the lovely Baldwin?" I didn't know what else to say. I had never even considered it, assuming he was married to the Baldwin via his general assistance for the duration. He'd need a job to move.

"I need a change, Neill. And they cut my check back—some fucking Republican thing or something," he tacked on, acting vague. "If you don't want to get a place together, fuck it; sorry I asked." He began straightening his books then, acting put out. "But can you lend me some money?"

"Well, sure, yeah. What do you need?" I pulled out my wallet.

"Fifty bucks." His hand was out, his eyes averted as I gave it to him. I didn't ask what he wanted it for. I'd lent him money before when he ran out. He was proud, and it humiliated him to have to ask for it. I didn't hold it over him of course, nor ever mention it, though I guessed he'd resent me every red cent in time anyway.

"Vince, you know if we were to get an apartment, we'd both have to get jobs and you'd lose your GA." As far as I knew, Vince was pulling in something like $500 a month on general assistance, a couple hundred of which went to the room and the rest ostensibly to food, though I was financing a lot of our meals—when he wasn't stealing our grub—off my existing student loan and my temp job while I'd had it. I knew the lion's share of Vince's government check went to drugs, which seemed delightfully ironic to me, considering the government's much-touted War on Drugs. The humor of the situation tempered my feelings of being exploited.

"I'll get a job once we get a place," he said. I'd never seen him look so unconvincing. *Maybe he's no better a liar than I am,* I thought. Even if Vince did manage to obtain a job, I considered cynically, who's to say he'd ever be able to keep it? I couldn't say any of this of course or he'd accuse me of not trusting him—an agent of the bourgeois capitalists out to prevent his happiness—and off we'd go into misery.

He seduced me instead, but that was more about the money than his feelings. Now that he was borrowing money, it was the same game as having offended me—well, not quite. It didn't sit as well with me as the apologetic version of sex, and I don't think it did with him either. The impetus was similar, but it played out different. It was like he gave his body to me when money was involved. He wasn't really participating so much as holding it out, like something in his hand, for me to take and use as I wished, while he checked out. It made me sad—*so he's a hustler after all.* Sometimes it even seemed he was that little boy in the basement giving his body to me as if I were his father, and that thought repulsed me. Other times, it was as if he gave his body *away* to me, as if he were asking me to take it from him—as if he didn't want it. I had a terrible vision once as I drove myself into him that he would love me to make passionate painful love to him and then slit his throat from ear to ear. It was a disturbing image and I was upset that I'd thought of it at all. And then it occurred to me that maybe it wasn't my fantasy at all, but his. I'd picked up on his nonverbal suggestion of it or something—a message I'd received, one he may not even know he communicated to me. But what was a message in the throes of sex? Was it a request, a game, or some kind of challenge? And who from? Him or me, or that which we made between us? Or was I just misinterpreting it? All I knew for sure was that I'd never be able to ask.

The next evening, gazing at the nape of his neck I so loved as he busied himself with dinner, and thinking of the scar that would cross his throat if I were to slit it—and then suddenly about the other one on his balls from where they'd removed his testicle, I asked him about his radiation for the last time, knowing he'd likely evade me or, if not that, fuck me in the good old angry-then-contrite way he used to before he was broke all the time.

"What about your radiation treatments, Vince, are you still going?"

"Oh, that's over. They gave me a clean bill of health weeks ago."

"Why didn't you tell me?" I didn't really believe him anyway, and as he busied himself with his back to me, I couldn't look in his eye to check his answer's veracity.

"Because you would have wanted to celebrate," he said impatiently, "and I don't celebrate that kind of thing. It wasn't a big deal either way for me."

I let it drop at that. I wouldn't have to ask again, having at least gotten a definitive answer in a sense. It meant he wouldn't be going back to the clinic either way. His health seemed yet another middle-class nuisance and he couldn't be bothered with all its requirements and demands. It was part of that "other world"—a world he felt no part of nor wanted any part of. He needed it only to steal from.

I'd only really looked at Vince's cancer scar once. I didn't dare ask to see it. The fact that it was in the locale of his sex organs, and then that it had to do with an experience he seemed angry over and dismissive about too—well, it wasn't an acceptable topic for discussion to say the least. So I only saw it when we were wrestling about and I ended up there peering directly at it, another jagged pink line on his wounded body—this one hardly conspicuous though, lost as it was in the folds of his scrotum. I reached out my tongue to lick it tenderly and I'm sure he never noticed, figuring whatever I expressed there was done solely out of lust. He never did hold my or anyone's sexual desires in very high esteem.

"I like your scar and your one ball," I said as he plopped a bowl of soup down in front of me.

"Well, you can't have it," he said, flashing that grin of his, which always meant *You can think about what that means, but I'm not tellin' ya.*

We went out to a movie that night, *Wings of Desire.* He smuggled a bottle of Glenfiddich in with him and he slurped at it while eating popcorn and watching the invisible existential angels wandering around, trying to encourage and prop people up, barely pulling it off, if at all. He liked the movie until the end when the angel decides to come to Earth because he's fallen in love with a human.

"What a fucking lame movie," he concluded.

"You liked the beginning."

He winked. "Yeah, but nothing ever ends right, does it, Neill?" He turned his head the minute he said it. He's not dramatic really, just confident that his enigmatic behavior is equivocal enough to keep you guessing.

He started talking about the rails again, and running from yard bosses; getting beaten up and mugged; having sex on flatcars with lost hungry boys, ostensibly not even gay. Then he was seething about "some crazy jackass" who pushed him off a flatcar once. I thought then that there was nothing ambiguous in Vince's world—that was what I'd liked about it; what I'd romanticized. I liked that it was simple and clear, with good guys and villains. It was like the hospital in fact, you always knew what needed to be done and you just did it. But why then did he wear that tattoo? *If the world is so black and white, Vince, why aren't you?* I thought cynically then that he was either the best argument against his own philosophy or I was just stupid and couldn't see. But that was part of his view too: Vince saw and everyone else was blind. He liked it that way, even as it made his place in the world impossible and love something utterly suspect and ultimately dangerous.

No wonder he hated the movie. He was one of those trenchcoated angels in black, looking down from a lonely tower. Oddly, I thought then, his suicide attempts were probably as close as he'd been to the world—truly fallen—and those had failed too. Love and death and all things human wouldn't have him, and so he climbed back up on his perch and spit on it all.

But you were my door, Vince, and I was yours. You can't see at all.

But he was good and drunk and he was running now down the street, laughing, and I didn't know whether to run after him or just let him go. I didn't feel *with him* at all. I was waiting for him; I didn't want to run after him anymore. No, I was waiting for him; waiting for a CAT scan of his heart to reveal that little ghost of a child; waiting for him to return from surgery, his tattoo scarred and reformed now into a heart with my name in it. I was not proud; I was not proud enough for him.

I caught up with him in front of the Baldwin, where he was sitting on the curb, staring into the gutter, and without looking up telling some man to "shut the fuck up" who was asking him something—perhaps for change.

"He ain't got no change, man," I told the guy and dug in my pockets for a quarter. "Here."

Vince was up and already inside, and I caught up with him at the elevator and rode the sad, rickety thing up six floors with him sitting on his haunches in the corner, smiling at the rug, lost in his own thoughts.

But when we got inside the room, he was all over me, and just as quickly he was pushing me away and going off to sit below the window, where he curled up eventually in his coat to sleep.

"I got another outbreak," he told me the next morning, coming in the door. I hadn't heard him go out.

"So soon?" I asked him, rubbing the sleep from my eyes. I suspected then for the first time that maybe he was lying about it, which made me wonder then if he'd ever had one. Could that be? I'd never seen it, hidden away under his long johns. It never left a scar. Could it have been a ruse to avoid sex? But him lying was less upsetting to me than that I suddenly was second-guessing him all the time.

"Maybe you should go fuck someone else for a while, Neill. You need to sow some wild oats anyway, or whatever the fuckin' stupid cliché is."

"I don't want to, Vince."

"Well, either do I." And he laughed, though it wasn't really a joke, just another vague dismissal.

We both became spectators of sorts from then on, it seemed to me. We spoke less. And yet there was a strange tenderness between us at times, vaguely reminiscent of Peter's convalescence. He'd take my hand at a crosswalk and hold me back from walking as a car rounded the corner, and then he wouldn't let it go for three blocks. Once he put eyeliner on my eyelids and dressed me up in clothes he'd stolen from some clubby shop—but we never went out. Another time he insisted on giving me a full-body massage. They were uncharacteristic things, and he did them in uncharacteristic ways that made me feel oddly distant and objective to him. Because whatever it was, and whatever he gave, he made a point not to look for too long into my eyes.

For my part, just being quiet and staying out of his way seemed to be the greatest kindness I could offer. Like always, I knew I could at least wait.

Then one night he seemed to lose all his energy for everything.

"Are you sad, Vince?"

"Nah," he said, but he was short with me.

"You seem a little down," I persisted.

"I'm not." He'd become less argumentative and just sort of irritable. His nerves seemed frazzled and he no longer bothered to set me straight in high style as was his usual way, nor to tear me down at high volume. I never thought I'd miss it, but perhaps *that* was the attention I'd gotten from him—and now it was denied me. He walked away more often than not or just said, "I disagree." He seemed not only disinterested in me now but somehow lost to himself as well, just going through the motions.

Instead of doing everything together now as we always had before, he'd taken to abruptly saying, "I'm going out for a while," and leaving me in the room, uninvited. *One day he won't even return,* I sadly told myself. Some part of him had already left. But I held out hope that one day he'd walk back in that door, all suited up, with the pack on his back even, ready once again to go. I kept telling myself to give him time, but I was losing patience.

I remember one day coming upon him when he'd gone out and I had too, maybe a half hour after him. I wasn't looking for him, but of course he wasn't someone you'd miss. He was walking out of a Walgreens drugstore, his pockets bulging with tobacco. Vince had that you-caught-me look on his face, as he hadn't expected me. I could see he resented my catching him, as if I'd followed him to do just that. But I resented him too, always having to take the heat for what he felt ashamed of. Vince and his shame, what a pain in the ass. I was suddenly sick of the whole game.

"What's up, Vince?" I could dodge the subject too; I didn't have to play my role forever.

"The price of tobacco, I suppose."

I resisted the urge to say "What difference would that make to you?" seeing in his eyes that he was goading me to do just that. I realized then that he really needed enemies more than he needed friends, and if he made the latter, he'd no doubt transform them into the former to justify his view of the world and his low assessment of those of us unlucky enough to people it. I smiled thinking if Vince hated all of humanity then he owed each and every one of them a good fuck as an apology.

He didn't try to read my expression as he normally would, saying, "Well, I got some other errands I gotta do. I'll catch you back at the room in a couple hours, OK?" He said it with an expression that seemed like he was looking forward to it, but I knew he wanted to be left alone. That form of insincerity was odd for Vince—why, you could even call it distinctly middle class.

I answered nonchalantly, "Sure, see you then," and watched him walk away, hunched over, a sad little thief. I thought him a wraith then in his long, tattered green army overcoat under the bright sun. He was like some sad fungus or moss—a night creature, primordial and dank, but the sun was achingly high now, leaving no place for his kind. And off he went to buy heroin, unbeknownst to me.

One night as we climbed into bed I could bear it no longer, and I vented my exasperation. "Vince, man, please talk to me. I feel far away."

"Well, you're right next to me, so you're wrong. Your perceptions are off," he said with derisive sarcasm. "I'm tired; let me sleep."

"Vince, things have been weird."

"Well, welcome to my life."

"I love you, Vince. You know that."

"Yeah, I know. My parents love me too, remember?" I rolled my eyes, angry and sad all at once. What was the use? So much for the wilderness—he'd packed it away in one of his slouched boxes or thrown it in the trash on one of his walks—perhaps he'd even nudged it over the windowsill, and the alley was now full of broken chunks of granite and fractured pines.

"What's that supposed to mean, Vince?" I called his bluff for a change; we were certainly getting nowhere. Why not have it out?

"Exactly what it says. Now let me sleep."

"Well, you hate your parents, so I guess you hate me?"

"That's not what I said," he curtly corrected me.

"I hate this. Insult me; do something. I'm not even here."

"Oh, you're here," he said with smug condescension, "and you're keeping me awake." Then he reached over and kissed me. "Sleep—everything's OK."

I wasn't placated, but his kiss at least was some kind of reassurance, as if he wasn't ready to burn it all down just quite yet. But even his kiss had changed, like how he'd spoken to me the other day on the street—he was just getting rid of me; he wasn't being sincere.

He was gone when I awoke; I didn't know where to. He'd taken to going out early mornings. He said he walked or went to the Meditation Center, but I knew that was bullshit. Whatever it was, he said he needed to do it alone, so I couldn't come. It was all part of how he was pulling away. I thought perhaps I should stop visiting altogether or at least take a few weeks off.

I got up and decided to smoke a joint. But I couldn't find any matches and I was digging all over and none seemed to be around. I started going through Vince's pockets, figuring that's my best bet, but I stopped abruptly when I came upon something I hoped to God I was wrong about in one of the big front pockets of his army jacket. I slowly lifted it out, anticipating it before it came into view. "Ah, Vince," I sighed, holding it in my palm, its bright orange top like a flame—*like his hair,* I thought, *the day I met him.*

Perhaps he's developed diabetes, I dubiously offered myself, in a reassurance of denial so absurd I almost laughed. It was as possible as the desperate hopes I'd had as a teenager that being homosexual was only a phase. I dropped the cheap drugstore hypodermic back into his pocket and tossed the joint out the window—another lost treasure for the growing pile down in the alley. He would push me out that window one day. The neon kept up its flashing as always, and its mindless and relentless rhythm made me angry suddenly, like a stuck needle on a record. "Fucking cork it!" I yelled at the mindless pulse of light, mimicking his cruel words.

And I suddenly felt so tired, emptied. I didn't know what to do, so I just left. I went home. Vince never called me there, leaving it always up to me to come find him at the hotel. I didn't figure he'd call now either, and wondered if he even still had the number from when he'd awkwardly scribbled it on a scrap of paper on the roof of my car that day we'd met. I saw it now in my mind's eye, lost between the pages of some book he'd probably resold somewhere, or in one of the pockets of a pair of his stained and threadbare Dickies. Wherever it was, I didn't imagine him turning the place upside down to find it.

Merging onto the bridge, I saw the piled stone madness of the city's towers in my rearview mirror and thought how one day an earthquake would knock it all down. I wondered then why Vince hadn't worn his coat out that morning. He always wore his army coat when he was out stealing. Wherever he'd gone, I guessed then it wasn't to steal. What had he worn then? That old red cable-knit sweater, the trashed letterman's jacket? I couldn't help feeling he'd left the jacket home just so I'd find what I'd found. But how could he have known I'd go looking for matches? Or did he just assume I'd grown suspicious and would rifle through his pockets? I'd never done that before, but he'd never gone out without his coat in the morning either. Another enigma to contemplate for eternity. *Vince and all his words and deeds will haunt me forever,* I thought then, *because I know, in his roundabout way, he's trying to tell me something.*

ॐ XXII

I spent the following few weekends with Peter, who was once again back in school, making his way through his junior year. My parents wondered what had happened to my burgeoning bohemian life—all those so-called friends—since I'd suddenly stopped disappearing for the weekend. But they respected my privacy and accepted my curt replies.

"Everyone's outta town," I'd say, walking out of the room. I could have said they were back in school, but I knew that would not only inevitably lead to their bringing up my failure to register, but it wouldn't follow as to why my friends were out of town. Perhaps I could claim they all went to school back East.

Mostly, Peter and I hiked—up through the hills that rose behind our house, down along the railroad tracks, and finally over to Shell Ridge, the next best thing to the mountains. It rose beyond the stucco walls of the new housing tracts out among the foothills bordering the state park, and once you crested the first ridge the town fell from view and you felt like you were hundreds of miles from civilization. Much of it was ranchland, but other than the occasional group of lolling steers or grazing cattle, there were just endless meandering fire trails linking up its old oak groves and curving up its grassy hillsides to the jagged, prehistoric fossil-encrusted ridge that gave it its name. It wasn't the Sierras, but once there the world slipped away all the same. It was enough. Enough of a wilderness to sustain Peter until next summer, I thought, since he'd had to sit out the backpacking season this year and had ultimately had to sacrifice the football season as well.

We headed up the main trail along the creek, which was all dry now, toward our favorite spot: a flat little meadow surrounded by hills and boasting the finest stands of mustard grass we'd ever seen anywhere. The stuff would grow as high as our heads in that one spot and its bright yellow flowers, bobbing on spindly, sparsely leafed chartreuse stems, always took our breath away. But that was in April or May. By this time of the year, they'd be gray-brown stalks, gone to seed and leaning into one another in great big heaps, a rather sad end to a glorious crop. We knew it would be that way, but something illogical in us always drew us there year-round regardless, harboring a vague hope that they'd be green and yellow and brilliantly alive.

When we reached the cattle gate that led into the glen, we registered the disappointment of the ruined field but were distracted by a ragged little coyote that was just now running off away up the hill, heading for a gully that cut into some trees. He'd stop and look back now and again as we watched him, just to let us know he wasn't afraid of us. It was always rare to see them—especially during the day— even though it was common to hear them howling far off somewhere at night.

Peter turned to me after the coyote was gone and asked me, "Did you ever see that guy again—from the radiation clinic? . . . What was his name?"

I hesitated. So here it was, and it had been left to Peter, like so much else, to bring it out of me. I felt the weight of it again in my stomach, but this time it felt almost like vomit and I knew it was finally time to tell him the whole story. "Vince," I responded sullenly, "His name was Vince." I paused and looked down. "Yeah, Peter, I did see him again."

"Yeah, I meant to ask you, but you know . . ." I nodded, letting him know I understood how distracted he'd been, or respectful, or whatever—he didn't have to explain himself to me. I remained silent, thus encouraging him to continue. "Was it like a date or . . ." The weight of it reached my chest then, and my eyes filled with tears and I couldn't answer him in words. I felt sad, not only about Vince and about myself, but that I'd never told Peter about any of it. He stopped then. "What's the matter, Neill? Did something happen?" He put his hand gently on my shoulder then.

I shook my head quickly from side to side, holding the tears back, and began to walk again. "No, it's OK, Peter. Nothing bad happened. I don't think. I've been hanging out with him for almost four months." I gave a small laugh through my tears.

"Wow . . . man, why didn't you tell me? So that's where you've been?"

"Yeah, there are no 'friends'," I said sarcastically, using my fingers to make quotes around that vague white lie I'd used all these months. "Peter, I just didn't want to bother you with any of this." I wiped my hand across my eyes.

"It wouldn't have bothered me, Neill. I told you I'm cool with it," he said innocently, but I hadn't meant "being gay" as the bother so much, but rather compounding that secret with yet another by adding some boyfriend I was sneaking around with to the mix.

"Well, I'll tell you all about it now, Peter. You'll be the first to hear."

"Well, hey, I think it's great," he said awkwardly, visibly confused. "Why are you sad? Did you break up?" He impressed me, as always, with his natural openness, and it brought a smile to my sorrowful face, which I figured he'd seen a million times on my mother.

We sat down on a log then, near an old collapsed wooden fence and a dilapidated salt lick, watching the cows grazing down the hillside and the wind in the now-brittle and ruined mustard grass—a few last seeds carried away. There were oaks scattered about in thick clumps, their leaves dusty dry, as they clung to the rocks that ran like a spine across the top of the hills. In the far distance, there were drier, golder hills with sometimes only single oaks on them rising like plumes of smoke against the blue sky beyond. I sat there, and that was our little campfire of sorts, and I told him everything.

It was sunset by the time I was through and had come to the hypodermic needle in Vince's coat pocket.

"You're going back, huh?" he inquired gravely.

"I don't know," I answered blankly, but I'd go back, just as he'd go back to the hospital and the sixth floor for special cases, though right then neither of us knew it. I hugged him close to me then with some vague sorrow about fate, or maybe just the raw deal of this life, which seemed then a painful and sorrow-making thing happening in an incredibly beautiful place. The incongruity seemed relentless, almost merciless. Life felt like a great and wonderful promise, unkept.

"I'm not gonna leave you with this, Peter. I gotta talk to the folks."

"Are you ready, you think?" I looked at the concern on his scarred face, studying the droop under his right eye, following each scar as if with my finger, to its source.

"Peter, I'll be OK." But I started to cry again, thinking to myself: *Who was ever ready, Peter? Maybe you. You're about the only one.*

"It's nothing compared to what you've been through, Peter. You've made me stronger and given me so much perspective."

"Yeah, well, all of it hurts, Neill. I don't think one problem is really any bigger a deal than another." I could only smile at his magnanimity. *The boy's a fucking damn good friend,* I thought to myself then, *and the wisest person I know.* My Dad's right: The kid can catch.

"I thought of you up there when we were in the mountains, Peter." He sighed at that. "I wanna go up there with you, first thing next summer." And he smiled, nodding his head, and as he did, I realized that he'd be taking me there more than I'd be taking him.

It was coming on dusk, so we gathered ourselves up and hiked down the trail, heading off for pizza and beer at a local dive. While we sat at the bar, sipping drafts, a fat man walked up to us and seated himself heavily on the stool next to Peter. A regular. There were no introductions as he settled in—but then, catching a glimpse of Peter, asked rudely, "What in the hell happened to you?"

Peter turned to me, with a tired look on his face, then took a deep breath and winked. I'd seen him do this before. The first few times had been hellish. The little boy in the museum who'd whispered too loud to his mother: "Momma, that boy looks like a monster." She *ssshhhed* him profusely, but we'd all heard it. My parents smiled wanly, attempting to let it blow over. You couldn't blame a kid, but Peter was furious, on the verge of rageful tears. He marched away, and I stated loud enough for the boy and his mother and Peter to hear, "No, he's not a monster. He's a Picasso—a masterpiece." The boy and his mother hurried off, while my parents looked away, subtly distancing themselves from me and my abstruse retort. Other patrons shuffled or smiled as acts of dissipation. But goddammit, I wasn't going to let Peter drown.

Then there'd been the little African-American kid at the public pool who very matter of factly asked Peter what had happened. The boy was sincere and direct, unafraid, and so Peter thought he deserved an answer. But he lied all the same, and it stung me that he, like my parents and I—ah, the whole world—was starting to avoid the truth because people didn't seem really interested in it, or if they were, they weren't quite ready for his tale. They wanted a good story. So Peter told more and more stories, his father's son. To the little black boy, he laid out an elaborate drama of a football game's final moments. "It was twenty-three to twenty-one. We needed that field goal, but our kicker was hurt and so we decided to go for the touchdown. I was the running back. I chipped away, with the final seconds, here a yard, there a yard. Our quarterback couldn't pass. It was up to me." The boy listened enraptured, his head tilted up to look at Peter, his jaw slack. Peter was gesticulating with his hands, acting it out, running back to pass, hunkering down to rush. "The other team knew that too. They double-teamed me, triple-teamed me. They tore at my jersey, they clawed at me, yanked on my face guard. As I crossed the scrimmage line, they crushed me into the ground and clawed at my flesh." The boy looked dumbfounded, and I was almost in shock. Then the boy looked at me, and I raised my arms as if to say "Who knows?" I don't think he believed Peter, but something happened during these stories, *some kind* of understanding bridged the mystery, and I knew it gave Peter confidence and strength.

And now here we are at the pizza parlor with a slovenly beer drinker in an ugly yellow CAT baseball cap and stained white T-shirt stretched across his swollen beer belly, just asking for it.

"I took a bullet in the face," Peter said matter of factly in response to the man's tactless inquiry. The man looked suddenly taken aback.

"Holy shit, how'd that happen? Drive-by?" I saw Peter stifle a laugh. My father was always imitating guys like this—guys he referred to as low renters. My father was an elitist of sorts but without the money or pedigree to back it up. I was disappointed in myself for almost laughing as well, but again, I too am my father's son. I've been taught to laugh at certain people. Now I was one of those people that got laughed at, just as Peter was. And yet, it felt OK suddenly to laugh too. It wasn't necessarily hatred. As long as we all laughed at one another, it could be OK. But could I laugh at Vince? Could I laugh at Paul? *It's whom you can't laugh at,* I thought—*there lie the problems.*

"I'm DEA," Peter blurted, sounding military and older than his years. He was after all only seventeen, though I guess he could pass for maybe twenty (this pizza parlor in fact never carded him, though from what we'd seen they didn't card anybody). Regardless, the guy bought it.

"Drug Enforcement Agency? You got hit in the line of duty?" he raised his voice, as if it was a personal affront to him as a patriot of his country.

"Took a bullet down on the border," Peter said in his best tough-guy routine, taking a large swig of beer.

"Buy this man a pitcher!" the slovenly fellow barked at the bartender. Now we were really getting results from Peter's story: free beer. We might manage a pizza as well, but did we want to eat with him? Or did he eat anything but the free bar pretzels he was gorging on from the bowl in front of him? "I can't hold a candle to you," and he lifted his glass to clink it against Peter's. Peter went along with it.

"And what do you do?" Peter turned the tables on him.

"Tool and die," he said, smacking his lips. "Tool and die, that's my trade."

"To tool and die then," Peter raised his glass.

"To the DEA!" He emptied his glass and poured them both a new one, offering me a glass as well. Then he continued. "So tell me everything, son; tell me how it happened. Tell me about our tax dollars at work." I sighed, completely over this Republican, patriotic bullshit, but it was Peter's performance now.

"We got in a chase, down near Nogales, with some drug runners." He paused for emphasis. "My partner, God rest his soul—" Peter crossed himself and bowed his head momentarily. My god, he was going to lay it on thick.

"Amen!" the man blurted. "Goddammit, you lost your partner." For emphasis, and to keep the engine running, he topped off our beer glasses.

"Jack was a good man."

"What happened next?"

"Once I saw Jack was a goner, I knew they'd likely be coming back for me. I had a pistol was all. We hadn't expected any trouble that day." Peter paused and took a swig of beer. He was getting good at this. "They did come back." And he looked the man right in the eye. "I thought about our children, our kids, you know? These drug runners are destroying the next generation." Peter was playing him now, and the man nodded emphatically in agreement.

"How many were there?"

"Six," he said in a deadpan voice, barely moving his lips.

"Jeeeeeesuz, how you'd get out of there alive?"

"I shot all six of them."

"With your pistol?" I knew Peter knew as much about guns as I did. He may have gone too far.

"Yes, I had eight rounds in it, and I took out all six drug runners." Luckily, the man didn't blink or ask for the make or model.

"Hot damn! 'Nother pitcher, please." Peter was beyond a tax-dollar-saving patriot now. He was a fucking movie star with a new fan.

"Not before taking a few hits myself, of course," and he lifted his shirt to reveal his scarred chest, the skin graft patches on his arms and belly. "I took two in the chest, one in the arm and another here in the belly, not to mention this one that blew off my cheek." Suddenly it was all too intense, and I wanted it to stop. With his shirt pulled up and all his scars revealed, I felt he was affronting his own dignity. I wanted suddenly to punch the tool-and-die man, cuss him out for making a freak of my brother. But then I just felt sorry for both of them, like life had made chumps of them both just now. I gulped down a beer and excused myself to go to the bathroom and throw cold water on my face.

By the time I returned, they were shaking hands and Mr. Tool and Die was soon to amble off. I pretended to look at posters near the telephone until he was gone.

I sat heavily back down on the barstool. "Peter, man, that was kind of intense."

"Yeah, I guess it was," and he rolled his shoulders. "You hungry?"

"Yeah, sure."

"He bought us a pizza," Peter grinned, guiltily.

"Shit," I chuckled.

"Hey, as I see it, he owed me after the way he assaulted me when he came in here. The fucking moron." So he was pissed, not just having fun. I nodded in agreement.

"Well, you don't gotta do that, Peter; you don't gotta show your scars to any bozo off the street." But he flashed a determined grin.

"Hey, man, I'm proud of these scars," and he lifted his shirt again. But I saw tears in his eyes then, as he added angrily, "I fucking paid for these fucking scars." He was almost shaking, but he composed himself and I tossed in a joke to help him out.

"You paid goddamn full price, kid," I concurred, imitating Tool and Die. "No fucking rebates, no goddamn payment plan, points . . ." And he burst out laughing, and I wondered then if my little brother Peter, the angel of light, was another shadow-clad Vince in the making. There was a flicker of darkness even in Peter, just as there was a flicker of light in Vince—that I thought with a sudden dread, was about to be snuffed out for good, to dissipate in a wisp of smoke.

CR XXIII

Three weeks later, I returned. I stood across the street from the Baldwin Arms probably twenty minutes, conflicted and debating with myself whether to go in. I might have been some dumb middle-class kid, but I wasn't sentimental or stupid and I knew I was no match for heroin. I didn't want to, or just couldn't, witness him becoming a junkie. That would be like losing an eye.

Sixth Street wasn't an easy place to stand and think. Panhandlers and the mentally ill accosted me; drug peddlers eyed me; loitering young men leered. On top of it all, it began to rain—just sprinkles at first, but the drops grew heavier and more rapid. There was nothing to do but go in, if for no other reason it was the nearest refuge, which was all the Baldwin could ever really hope to be.

"Hey, long time," the Arab greeted me.

"How goes?" I gestured to him, raising my head as he leaned down to flick the switch for the elevator. "What's your name anyway?" I don't know what made me ask. Maybe I was just tired of the alienation, or maybe I was stalling before going up.

"Amar," he announced proudly.

"Amar," and I nodded. "Neill," and I pointed to myself and he nodded back.

Someone had drawn a "6" with a black felt marker on either side of the glowing 6 of the elevator panel, perhaps Vince. That lightened me somewhat as I had to laugh at it. I hesitated before stepping out, thinking I'd see him waiting, having heard the rattle of the elevator's jarring door. But I knew he wouldn't be expecting me necessarily, and when I stepped out into the dark hallway, the dust motes were all empty. The hallway was strangely quiet, with just the din of the street bleeding in through the windows at either end, an occasional cough or snore, a murmur.

When I knocked at his door, there was no answer. Which made me panic momentarily, arousing my worst fears. Amar would have said if he'd checked out. He must have been asleep or on an errand or something; maybe in the bathroom down the hall. But I didn't want to go looking for him, so I banged on the door harder. Nothing. I collapsed in a heap, my back against the door, a little angry and worried, and a little sad. Perhaps I should just leave; perhaps *he* has already. If I left, I wouldn't feel I'd be abandoning Vince since he was already profoundly abandoned and sort of undesertable, really. He'd be the first to tell you that he didn't need anybody, least of all you. He'd never lean on anyone enough to be abandoned, or so he told himself. In his story, his parents had set a precedent for what love was supposed to be so that he'd be sure not to let himself ever get fooled again. But he'd been slipping with me. Or the foundation had. It must have been time for Vince to close ranks, to get serious. He knew what love was: love was a transgression; love was a thief. And so, it followed, was I. And I was a thief who'd lay there in wait.

I sat there ten minutes and then I heard a sound, like the sink tap had been turned on inside his room and water was running. I listened to make sure it was coming from behind his door. It sure sounded like it. I banged again and heard then his tired voice: "What?"

"Vince, it's me, Neill."

"Neill, what the fuck?" He opened the door. He looked disheveled and pale. "Where the fuck have you been?" he demanded, the brow furrowing, but almost halfheartedly, like he was playing a part and didn't really care or mean what he was saying.

"I needed time. You needed time."

"Don't tell me what I need," he said dismissively, walking back into the room, expecting me to follow. But I just stood at the open door.

"I missed you," I said pliantly.

"You shouldn't," he said snidely.

"What do you mean?"

"Always what I say, Neill," and he looked scoldingly at me.

I looked at his tattoo momentarily then, thinking how what he says is harder and harder to decipher. "Don't you miss me?" I ventured.

"I don't miss anyone or anything," he said without passion, looking for something on the floor. He looked up quickly then and caught my glance to his forearm, pulling his sleeve down reactively. But I saw the bruise first. It was like a new tattoo, but this time its statement was clear. I wasn't shocked or horrified, so much as just sad. I knew it would be there—or somewhere. I felt then like I'd been vaguely worried about it forever, like getting a brain tumor or being in some horrible car accident. That bruise was the letter of verification and it filled me with dread and sorrow, as Peter's bad results always did. Well, I didn't have to wait and worry anymore at least. Now I knew. It had come to this. It's heartbreaking to see that arm in my mind's eye now. The bruise in the crotch of his elbow, just beyond the long pink scars of his attempted suicide. Is this where they all lead, these scars?

"So, do you want to talk about it, Vince?" I said as carefully and kindly as I could.

His jaw dropped, and he turned to me, bristling. "Talk about what?"

"Come on, Vince," and I approached him, but he repelled me with his glare.

"So you came back here on some little social work visit, eh, Neill?"

"No," I stated, "are you afraid of me?"

"Fuck no." And he laughed out loud.

"Then talk to me, Vince!"

"I've said way too much already. You talk for a change," he said tiredly, lighting a cigarette and going to the window to sit. He struggled with the window for a bit as it was jammed. Suddenly, up it flew and *Moby Dick* dropped six stories.

"Oh well."

I shut the door behind me and sat down on the bed. "Well, Vince, I've missed you and I've worried about you and I just want to help you if I can or . . ."

"Help yourself, Neill, fuck." And he threw the barely smoked cigarette out the window and got up.

"Well, I'm not gonna sit here and not talk about it. I'll just leave."

"Go ahead; get the fuck out," he said then, dismissively. "You've got nowhere to go. I knew you'd come back." Then he looked me

right in the eye, as he added audaciously: "You need me more than I
need you." Reconsidering, he revised his comment. "I don't need you
at all. I just tolerate you."

I was stung by his coldheartedness. But I couldn't turn to leave any
more than I could believe him. And I couldn't cry because he'd get
mad at that too. Nor could I apparently talk to him about junk. I
didn't know what to do. Why was I suddenly the cornered one when
he was the one who had the explaining to do? Because. It was always
that way.

"Well, why do you tolerate me?" I managed to squeeze out.

"I tolerate a lot of things." That was as good as saying I'd joined the
list of all the awful things in the world he had to put up with.

"Vince, for God's sake," I said, exasperated and desperate.

"Make it for Christ's sake; it's a little more human—and certainly
more tragic," he said tiredly, leaning on the edge of the sink, adding
as an afterthought: "That's your forte, right?" I suddenly felt I had to
go. I'd had it. I couldn't stand here and take his abuse, and maybe the
sooner I tore myself away the better.

I got up then, visibly pissed off, muttering, "Fuck it," but he
jumped up then and in one fluid motion—where had this sudden bolt
of energy come from?—he blocked the door.

"I'm making you dinner, Neill; don't leave yet."

"Yet?" I said, miffed.

"Get the fuck over yourself. I can't protect you forever. I'm tired of
protecting you." He was protecting me? From what? "I need some
fucking money, Neill. Do you have any?" Was this why he wanted to
keep me around for dinner? I didn't like the desperation in his eyes
and all his vagueness.

I plopped back down on the bed. "No, I'm not giving you money
for drugs, Vince. No," I answered stubbornly.

"Just asking. You don't have to give me any money. I can get it
elsewhere. Doesn't hurt to ask, right? Like they say in the fucking Bi-
ble, right? Ask and thou shalt receive."

"I'm not lending you any more money, Vince."

"Then you're not getting any sex, since I'm just your whore anyway," he quipped sarcastically and maliciously. I wanted to lash out at

him and tell him what a sad excuse for a whore he was then, but I held my tongue. I hadn't come back here to argue with him. "You want soup or some pasta?" he asked, changing the subject.

"Neither, Vince. I just came back here to maybe talk to you, but I can see that that's not a great idea. I don't want to have dinner with you." Then he started yelling all sorts of shit about how I'd just left and who the fuck did I think I was coming in here and putting demands on him and expecting him to miss me?

"Who the fuck do you think you are?" he got loudly in my face, like a German shepherd baring its teeth. Then he started shaking and blubbering with tears.

"Vince, what's wrong?" I asked, alarmed, getting up.

"Don't touch me!" and he backed away as I approached him. "You have to go; you have to leave here."

"I can't leave, Vince," and I felt my own tears welling up, but this time I wouldn't let them come. "I came back here because I wanted to see you."

"Well, see!" and he held his arms out wide, his expression cross again. "Now you can go, you got what you fuckin' wanted."

I plopped down on the floor then, and looked down at the carpet. "I'm sorry, Vince. I shouldn't have just left, but it didn't seem . . ."

He cut me off. "No, you shouldn't have come back is what you shouldn't have done." Perhaps he was right. But he must have known as well as I did that I'd be back. I decided to say nothing more. I couldn't talk to him; I couldn't touch him. He pulled out the hot plate and cooked me up a can of soup (I'd never witnessed such a lack of culinary inspiration in him) and put it unceremoniously on the floor in front of me with a bottle of red wine and a corkscrew. Then he sat opposite me and pulled out his cigarette-making paraphernalia. I didn't ask why he wasn't having any soup, figuring perhaps he'd decided to poison me. That would probably be the only way to get rid of me at this point.

He involved himself with the manufacture of his cigarette, giving it his full concentration. I watched him shake the little bit of the tobacco out of the blue Drum bag and onto the paper, spreading it out expertly. It reminded me a little bit of making a campfire. Well, this is his mountain—Mount Baldwin. He carefully rolled it up, licked it, turned the ends, looked across at me coldly, got up, and went to the window where he lit it, and taking a puff, exhaled for what seemed like the longest time.

"We need to go up to Polk Street," he stated.

"Why?"

"We just do. Can you drive me up there?"

"Well, yeah, sure, but why?"

"Neill, you ask way too many questions," he said impatiently. Suddenly losing it, he yelled at me: "Fuck, can't you just give me a fucking ride?" As quickly as his temper had flared, it subsided, as he added, "Forget it; I'll take the bus."

"It's pouring out there, Vince. I'm not gonna make you take the bus," I sighed resignedly, and then added meekly: "Come on, I'll drive you."

It was raining hard as we drove the black, oil-rainbowed streets the seven blocks up Polk Street. He refused to speak to me in the car, commanding me to "Drive!" whenever I ventured a question or tried to make conversation. But I knew where we were going.

"If we're going to get you heroin, it's OK," I commented to him.

He made no response; he didn't look at me or acknowledge the statement in any way. I was wrong to know; I was wrong to have brought it up at all. I was prying and invasive. I was just a middle-class bastard always hemming him in. *Well, fuck him,* I thought, and yet I loved him and was willing to accept even this. I'd never leave him—I'd seen the boy in the middle of the night who was frightened and grateful for my friendship and who loved me with whatever heart he had. I'd wait for him. I'd drag him back up into the mountains, tie him to a rock like Prometheus, and just wait. My mother and father and I weren't giving up on Peter and I wasn't going to give up on Vince. As if the two situations were the same. Well, on some level they were. Because I realized in that moment—even through all my growing cynicism—that I was totally committed to Vince. Why else would I follow him into this abyss?

"Pull over here," he commanded me, opening the car door and hopping out before I'd completely stopped. Hurriedly crossing the sidewalk, he nervously rang the buzzer and waited without opening his umbrella, looking pensively up and down the street, before he heard the buzzer respond and pushed the gate in to enter.

I found a parking spot across the street after circling the block twice. I sat and waited, watching the street through the driving rain, and realized then that two blocks up the street behind me was the very intersection where I'd seen the man with the poodle so many years ago. Was this the flower that bloomed here on the same spot all these years later? A poppy no less.

Ten minutes later, I saw Vince running up the street, looking like he was in trouble. I rolled down my window and screamed his name and, running heedless through horn-blaring traffic, he came. He looked so desperate, pelted by rain, little and skinny, like a frightened animal. He yanked the door open violently and hopped in.

"Drive, go! Come on, go!" he banged on the dashboard.

I carefully pulled out and, revving the engine, shifted gears and headed down the street. I watched the rearview mirror but saw nothing. I looked at him, soaked to the skin by the downpour that had met him as he departed the building. He was visibly in a panic, nervously shaking, overanimated, and ghostly pale. He looked pathetic, a terrified little boy, and I felt sad for him as he grabbed my free hand and clutched it hard.

We found a parking space near the hotel and though I tried to hurry him along he walked slowly now, in a daze. I just figured I had to get him home and settled down before I figured out what the hell had happened.

"Come on, Vince, you're soaked."

But he only stopped in his tracks, still shaking.

"What the fuck happened, Vince?"

"They jumped me . . . they took my money . . ."

"So you didn't get what you were there for?" I was trying to be politic in not saying the word.

"No!"

"Calm down, Vince; it's OK." I didn't know what else to say. "I got money."

"No, no," he waved his arms. "I poked one of them in the eye with my umbrella and bashed the other over the head with a big glass ashtray. There was fucking blood everywhere. I went crazy, and then I just ran," and he was shaking again, crying and falling into me, clutching my shoulders and burying his face in my sternum.

"It's OK, Vince; you're safe now," and I looked over his shoulder, into the street that was gray and dreary with rain. "Do they know where you live?" He looked up at me then and his face lost all its animation, the tears stopping abruptly.

"They got nothing to do with anything, Neill. You don't fucking get it." He stepped back then and pushed my chest halfheartedly with both his hands and walked toward the door of the Baldwin. He'd stopped shaking so much, and some color had come back into his face, but he was now wholly withdrawn into himself. And it was then that I realized my mistake. He wasn't afraid of them; he wasn't afraid of anybody. Vince was only afraid of himself. I remembered then those moments where I'd witnessed his violence: On the fire escape, and when he'd thrown the shoe at the old Christian drunk. Each time he'd gone pale and shaky, vanishing inside himself, just like he had now. I thought also of his boyhood story of being tackled by the cop, that satisfaction it had given him. And I thought how he'd probably have gotten more satisfaction if I'd thrown him hard against the chipped cement facade of the Baldwin. But I was a sucker for tears.

I was standing in the rain now, dumb, my jaw hanging down, paralyzed by my sudden understanding and regretting how stupid I'd been, remembering everything he'd told me. It all dawned on me, poured down like the rain, and I saw him, the ghost of him, wraithlike wandering the world, terrified only by himself and what he was capable of. I'd offered no comfort for that. I'd miscalculated badly from the start. His problems had nothing to do with sex, as I'd so smugly assumed, and everything to do with violence and loss of control. And they didn't have anything to do with me either. He wasn't afraid that *I* was like his father; he was afraid that *he* was. I *was* a dumb middle-class kid, and he didn't want my love unless I understood him, and I think just now he'd completely given up any hope of that ever happening.

So I ran to catch up with him, hoping to find some way to let him know that I understood. But I felt small suddenly—terribly powerless and small. He was right that he couldn't help me, and now I was learning that I couldn't help him either. It's back to "hang in there," the sad consolation and default of love. *Well, that's enough,* I thought, as I ran across the Baldwin's antiseptic lobby.

I missed his elevator, and when I reached the sixth floor and ran down the hall to his room, I found the door ajar. He was already crashed out on the bed, wholly spent—I guess they'd given him at least a taste of smack before jumping him. I undressed him because I had to do something; I wanted to do something for him, be of some use. He never woke through any of it, as I pulled back the bedspread and lugged him onto the sheets, tucking him in. Then I climbed in beside him to sleep. I held him, but it felt worthless suddenly. Who was large enough to hold Vince, to encompass his pain—to squeeze it out of him in a never-ending embrace? Not I. Where was the power or person who could hold this exploding star? Even the wilderness had failed him. Or had it just been because he'd gone with me and I ruined his chances?

I awoke with a start hours later, hearing his voice, that voice of deep in the night: "I love you." But his breathing was that of sleep, so perhaps I dreamed it. I told him the same back and I knew he heard me—that part of him heard me—and he knew. He knew I did; he'd always known.

But I should have said, "I understand you" because that's what he wanted. It wasn't love he was after, was it? Well, understanding was a kind of love too. The problem with love was that it was different things all the time, and we guessed and we hoped that we guessed right. And I was terribly afraid then that I'd guessed badly wrong with Vince and now it was probably too late. I looked at him then, his lower lip out in the pout of sleep, and his tattoo bluntly mocking me. *Why'd you have to be so vague and mysterious, Vince? Why didn't you just explain everything to me? Why'd you have to go back on junk and go crazy to tell me how to love you? Why am I so fucking stupid, and why didn't I listen before it was too late?*

But the bigger question was: *What do I do now? What does he need? And how do I love him now?*

Should I hit him? No, that would have been giving him what he wanted. But as he'd done for me out in the mountains, I knew the right thing to do was not to give him what he wanted, but what he needed. Which was what?

I found out when I woke up. And I understood, so there was no need to forgive him. I looked around and registered the room's emptiness. I looked at the little table where the hot plate had sat, then toward the corner where he'd kept his boxes. There was the other little table that he'd made into an altar, wiped clean. My pants had been pulled from the chair and they lay now on the floor with the pockets sticking out, so I knew he'd taken my keys. I laid there for a while and I could still feel him, and I wanted to feel him one last time.

Vince only stole from the people he loved—they deserved it, after all. They were the source of his pain. They pushed him to it. I wasn't surprised, and I even felt oddly proud and select to have joined that exclusive club. It was like his final gift. Because I'd have ruined myself for love of him, he did me the favor of leaving forever.

I got up and got dressed, and as I left I didn't close the door. Let the neon and the dust motes welcome whatever broken—hell, maybe even lucky—soul that needs this place next. But I did turn before leaving, remembering how in *Dharma Bums* Gary Snyder always thanked and blessed his campsites before he left them. How should I do so now? I wondered, before remembering Vince's lama and how he held his hands in prayer fashion at his heart. I tried that, but I was a Catholic boy, so I genuflected instead, crossing myself and wishing Vince all the best, leaving him there in that time and place enshrined now and forever: Our Lady of thievery and junk—and fine cooking, and bitter irony, and cruel snippy comments, and that small voice too from deep in the night; patron saint of all the fucked of the world; the god of great ideas and grim prospects; fire from his head and molten lava from his handsome loins; the sad god of brilliant inspired sermons on the hideousness of the human mind and its civilizations; Our

Lady of All the Sorrows and All the Wrong Moves, assumed finally into heaven. Or cast out, forever to wander. It's all the same. A one Vincent James Malone, wholly at large and for good.

I let myself cry on the elevator and sucked it up when I reached the lobby.

Amar was away from the desk when I came down, and I was glad of it. I walked out and never saw Amar or Vince or even the faded grandeur of the old down-on-its-luck Baldwin Arms ever again.

I wanted to keep walking, and so I headed south into the warehouse district where we'd first walked together, passing the coffee shop where we first met, and seeing that the Japanese plum trees were bare branched now, the piled purple refuse of their leaves lying at their roots, the color of old dried blood. The café and those trees looked so out of place, lost among the vaulted brick hangars and hulking factories, which seemed lost themselves, like hollow headstones in the middle of a modern steel city. As I waited for the light to change, I thought of how those trees always bloomed too early; then when it next rained, their blossoms were torn away and littered the street with drifts of pink flowers that kids would carelessly kick through.

The light turned and I walked on, down into the old rail yard meadows, the ridges and peaks of downtown shouldering together behind me. But soon it grew cold and the fog was rolling in ominously to swallow it all besides, so I bid a hasty farewell to his wilderness and hurried back to the underground to make my way home, where I knew a little better how to love and where, it turned out, there was still something for me to give.

ℭ XXIV

Vince never came back. But cancer did.

Vince had been gone two weeks and then this. But they didn't want Peter's eye. Or *it* didn't want his eye. And that was the damn good news in all this because it meant my mother could get up and fry eggs and clean house and get dressed and make the trip into town. And she could cry and worry and obsess. Because she was here. All because of that eye. I needed it too, having, in a sense, just lost the other.

We ended up back on the sixth floor with Peter after surgery. But the others were nowhere in sight. There were new special cases this time around. I wondered—I suppose we all wondered—what happened to Ryan and Mrs. Granger, the junkie and the rest of them. But we hesitated to ask and no one offered explanations.

The other nurses had all transferred, but thankfully Susan was still there.

She popped in the minute he was brought up from the recovery room. "My long lost love," she joked, "you came back for me." And she smiled theatrically, while we waited for the punch line. "Well, you're too late, you cad—I'm engaged!"

And she was, and we congratulated her. But even that news was somehow sad. We knew it meant her days here were likely numbered; and it hinted yet again at what felt so heavy in the air—that everything was changing, moving; that even, as sad as it was, our little neighborhood of special cases from a year ago was like some nostalgic pastoral that we missed and longed somehow to recapture. Because the sixth floor was now altogether quieter; the hope for Peter more guarded. Susan didn't speak to me separately as she had last time, when she'd shared her feelings and anxieties about Peter. Peter seemed the only one who remained undaunted, in fact. And if there weren't fun people on his floor this time, he'd drag himself and his IV pole onto the elevator—totally against hospital policy—and go visit the pediatrics floor, which was forever cheerful no matter how grim those kids' prospects might be.

He befriended a little girl with leukemia named Jenny who promised to marry him if he'd wait for her to grow up. She was bald of course, and gray, as are all kids in her situation—that strange other race of children. Jenny and Peter would leaf through magazines, making their wedding plans, picking out food for the reception, drapes and furniture for the house, cars for the driveway, and even names for their kids.

Then one day Jenny suddenly took a turn for the worse, and just as suddenly died.

"That's the first time someone's died around here that *I* didn't feel ripped off," Peter said to me. "Poor kid."

I looked at him, unsure of his meaning.

"She was eight, Neill. I always thought I was young. Man, she was *eight*."

"Well, you married her, Peter. She got to have that."

He sighed, half-laughed. "Yeah."

We sat there together in the sunroom quietly, he in his hospital pajamas, holding the IV pole like a trident. And we felt we were lucky. We knew we were.

I grew closer to my mother again, but we didn't seem like a team so much anymore. We were two old hands on the same shift and we worked together fine, but something had happened since last time that had uncoupled us from each other somehow. Cancer had broken all of us in different ways. She seemed tougher to me now, more resigned, but still hopeful. She carried her rosary always now, clutched it a little too desperately, as Vince had gripped me on the sidewalk in the rain. We'd gone through different doors to find our way out, or in, or whatever grief does. But we still ended up here, in the very same room.

I'd imagined she'd never forgive me when I told her I was gay, and over the months that I'd been seeing Vince I'd grown increasingly angry with her. I felt as if a crevice, a crack had begun, and then it grew wider by the day, like one of Peter's scars that kept pulling apart. I began to resent her finding comfort in her religion, seeing it was the same one that had offered none to me. Like her church, I figured she'd shame me, scold me, maybe even blame me for this fire that had rained down on her Sodom. But I knew when we got the latest bad scan that it was time she knew.

I only worried about the scar it would leave. But I figured if cancer happened to a family then maybe being gay did too, and it wasn't as much about *me* as I'd always thought it had been. And maybe it was even part of all this. What this cancer wanted from us. Like an angry god that had demanded blood from her youngest son, vegetables and sports commentary from her husband—and from me, the truth. They'd all made their offerings of appeasement—all but me.

I cornered her one day in the hospital cafeteria, the day after Jenny's death. She'd been devastated and looked weak-kneed at first, but she'd marched out into the hallway and paced back and forth with her rosary, reminding me then of Ryan and his heavy metal—and of Vince and his junk. She came back and reassured Peter that his cancer, being localized, made him lucky, and he shouldn't be discouraged that Jenny didn't make it. But she was reassuring herself. And I reassured her with tea, as always. But I just had a sudden sense that time was running out and the sooner I told her this, the better.

"Mom, I need to tell you something. I don't have any friends in San Francisco."

"What?" she asked tiredly, worn out, I think, from trying to make sense of Jenny's death. She looked as concerned as she could, considering. I looked at her a long time and I thought it jumpstarted some part of her—some part I was looking for that could take what I was about to tell her, that has taken all this. But how long could it hold? How strong was the little brilliant-eyed child who lived deep within her like the one in Vince, both of them so burdened by all they've withstood? Was I about to reach her, or just deliver the final blow? But I didn't seem to have as many choices about such things nowadays, so I just proceeded.

"I love you, Mom," I said, and she reached out for my hand then and clasped it with gratitude, thinking there was nothing more coming. "I don't want to hurt you, Mom," I said then. And I remember her collapsing to the kitchen floor after the bad CAT scan all those months ago.

Now she looked concerned. "What is it, honey? You could never hurt me." Hadn't she said something similar about the queen in the blue pantsuit on the street all those years ago? *Oh, you'd be surprised, Mom* . . . But she'd been right then, and maybe she still was.

"All that time in San Francisco—well . . . I was seeing a guy." *Done,* I thought, trying to keep eye contact. But she still looked perplexed, not yet getting my meaning. She probably thought I meant a therapist or a drug dealer. "Mom, I'm gay."

Her head sort of jerked back momentarily, as if she were just given smelling salts, before she said, "Oh, honey, that's nothing. I thought you were going to say something terrible had happened." I'd assumed that's what this would be to her, but I'd guessed wrong.

"That's it?" I questioned her, sighing a breath of relief, but feeling at the same time disappointed, considering how long and hard the journey to this cup of tea had been. It had been "something terrible" to me for years, and I felt in that moment that she didn't understand what I'd just said, or it hadn't registered, or maybe she didn't care how much I'd suffered with it.

"I love you, honey," she said, and she squeezed my hand again. But then she suddenly looked worried. "I hope you've been careful," she pleaded for reassurance, obviously referring to HIV.

"Of course, Mom."

Suddenly she became upset, and her face began to slide. Here was the collapse I'd both feared and yet would not be satisfied without. "Please," she added, a terribly worried look on her face, "I couldn't take that after this." But I understood then just how basic everything had become for her. As long as I didn't die or get sick, she could handle anything.

"Ah, Mom," I sighed and reached out for her hand. "Don't worry about that. Nothing's gonna happen to me." I realized, in that moment, that Peter had not only paved the way for me to accept this, but he'd done the same for her.

"Oh, Lord, I hope it isn't something I did," she inevitably said. It made me a little angry how quickly she'd shifted the focus onto herself, but I was through with feeling cheated by the world and reminded myself that the better part of love was in the giving.

"No, Ma, it had nothing to do with you." And then I had an uncanny thought that made me smile. "And if it did, I thank you for it with all my heart because I think it's a kind of good luck." And I squeezed her hand back as she smiled that sigh-heavy smile.

I didn't know if she completely understood my meaning, but I didn't know how to articulate it and I didn't want to go off and explain some crazed theory that cancer and being queer and heroin were blessings rained down upon us that led us where we needed to go.

"Can we meet your friend?" she said then, uncomfortably, I sensed, but she was always well mannered and she couldn't have not asked.

I thought of Vince, and I wished I could say yes, but of course I probably wouldn't want her to meet Vince even if he were still around. "No, Mom, he's gone—gone away," I said, averting my eyes. She didn't need to know the details, now if ever, and I'd said enough in how my face must have looked just then.

She took a deep breath then and readied herself to get up, wiping her hands on the little checkered napkin, but I stood up and held her shoulder. "I'll clear the table, Mom."

As I pushed our Styrofoam cups and wadded-up napkins into the swinging refuse door of the receptacle, I felt the strange satisfaction of generating trash—an odd and humble feeling of accomplishment. When I returned, she was composed, and asked me: "Have you told your father?"

"Oh, I don't know about that," I responded, but I knew I must. "I've told Peter," I said, and she smiled softly, thinking again, I suppose, of sentimental brotherly love, "but I'm afraid Dad would have a heart attack and die." I was racking my mind for some way to make such news funny, but I couldn't see how. Athletic metaphors didn't look promising either. Maybe I could tell him at the screen door so at least he'd have the garden to escape to.

"Yes, he might," she answered, looking pensive and somewhat alarmed even. And then, completely out of character, she added, "Oh well, if he has a heart attack, I'll take care of him."

There was a pause. She sounded more like him, I thought, than herself. She'd supplied his joke that I couldn't find. And then we both burst out laughing. And we laughed full and with great relief, and it was as if for a moment we weren't mother and son; we were two nurses on our coffee break, blowing off steam. We laughed heartily together; we laughed for all the times we didn't laugh when Peter was ill, for all the foolish escapades of my father over the years—we laughed because somehow she'd been through *it* with my brother, and, really, nothing could possibly faze her now. We laughed because we could. And we felt lucky. In some strange way, she'd crossed over; she was stronger than I thought, and I knew then my father he would be too. I'd underestimated them all.

Two hours later I was waiting for my father at the bus stop down the hill.

He was surprised to see me waiting, of course, and even more so when I gravely said, "Hi, Dad, can we get a beer?" He looked perplexed, and I knew I shouldn't be cryptic with his son in the hospital up the hill, so I added, "It's not about Peter; it's about me, OK?"

"Sure, OK," and he nodded his head, "let's get a beer."

We ended up at The Jackpot, a dive a block or two farther on, which the proprietor opened, so the story goes, with the proceeds from a big win in Reno. I knew the place because Vince and I had been there once, though we'd financed our evening on either my student loan or his GA, I don't remember which.

I eyed a corner booth and went for it the minute we stepped inside. He caught up with me as the waitress arrived to card me and take our order.

"Draft, please," I sheepishly requested. He, meanwhile, embarked on an elaborate question-and-answer interview with her regarding what kind of vodka they had, and what kind of tonic, how fresh the lemons, ad infinitum. He smiled at me when he was through with his order, satisfied with his meticulous efficiency.

"Dad, I have something I gotta tell you, and it has nothing to do with the car." I'd been dodging his questions regarding that subject for two weeks, claiming it was languishing in an auto shop's parking lot somewhere as I didn't yet have the money to pay for its repairs. I'd kept it all as vague as possible, but once he'd gone so far as to ask me the name of the shop. "Uh, I don't know, Malone's Mufflers . . . or something." I was surprised I'd even said it, but I was a poor liar and I always got around that by throwing in at least some morsel of truth.

"OK," he said slowly, speculating. "Is it about school then?"

"No. No, I don't want to talk about school."

"OK, shoot." And he scooped up a handful of peanuts and began popping them into his mouth from his fist. He was so normal, and yet so odd, he struck me as almost ridiculous sometimes. But a lovable ridiculous.

"Dad, listen, I . . . I've been having some trouble sharing this . . . and I need you to just listen to me for a minute." He looked at me, closed-lipped with his brows arched, to communicate his compliance. But just then our drinks arrived and so I had to shove it back down momentarily, yet again.

I waited for him to take a sip of his drink. While he did, I overheard some sporting event on the TV in the distance and wondered if I could do this. I knew my father was a coach and a jock at heart. What was he gonna say? "Well, go get 'em sport—fuck your way to the top"? More likely, he would say, "Win some, lose some," speaking more to himself than to me. I was never much of an athlete; I was the problematic benchwarmer he'd tried not to draw too much attention to. But he never made fun of me, and he wouldn't now. I was grateful at least for that. And if my mother took it as well as she did, why was I so worried about it breaking him? He had already proved he was tougher than I thought, and although he was certainly going to have some more gardening to do, this wouldn't kill him.

"Dad, I've struggled for years wanting to share this with you, and—" He looked at me quizzically then, empathetically, and I knew I was being way too melodramatic, drawing this out, so I had best belt it out. "What I asked you to come here for, Dad, is to tell you that I'm gay. And you need to know that." I said it fast, like I was taking foul-tasting medicine, to get it over with. It was harder with him; I couldn't reach out and hold his hand or cry or any of that as I could with Mom. "Get in the goddamn pool!" I heard Max's voice.

He just said nothing at first, took a sip of his vodka/tonic, popped a peanut, all the while looking down at the table. I gulped down a draught of my beer, swallowing hard, staring at his averted face, waiting for the silence to break, grateful he hadn't seized up in cardiac arrest.

He looked up, businesslike: "Are you sure?"

"Yes, Dad. I wouldn't be telling you this if it was just some crazy idea of mine," I said tiredly. I suddenly regretted my tone, but he gave me an affected smile, which seemed a sort of forgiveness for it, or perhaps an apology for what he'd just said, or something. I wanted to get up and get out of there.

"How long have you known, Neill?" he asked me then, almost softly.

"I don't know . . ." (But I did. And I remembered his words from that very day I first knew, ten or more years ago on Polk Street. I could see his grinning face, hear his words: "Look, boys. Look at the fag, over there with the poodle.") ". . . ten years give or take."

"I always knew you were different," he said philosophically then, sounding like he was maybe reminiscing too. His face looked sad.

"Why didn't you treat me different then?" I responded, almost angrily.

"I didn't think it would be right. I didn't want you to feel like I thought you were different." Of course—a coach treats all his players the same. He didn't want a benchwarmer, let alone a fairy, but he wouldn't draw unnecessary attention to the fact. He just left them on the bench.

"Well, I'm glad you knew I was different. And now you know why," I stated flatly, unable to conceal my disappointment.

He looked at me with a great sadness then that I'd never seen in him. He too was just a boy suddenly. I knew so little of his childhood. He never spoke of it; its loneliness. He always deflected our questions by praising his Aunt Mary for taking him on when he'd lost his parents, thus shifting the conversation away from himself. I never knew what kind of boyhood he'd had. There were those small hints in the basement, among the crates and treasures, or when he told his stories of the games he'd invented as a kid with milk tops or whatever. I knew he'd had a rich imagination then. He'd obviously been a lonely child, and a brilliant one, and I'd always felt close to that part of him when he told me those stories of his. It had been enough somehow, when I thought back on it, even though I'd wanted more then.

He was just looking at me, and for a minute I thought he was going to tell me that he was gay too—and who knows, the world had opened like a flower and it was bigger and more varied than I'd ever dreamed. I almost reached out to grab his hand and say: "Remember—remember that machete we found? Remember the lies you told me?" But everything was hesitation between us and another moment of possibility, I feared, would pass.

But he spoke. "I'm so sorry that you suffered with this for so long alone. I'm so sorry there wasn't something I could have done to make it easier. To help you not be so alone." I was utterly surprised at this. It was as if he was apologizing to me. "I love you, son. I'm sorry if I haven't been the father you wanted." I suddenly felt a rushing inward of something because it wasn't just me telling him something new. It was as if some old layer of wax was melting off his face, or falling like a screen that had stood between us.

What was I supposed to do? Cry? I shoved it back. But I wondered if I did so for his dignity or for my own. I was all business, my father's son, as I answered him, "I appreciate that Dad," averting my gaze and staring into my beer glass.

"Well, we should get going," he finally said.

We both got up, but as he did, the back of his suit coat caught on a nail or something behind him and he awkwardly pulled himself out of his coat to try and detach it. "Oh, for God's sake." I thought then of Vince's retort—"Better make it for Christ's; it's more human"—which was what my father was suddenly. He yanked it and I heard it rip. He was such a frugal man; it was completely unlike him and I just watched as he put it on like nothing had happened and walked ahead of me out the door. I was grinning at how unintimidating he really was; a clown without ever letting on. My mother would have scolded him and called him a fool for ripping it—would have, six months ago perhaps. I didn't think she would care this time either.

I felt suddenly that I was letting him down, when all this time I had assumed it was always the reverse. And I had figured he was going to once again let me down today. But he hadn't, not at all. I caught up with him at the door and put my arm on his shoulder to stop him. "Hey, Dad, I love you too. You're a good dad and always have been. You've got nothing to apologize for."

I thought I saw his eyes glisten, but he wouldn't let on as he cheerily grabbed me back. "We'll be all right, Neill; we'll get by. It's round nine in a . . ." And he was off.

❧ Epilogue

When Peter rises from his bed and the CAT scans turn clear as the waters in Illilouette Creek—stones and little rainbow trout glisten, their spots and texture clear through the wobbling water—we will go again up into the high country and be together there. We will meticulously pack our backpacks with every little tool and convenience. In silence we will prepare. And we'll drive in the black dawn across the great valley, scattered with stars and distant lights and the occasional invitation of fast-food coffee, gasoline, and donuts.

As we have a dozen times before, we will wind into the pine-studded stone places where no one lives, and into the dreamtime of our wilderness world. Patches of snow will blink from shaded glens and the sun will shine brightly across rushing rivers and stone. Dark firs will lean into the road, curious at our return, and pines will thrust like fists into the air amid the cheers of wind, goading us onward.

A uniformed ranger, last sad semblance of rules and society, will issue us a permit from his little brown cabin or booth, with his creamy green truck parked outside. We'll listen to him recount the rules we already know and then we will leave him there and move outward and upward, higher and higher, like birds or phoenixes rising.

We'll leave the car—who can guess the make of it, for like so much else the VW is gone forever—dwarfed at the end of a dirt road where a trail leads into the high nowhere. Through the forest we'll march, an "x" on our map at a river crossing or a lake ten or fifteen miles in to mark the place we'll camp—far enough so that no one else will be near. And if we take a wrong trail or are tempted by other paths, that's OK too; we don't care—one place is as good as another out here.

We'll walk in silence up the canyon, in our own thoughts. I'll remember Vince and wonder about him—wonder if, wherever he is, he ever remembers this place: what it gave and what it took. Behind me, Peter will worry perhaps about the cancer and about the false prosthetic palate he now wears that must be cleaned carefully, and can he do that here without a bathroom? Perhaps he will remember too what is lost: that limits have been carved into his flesh as they have been carved into my own heart; that we are growing older; and that dreams are harder work than they once were, and different. That one world has died for us, and some other beckons us on, as yet unknown.

The trail will be littered with pinecones the size of my boots. Broken logs will block our path and we will climb over them, determined as the insects that have made great mazes on their blanched white trunks—maps left behind by mystical termites, their secrets revealed. The scars upon the face of my brother. But what secret route do these endless and undecipherable maps convey? Where do they go? What promised land sought the termites? And are they there now? Will we reach it as well?

Through the trees we will spy other dying things full of life: the filtered light on ponds slowly turning them into reedy, green meadows; forlorn brambles suddenly pocked by green rashes of buds. Passing a patch of snow, We listen carefully and hear it melting: a drip, a baby salivating, the slow crystalline collapse of a precious thing and the beginning of some other. Ten feet away, the dirt will be dry as desert, the pines all dusty among big, glaring, diamond-studded granite boulders.

We'll round a clump of rocks and a vista will open upon faraway peaks capped by snow, their long slashing lines of forest running down the watershed clefts and along the steep streams that surrender into waterfalls as they descend. We'll see a lake far below us, mirroring the few clouds in the sky, and it will make us want to swim; we'll wipe away the sweat from our brows, thinking of its coolness. We'll traverse the slope down toward it, tracing steep switchbacks, all the while taking in the heartbreaking views laid out miles across the canyon, spotting brook-crossed meadows and steep slopes of bright green manzanita with just a touch of red, evidence of their singular bark. Mostly there will be trees—endless dark and green mountains of pine and fir and cedar trees that will make us think there's plenty of room and plenty of everything for everybody. High up toward the peaks, among the snow fields, a few crazy or courageous trees manage to crookedly hang on, and making it hard for me not to voice a word of encouragement for what they've taken on, or what they've been called to face. "The kid can catch . . . and ain't it grand?"

We'll find a chartreuse, flower-strewn meadow, buzzing with crickets, when the sun is high, and we'll stop for lunch. We'll smile at each other, say stupid things: "This is great" and "It's been a long time." I'll have the urge to tell him I love him and even to cry, but I won't let myself, preferring this open silence that we share with the mountains, and remembering not to ask for too much. He'll marvel at the beauty, amazed he made it back.

As if it were an echo, I hear my own words: "Peter, did you really think you'd ever make it back here?" I can only see his eyes, and he doesn't answer. The longer I imagine his face, the more he disappears into the wilderness surrounding him. He's scarred like the land—stone cleaved, carved by glaciers. Because his face has changed so, I no longer believe in it, as I no longer believe in any of the faces of things. The seed looks nothing like the flower.

Peter is ancient and earth now; he's a something; he is the valley of Yosemite laid out before me, breathtaking, a gift from primordial glaciers. He has become that which I love. He has always been it. He is the prize I have sought here, that has returned with me, and that on this day bridges the two and makes the world whole. An original face, that I saw in Vince once, that I sought in my father and longed for in my brother Paul, that sighed heartbreakingly from the visage of my mother—all so I'd know there was no easy route to it.

I imagine no more words.

We'll find a clearing near the lake, lean our packs on boulders, and hang our sweaty clothes on pine bows, anxious to dive into the frigid, bracing waters of the lake. We'll hoot and we'll swim about briskly, trying to keep warm. We'll race off to a little island of stone and scraggly pine and manzanita, where we'll scurry ashore from the cold water to lay out and dry under the sun before diving back in and swimming and splashing about all over again on our way back in to the lake's shore.

Later, I'll watch him hang the food, build the fire, lay out his bag, and sweep away the pine needles as I prepare our dinner, the sun so low and lost in the columns of pines that it lays out a vast landscape of shadowy bars imprisoning nothing and no one.

And when the light is gone, we'll sit by the fire and tell each other wondrous lies, and through the dancing flames I'll see his crooked smile and he'll see my tears, and together we will know that we are born.

ABOUT THE AUTHOR

The poetry of **Trebor Healey** has appeared in dozens of literary jour-
nals, including the *James White Review,* the *Chiron Review, Long Shot, The
Santa Barbara Review,* and *Evergreen Chronicles,* and has accompanied the
films *Penny Arcade* and *Peep Show in G.* His fiction has been featured in
the *Harrington Gay Men's Fiction Quarterly* (Southern Tier Editions) and
has appeared online in the *Blithe House Quarterly, Lodestar, Ashé!,* and
Tina. Healey's work has also appeared in *Queer Dharma: Voices of Gay
Buddhists* (Vols. II and III), *Wilma Loves Betty and Other Hilarious Gay
and Lesbian Parodies, Mama's Boy: Gay Men Write About Their Mothers,
Signs of Life, Pills and Thrills,* and *Beyond Definition: New Writing from
Gay and Lesbian San Francisco,* for which he served as co-editor. He can
be reached at <www.treborhealey.com>.

SPECIAL 25%-OFF DISCOUNT!
Order a copy of this book with this form or online at:
http://www.haworthpressinc.com/store/product.asp?sku=4832

THROUGH IT CAME BRIGHT COLORS

_____in hardbound at $26.21 (regularly $34.95) (ISBN: 1-56023-451-2)

_____in softbound at $14.96 (regularly $19.95) (ISBN: 1-56023-452-0)

Or order online and use Code HEC25 in the shopping cart.

COST OF BOOKS_____

OUTSIDE USA/CANADA/
MEXICO: ADD 20%_____

POSTAGE & HANDLING_____
*(US: $4.00 for first book & $1.50
for each additional book)
Outside US: $5.00 for first book
& $2.00 for each additional book)*

SUBTOTAL_____

in Canada: add 7% GST_____

STATE TAX_____
*(NY, OH & MIN residents, please
add appropriate local sales tax)*

FINAL TOTAL_____
*(If paying in Canadian funds,
convert using the current
exchange rate, UNESCO
coupons welcome.)*

☐ **BILL ME LATER:** ($5 service charge will be added)
(Bill-me option is good on US/Canada/Mexico orders only;
not good to jobbers, wholesalers, or subscription agencies.)

☐ Check here if billing address is different from
shipping address and attach purchase order and
billing address information.

Signature_____

☐ **PAYMENT ENCLOSED:** $_____

☐ **PLEASE CHARGE TO MY CREDIT CARD.**

☐ Visa ☐ MasterCard ☐ AmEx ☐ Discover
☐ Diner's Club ☐ Eurocard ☐ JCB

Account # _____

Exp. Date_____

Signature_____

Prices in US dollars and subject to change without notice.

NAME_____
INSTITUTION_____
ADDRESS_____
CITY_____
STATE/ZIP_____
COUNTRY_____ COUNTY (NY residents only)_____
TEL_____ FAX_____
E-MAIL_____

May we use your e-mail address for confirmations and other types of information? ☐ Yes ☐ No
We appreciate receiving your e-mail address and fax number. Haworth would like to e-mail or fax special
discount offers to you, as a preferred customer. **We will never share, rent, or exchange your e-mail address
or fax number.** We regard such actions as an invasion of your privacy.

Order From Your Local Bookstore or Directly From
The Haworth Press, Inc.
10 Alice Street, Binghamton, New York 13904-1580 • USA
TELEPHONE: 1-800-HAWORTH (1-800-429-6784) / Outside US/Canada: (607) 722-5857
FAX: 1-800-895-0582 / Outside US/Canada: (607) 722-6362
E-mailto: getinfo@haworthpressinc.com
PLEASE PHOTOCOPY THIS FORM FOR YOUR PERSONAL USE.
http://www.HaworthPress.com   BOF02